# THE JVLIVS CÆSAR MVRDER CASE

# THE JVLIVS CAESAR MVRDER CASE

by

Wallace Irwin

With an Introduction by

Richard A. Lupoff

RAMBLE HOUSE

©1935 by Wallace Irwin

ISBN 13: 978-1-60543-037-9

ISBN 10: 1-60543-037-4

Published: 2007 by Ramble House
Cover Art: Gavin L. O'Keefe
Preparation: Fender Tucker

*To*

BENITO MUSSOLINI *and* ADOLF HITLER

THIS BOOK IS AFFECTIONATELY DEDICATED
WITH THE AUTHOR'S FEELING THAT
IN DISTANCE THERE IS SECURITY

# WALLACE IRWIN
## AND THE JULIUS CAESAR MURDER CASE

Wallace Irwin was born in Oneida, New York, on March 15, 1875. A few months later he moved to Leadville, Colorado along with his parents and older brother, Will Irwin. Fast forward a couple of decades and both Irwin brothers are attending Stanford University in Palo Alto, California.

Will and Wallace both went in for satirical journalism and both were shortly expelled by Stanford for lampooning their professors in campus publications. This was probably not the first instance of its sort, but it is surely an unusual achievement, for which the Irwins should be fondly remembered.

Leaving Stanford, Wallace Irwin traveled a few miles north to San Francisco, where he wrote comic sketches for the old Republic Burlesque Theatre. He applied his journalistic talents in behalf of *The San Francisco Examiner, News Letter,* and *Report.* He then became editor of the onetime prestigious *Overland Monthly.* His forte was humorous verse, particularly sonnets written in what the University of California Library calls "tough American slang."

This led to the publication of Wallace Irwin's first book, *The Love Sonnets of a Hoodlum.* In later years he would add more books of light verse, but his greatest success came with a series of humorous pieces for the old *Collier's* magazine, an immensely influential slick weekly. Titled "Letters of a Japanese Schoolboy," these stories provided a satirical look at American life from the perspective of an immigrant trying — with at best mixed success — to understand a strange new world.

No fewer than four volumes of these ongoing memoirs by the fictitious Hashimura Togo were published. The imaginary Mr. Togo was immensely popular. Wallace Irwin's fans ranged from Gelett Burgess to Mark Twain. In later years, Irwin would be criticized for his caricature of Japanese-Americans, but in Irwin's own era such ethnic humor was commonplace. Hashimura Togo was brought to the screen as early as 1917, when he was portrayed by the great Japanese-American actor Sessue Hayakawa.

In 1923, *Time* magazine ran a profile of Will and Wallace Irwin, their respective wives and their niece, all of whom were pursuing successful literary careers. The anonymous reporter for *Time* (he signed his work simply, *J.F.*) offered this description:

"Wallace Irwin is short, stoutish, always smiling through his glasses and snapping his eyes as he talks in little grunting periods. He will slouch down on a couch, then tell you a story as though it were being shot at you from some great distance."

By 1935, at age sixty, Wallace Irwin was far from slowing down. To his humorous writing, both in verse and in prose, he had added more serious novels. He had written well over a score of books when he produced *The Julius Caesar Murder Case.* The fact that his own birthday fell on March 15, the fatal Ides of March, may have inspired him to write the book.

He may also have been feeling nostalgic for his old days as a reporter, for the protagonist of this new book, Publius Manlius Scribo, is a reporter for the *Evening Tiber.* Through the eyes and in the voice of Mannie Scribo he goes out of his way to lampoon craven editors, ruthless publishers, and Roman politicians.

He also manages to include offensive caricatures of blacks, Greeks, Jews, Britons, gays, Chinese, and little people. If Wallace Irwin was a bigot, at least he was an equal-opportunity bigot. But in fact, careful reading of the book would suggest that the author was merely utilizing the ethnic stereotypes that were so popular in his era. If fish are unaware of the water in which they swim, Wallace Irwin was so thoroughly immersed in a culture of stereotypes that he simply took for granted the images he perpetuated.

Wallace Irwin continued to produce books for several decades. He moved to the hamlet of Southern Pines, North Carolina, where he died on February 14, 1959.

*The Julius Caesar Murder Case* was surely not the first novel set in ancient Rome, nor was it the first literary murder mystery. But it is surely one of the first instances — perhaps the very first — of a genre that has come to be known as "toga mysteries." It is indeed a detective story cast in the classic mold, and offers a solution that is as logically plausible as it is surprising.

First published by the D. Appleton — Century Company in 1935, there is no indication of any later publication until the present Ramble House edition. Copies of the Appleton edition are seldom seen and a copy in dust jacket was recently offered by a leading book dealer for $550. Gavin O'Keefe's new design for the Ramble House edition of *The Julius Caesar Murder Case* was inspired by the clever but regrettably anonymous dust jacket of the 1935 publication.

— Richard A. Lupoff

## BIBLIOGRAPHY

NAPOLEON III.—*Histoire de Jules César*
RING LARDNER.—*How to Write Short Stories*
W. A. BECKER.—*Gallus*
*Encyclopedia Britannica.*—BIF to COG
THEODOR MOMMSEN.—*Die Geschichte des römischen Münzwesens*
S.S. VAN DYNE.—*The Green Murder Case*
ANONYMOUS.—*The Yellow Murder Case*
————*The Blue Murder Case*
*Congressional Record, 1876-79*
GUGLIELMO FERRERO.—*Cæsar*
S. LEWIS.—*Elmer Gantry*
DELORME.—*César et son contemporains*
DEFOE.—*Robinson Crusoe*
MARY ROBERTS RINEHART.—*The Door*
JAMES ANTHONY FROUDE.—*Cæsar*
EDGAR WALLACE.—*The Four Just Men*
MARK SULLIVAN.—*Our Times*
DASHIELL HAMMETT.—*The Maltese Falcon*
HARRY STEPHEN KEELER.—*The Box from Japan*
ANON.—*The President's Daughter*
HARKNESS.—*Latin Grammar*
CYRIL E. ROBINSON.—*The Roman Republic*
ANTHONY ABBOT.—*The Night Club Lady*
ELLERY QUEEN.—*The American Gun Mystery*
EDWARD LUCAS WHITE.—*The Unwilling Vestal*
HAROLD WHETSTONE JOHNSTON.—*Private Life of the Romans*
PETRONIUS.—*The Satyricon*
SHAKESPEARE.—*Julius Casar*
SUETONIUS.—*Lives of the Cæsars*
ANDREW FLECH DOUGHBEER, M.D., PH.D., Litt.D.—*100 Lessons in Sex*

# I

EARLY in the afternoon of March 12th, in the year 44 B.C., Publius Manlius Scribo, star reporter and sports columnist on the *Evening Tiber,* came down from the local room and started out to solve a murder.

In Rome, where homicide could reach magnificent proportions, the taking off of J. Romulus Comma didn't, in the young journalist's opinion, amount to a hill of beans. Q. Bulbus Apex, city editor and owner of the world's first experiment in daily journalism, had about agreed with him when he gave out the assignment; but the sour little man, whom the reporters called Boss to his face and Old Calamity to his back, believed in dishing up the lesser crimes as tiny hors d'oeuvres before the big, hot news.

Just now Mannie Scribo had found Old Calamity in his usual place, dictating to about twenty-five slaves, who copied his words, with more or less accuracy, on small tablets of wax-covered wood; the men-about-Rome were already calling his daily a *tabloidium,* abbreviated to "tab." Old Calamity was stripped to his undershirt, the sleeves rolled up to his scrawny shoulders; he wore a green shade to save his weak eyes and chewed at some sweet root the doctors had given him to cure his asthma. Creak-creak-creak went his stingy little voice, giving forth an editorial:

> ". . . trouble with us Romans is, we never learn anything. We've gone pie-eyed over Democracy, and here we are again, tied up in a knot and yelling, 'Give us a Dictator!' What's happened to the Roman memory? We've forgotten Dictator Sulla and how, the day after he faded out, a yellow dog wouldn't lift a hind leg to salute his statue. . . ."

The practical-minded Mannie Scribo, listening, said to himself, I wonder if Old Calamity's trying to get himself crucified? The editor looked up, dropped the stylus he wore habitually over his left ear and snarled biliously, "Well?" Then, after an acid pause, "Bring anything down from the Capitol Building?"

"Yeah." Almost blithely the reporter flipped out some closely written tablets. "And I've got a lead on a little murder story—"

"Don't want it," snapped his superior.

"This one seems sort of screwy. It's just an item, but—"

"Oh, come here." Q. Bulbus got up and beckoned toward an inner sanctum in the rear; testily he let his scribe into the shabby cubicle of chipped marble, cluttered with broken tablets and scraps of papyrus; a wine jug and cups sat on a table.

"I hate to bawl you out," he moaned, pouring himself a slug of cheap stuff, "but we're working high pressure—circulation went up to two hundred and twelve this week. I'm most dead. Listen—confidential. I'm after a shipload of Grade A Egyptian papyrus. Get that? When a big enough story breaks, we'll knock their eyes out with the first paper edition ever published. . . . Got to keep up with the times, boy . . . be modern, see modern. . . ." He waited for his asthma to subside, then asked sharply, "Well, what's the murder? What about it?"

The young reporter was very handsome and collegiate in his new tunic; had they worn collars in those days, Manlius Scribe's virile beauty would have favored the Arrow type. Now he smiled confidently and said:

"That's what I want to find out. The dead man's P. Romulus Comma."

"Oh, that little theatrical squirt?" obviously disappointed.

"Yeah," agreed Manlius. "General producer of Pompey's Theater. Lived in a small *bungalorium,* 'way out on Hesperides Avenue. Found this morning on front porch—throat cut—amateur job. No attempt at robbery."

"Why bother me?" asked Q. Bulbus, unimpressed.

"But listen, O Boss. Pompey's Theater is Cæsar's own property, and Comma was one of the Big Fella's pet poodles."

"Then it's Cæsar's funeral, not ours."

"All right. Suppose the *Daily Astra* takes a notion to play it up," said Mannie, mentioning a weak rival which had suddenly appeared in imitation of the *Tiber.*

*"Pons asinorum!"* snifted Q. Bulbus contemptuously and held a crabbed forefinger an inch above a crabbed thumb. "Give the story that much."

"Then here's something else again," drawled Mannie Scribo. "I got my tip at Police Headquarters, off the desk sergeant, who was plastered to the hair. Believe it or not, they're all celebrating down there because ex-Sergeant Kellius of the Homicide Squad is now Chief of Police!"

"Who? Kellius? That fallen arch?"

"Fact. Caesar called him in at midnight and promoted him. Don't ask me why. And is Kellius a changed man? Baby! When I was getting the Comma story from the pie-eyed sarj, in struts Kellius, swole like a poison pup. 'From now on,' he roars, 'no more *Tiber* reporters. Show this person out!' Meaning me, O Boss. Tie that in a Gordian knot."

"The Dictator's started muzzling the press," mused the editor.

"Somebody's being protected in this case," said Mannie. "How come Kellius snubbing me all of a sudden? After what I've done to help the Department solve a lot of crimes, like the H. P. Hippolitus poisoning case and—"

"Go on hating yourself," said the Boss sadly. "But this Comma killing isn't news exactly; it isn't big or queer enough."

"If a man bites a dog it's news, you mean?" asked Mannie, for the first time in newspaper history.

"Pretty good! I'll remember that." Old Calamity's chuckle sounded like a bad cold. "The story's too late for today, anyhow. Now, get out. And bring me that much." Again the inch-mark between thumb and finger.

And so it was that, with a careless flourish of the hand, P. Manlius Scribo went out for the needle that grew into a bloody sword.

At the street entrance a weedy giant with a weeping moustache above a servile tunic stepped out and helped Mannie on with his stylish winter toga, pipeclayed to a dazzling white. This attention gave our young man a tremendous thrill in the seat of vanity. It was great to have a slave, even if he couldn't afford one—what reporter can? The fellow was a Briton whom Mannie had bought this morning at an auction of slightly damaged gladiators. He had cost the equivalent of forty American dollars. He wore his nose at least one degree higher than the average Roman nose; he had knotty hands and feet, and an Adam's apple which, for some odd reason, seemed to match them. He'd be useful as a valet, maybe; and in the newspaper game you never can tell when a gladiator will come in handy.

"Hully up, boy, go-fetchum litter," said Mannie in his best pidgin.

"If you don't mind, sir, I speak Latin," said the British slave sadly. "And I have taken the liberty of engaging you a rather fast litter. The charge will be two denarii to the Wall and back."

"Wonderful! Do you read minds in Briton?"

"No, sir. We are not interested in other people's minds."

The master, having thus been put in his place, decided that the man would turn out fine, if anybody could ever pronounce his barbarous name.

"Say, what's your name again?" asked Mannie confidentially.

The slave said it twice, repeated it four times.

"Awfully sorry," said Mannie, "but that isn't a name. It's just a voice exercise. Know what it sounds like? Ha-ha. Excuse my laughing. But, the way you say it, it sounds like *Smith!"*

"Exactly, sir! You have it!" said the slave, brightening.

"What? Sm—Sm—Smith?"

"If you don't mind, sir."

"Actually? But Smith doesn't make sense. I might fix it around, though—I might even call you Smithicus. . . ."

A short parade was coming down the narrow street and stopping at the *Evening Tiber's* door. Lictors with fasces, centurions with swords, a rabble of "clients" (Roman bums who followed great men about, bawling their praises) gathered around a splendid litter, graven with the insignia of the Republic. The consular litter! This, then, must be Mark Anthony in person.

Mark Anthony it was, tall, curly-haired, rubicund, professional good fellow, who swung himself out as one dismounting from an awfully sporting war chariot. Julius Cæsar's dummy Consul, the Administration's handshaker, was in the uniform of a general of the Legion, one of his affectations that didn't impress Mannie a bit. Mark was getting rather fat.

At once the Consul's quick eye spotted the reporter, and he came forward with the smile that made him the most popular figure in Rome.

"Hail, Manlius Scribo!" he sang out, laying a jolly hand on the young fellow's shoulder. "Hail yourself," Mannie wanted to say. This was Anthony, who prided himself on knowing everybody. But it wasn't like him to be visiting the office of a humble editor on this busy day in Roman politics. Anthony was still patting Mannie on the back. "Apex is making a great thing of the *Tiber,* isn't he? Fine. Rome needs pepping up. And I'm bringing him a little news of my own. I've just fetched a boatload of papyrus over from Egypt. Came as ballast."

"Break it to him gently," sighed Mannie, "or he'll die of joy."

This wasn't a joke, either. But Mannie Scribo, being a born detective, smelled a bribe. Anthony kept on laughing, showing his fine, fierce teeth. "Ho-ho. I want to see the *Tiber* get ahead." Queer, considering that the *Tiber* hadn't let the Administration alone since the sunny morning when Caesar had appointed himself Dictator for life.

"Maybe the papyrus'll do some good," went on Anthony, his pop-eyes trying to look thoughtful. "Keep 'em amused. That's my slogan. Scribo, I'm crazy about your sports column. Not letting up on that, I hope?"

"I'm on a murder case today," said Mannie experimentally.

"Really?" The quiet way he said it was worth twenty pages of testimony. "Not that Comma murder, by any chance?" When Mannie nodded Mark Anthony plunged in a bit too eagerly, "My boy, if I were a journalist I wouldn't clutter up my pages with such sensational rot. Who's interested in retail killings? The average gladiatorial show is twice as dramatic. And you ought to stick to sports. You do it so well."

"I cover the water-front," grinned Manlius.

"Meaning?"

"That what I'm sent out to get I get."

"I admire your spirit." Anthony fumbled with his sword hilt. Had he been born two thousand years later he would have brought out his cigarette lighter. "Look here, Scribo. With your training and natural gifts, why waste your time with a little squirt of a *tabloidium?* You belong in politics. There's a vacancy in my office; in six months I'll make you an ædile. Suppose you forget this what-you-call-it murder case and hop into my litter. I'll put you to work, right away, for three times what you'll ever get here—"

"Thanks awfully," said Manlius, "but I cover the water-front."

"I like your nerve," smiled Anthony.

"And I like yours, sir," smiled Manlius.

So Cæsar's popular yes-man, jaunty and unruffled, mounted the stairs. He was intending, no doubt, to bribe Q. Bulbus Apex with a shipload of papyrus. Why? For the same reason that he had offered a large public career to Mannie Scribo. To keep the *Evening Tiber* from probing too deeply into the death of J. Romulus Comma.

Mannie Scribo, bobbing along in his hired litter, his British slave at his side, had time to reflect on several things. Papyrus. A shipload of papyrus. From Egypt. How did Anthony get papyrus from Egypt? Through Cleopatra, as sure as archery.

There was a funny triangle up there on Janiculum Hill where Cæsar, Rome's all-powerful Big Fella, had brought the trouble-making little Queen of Egypt and established her in a love-nest worth a Persian king's ransom. Cæsar, once the small end of the Big Three, had managed the untimely death of his fellow tyrants, first Crassus, then Pompey. This had given the Big Fella a chance to elect himself Dictator by acclamation—his own. With the Republic in his lap, as it were, he found time to start a really first-class scandal.

The work of mopping up that part of the world which Rome hadn't already laid flat, called Cæsar to Egypt. The boy Pharaoh had escaped from his throne and was returned to Cæsar in the form of a mummy. When Cæsar asked for Pharaoh's widow, the priests of Isis had said, "We guess you mean his sister," in their artless Egyptian way. Her name was Cleopatra, they said, and she had her points. But one day, so ran the tale, the Conqueror of the World sat alone and bored in his apartment at Alexandria. Two slaves entered with a long roll of carpet; swiftly they unrolled it, and out jumped a sprightly little lady who might have entered the beauty contest as Miss Nudist. She wore nothing but her hair, like smouldering fire, and a remarkable blue amethyst ring on her thumb. "I have come to make peace," she said, and that was Cleopatra's little joke.

For two years now Cæsar had been keeping his legal wife on a dole, in some obscure boarding house at Pompeii or Baiæ. Meanwhile, Cleopatra reigned in her palace on the Janiculum Hill. She entertained quietly—men mostly. The old fashioned Roman matrons called her "the Levantine Squaw," and sniffed their haughty noses. And if Cæsar noticed the too frequent appearance of Mark Anthony around the lady's establishment, he made no sign. Queer cuss, Cæsar. Strangely tolerant about some things, and generous with his friends.

Thus reflecting, Mannie Scribo looked out of his litter and studied the damaged British gladiator, walking at his side.

"Now listen, p*or,"* he said, "are you dumb as you look?"

"I dare say, sir."

"Dare what?"

"Say, sir."

"Smithicus, if you follow me round and make good, some day I'll turn you loose. But take my tip. Get rid of that London brogue. Nobody but hicks talk that way. When you're in Rome—"

"One should do as the Romans do, sir."

"Sacred Vulcan! How long did it take you to think that up?"

The Briton hid behind his walrus moustache and seemed unable to reply; Mannie's mind reverted, for an instant, from crime to love. Love, he reflected, was worse than liquor, the way it got some men. Look at Cæsar; the Egyptian wren had wrapped him around her finger. Yeah. And as for Mannie Scribo, no *puella* in the world could do that thing to *him.* Almost regretfully he remembered the girl with the silver wig. The look she gave him the other day when he tried to pick her up, coming out of Cato's Sandal Shoppe. Blue eyes that could freeze to ice. But not naturally cold. G. Lucifer, but Mannie had gotten even with her last night, when he saw her stepping into a litter with a Greek dude—one of those Athenian male violets. She'd looked straight at Mannie and pulled a funny little smile. He had pretended to be looking at a statue on the top of the Temple of Jupiter. That's the way to treat 'em. Rough. But with a face like that, and those eyes. . . .

Mannie shook off these weak thoughts and saw that his litter had reached the Forum. The law courts were going rather languidly, for it was now the hour when Rome took its midday snooze; but around a few second-grade lawyers, belching orations on the Rostra, a small mob of unemployed applauded, hoping for a free lunch. With the cynic keenness of the newsman, Mannie noticed a lot of things. The Capitol Building was closed for repairs. Another Lucullus Bros, botch job; Uncle Lucius Lucullus ate himself to death three years ago, but his racket went right on. That was the golden rule of Rome; get the job and get the coin. Why not? Manlius was born nearly two thousand years too early to think of Tammany Hall, but his soul felt out into the future and made him smile. And there was Cæsar too, if Mannie had but known it, who had reached into unborn time and stolen a page from Hitler's book. Almost the first thing the Big Fella did, after he took Rome with a handful of centurions, was to break open the State Treasury, under the Temple of Saturn, and cart away a few tons of gold bullion. . . .

Hello! Look at that. Fatty Cassius and Mealy-mouth Brutus, arm in arm, were passing up toward the Senate office buildings. What did these two see in each other? Brutus, a weak-chin, but not a bad sort, in spite of the way he was always harping on My Noble Grandfather, had picked a funny chum in Fatty Cassius. Nobody really liked Fatty, social climber and wire-puller. And what was Fatty trying to put over now? What was he getting a poor simp like Brutus into? Rumors about Cassius and his ambitions were as common talk in Rome as the buzz about Cæsar's wanting to be king. Cæsar. The gods love a bright target. And what a newspaper story it would make if Brutus and Cassius really steamed up enough courage to get rough with the Big Fella and grab the works. . . .

His eyes on the two white togas, Manlius was surprised by another figure in white. A vestal virgin glided out from behind a pillar. It might have been an accident, but their meeting had the neatness of design. She came in the way of Brutus and Cassius. One of her hands, the right one, stole out of her pure robes; it moved twice, up and down. Twice up and down moved the hands of Brutus and Cassius.

Mannie's brain, sensitized to Rome's every gesture, read meaning into the sly play of hands. Vestals, by all their vows, never signal to men. Brutus and Cassius . . . what was she trying to tell them? Rome was full of echoing shadows, disconnected danger signs. The queer friendship of these two pretors; the vestal's warning; Anthony and Cleopatra; the lone corpse of Comma. Yes, and Cæsar alone, too, as genius must always be. The Big Fella was certainly getting touchy about public opinion, or he wouldn't have sent Anthony around to bribe Old Calamity with a shipload of papyrus. Whose papyrus? Cleopatra's? Whew! The mean look Anthony gave Manlius when he suggested that Cæsar's assassination might be big news. And Anthony's funny little blink at the mention of Comma's murder. Trying to hush it up. Yes, and Kellius, suddenly promoted to be Chief Husher. Why?

Curiouser and curiouser.

"Say, can't you boys speed up a little?" asked the journalist-detective, leaning out of his litter. It might be better to get out to the *bungalorium* before Kellius took a notion to move the body. Even in politics-ridden Rome bodies did get moved, after a while.

At a street corner stood one of Cæsar's new policemen with a scarlet tunic and gilded scales on his kilt-straps. He was regulating traffic—another of Cæsar's pet ideas. But even though the policeman retained his Roman calm, West-going and South-going litters were in a shaft-locked huddle. Wherefore Smithicus spoke up in his quaint London brogue:

"It might be a good idea, sir, for the policeman to have two torches, a red one and a green one, by way of signaling."

"When you give a Roman two torches," said Manlius, "he usually starts burning down the town. Where'd you get the bright idea?"

"A clerical gentleman, a Druid priest, sir, mentioned it to me."

Traffic was moving again, and Manlius, who just now had been so feverish for speed, shouted, "Hey, stop!" and reached out to seize the front pole of another litter, passing in the opposite direction. What a stroke of luck! For behind the elaborately golden curtains he recognized the face that all Rome knew. Hesiod, the comic actor. Hesiod, Cæsar's favorite and the late Romulus Comma's most intimate friend. Golden curtains parted, and Hesiod's Grecian profile snowed, wrinkled with annoyance.

"Oh, hello!" he said, smiling, because actors mustn't be unfriendly with the press. "I took you for a Neapolitan bandit. Just got back from there two hours ago. Anything I can do for you, old man? I've been away so long I'm rushed to death. Drop in pretty soon and I'll give you a good story about the Theater of Dionysius at Naples. I opened it officially, you know, on the Nones of March. My boy, I panicked 'em. Must tell you about it. Well, I'll be seeing you. Must rush over to the theater. Papa Comma's calling a rehearsal."

All in one breath, the way Hesiod was when he talked about himself. But Mannie still clung to the comedian's litter.

"Hesiod," he said, "you won't find Comma there, I'm afraid."

"No? Why not? But I had a special message from him. That's why I hurried back to—"

"Comma's dead."

"Dead?" Hesiod's handsome face turned to a mask of horror. "Dead? Oh, my poor friend. I was afraid of that."

"Afraid of what?"

"Some terrible worry. He told me everything—but that." Hesiod's jeweled hands went over his eyes. "He drank too much. He worked too hard. His heart. He had fainting fits—"

"This wasn't a fainting fit. I hate to tell you, Hesiod. It's pretty tough. But he was murdered last night."

*"Eheu!"* The funeral cry. Tears were running down the actor's sensitive, emotional face. "Ah, that good man! Ah, my only real friend! Who could have hated him so?"

"That's what I'm trying to find out," said Manlius.

"I'll give my private fortune—I'll take this to Cæsar himself. The shade of my friend shall be avenged—"

Then the harsh voice of Cæsar's policeman, breaking through and waving his short sword. "Wadda ya think y'are? Good morning, Hesiod." With the deference all Rome showed its favorite actor—"Afraid you'll have to move the boat, sir."

Hesiod drew the curtains. Two litters took their separate ways. In cadence with the joggling of the poles Mannie Scribo was reflecting. Comma was a worried man. Worry drove him to drink, possibly to fainting fits. Hesiod personally would put the case before Cæsar. All right so far. But why was Cæsar's precious Kellius doing all he could to block investigation?

## II

BECAUSE it was P. Manlius Scribo's business to know his Rome, he soon located MMCXIV Hesperides Avenue along a row of smallish marble shacks, each looking exactly like the next one; they were constructed by the mile out of scraps of building material which Lucullus Bros, had stolen liberally from Cæsar's now Capitol. "Home of J. Romulus Comma," chipped in black marble over a door, identified the tragic *bungalorium.* The morgue wagon, hitched to a pair of mules, stood at the curb; as if by prearrangement the door of the small house swung open on its wooden post; heavy shoes were scuffling as four stalwart policemen carried on their shoulders something long and human-like, draped with a brownish cloth. Brushing the reporter aside, they carried their burden over to the wagon.

"What's the idea?" Manlius was protesting emptily against this high-handed procedure when Chief Kellius himself, pompous in his new brass helmet and brilliant uniform, came swaggering out.

"Good morning, Manlius," said Kellius in a lofty key, his enormous face looking down. "A little late, I see."

"And you a little earlier than usual." Mannie resolved to take no lip off this dull policeman whom, as a humble sergeant on the Homicide Squad, he had helped through many tougher cases than this. "Hail, O Chief of Police! *Princeps Politicorum* is, I believe, the official title. You're getting kind of fat, Kelly. Maybe you'd look better wearing a senatorial toga—covers up the bay window."

Instead of being offended Kellius swallowed the compliment.

"As a matter of fact," he admitted, "the Dictator has me on the list—hmph—for a knighthood."

"You can't keep a good man down, as the lion said when he coughed up the Hebrew martyr. How 'bout this corpse, Kellius? When did the Department begin refusing to let the press look upon the dead?"

"Since I went into office," replied Kellius stiffly. "What's this sudden curiosity about Comma, anyhow?"

"You tell me," suggested Manlius, determined to keep his temper.

"Seems to me the *Evening Tiber* is pretty hard up for news, wastin' its time with a little flash murder."

"Yeah. Mark Anthony said something like that today."

"Huh? Mark Anthony?" Kellius, having served his time as a city detective, had a face like an open book. It showed that he was startled, if not scared.

"And by the way," persisted our reporter innocently, "it seems to me, O Chief of Police, that you've gone quite a distance yourself to look into this little flash murder."

"Whose case is it—yours or mine?" asked Kellius, puffing.

"Here's the answer. It's yours now, but it'll be mine before you know it."

With a jaunty wave of the hand Manlius started into the house.

"Nobody, reporter or no reporter, goes in there without my consent," growled Kellius, blocking the way.

"Which I have, of course," Manlius showed his police pass.

"Guess again. Try it, and you're under arrest."

"Thanks for the tip."

Very obediently Mannie got back into his litter and watched the Chief lumbering into his own. The dead wagon moved, the Police Department litter moved, and Mannie ordered his bearers to follow; but at a tangle of side streets just outside the Wall, he commanded crisply, "Go back to MMCXIV Hesperides Avenue, and make it snappy."

Because all Romans were bribable, the cop on guard at the door accepted something out of the *Tiber's* expense account. The expense account was useful again inside the atrium, or parlor, where it required three pieces of silver to persuade a sergeant.

"You saw the body?" asked the inquiring reporter.

"Yeah."

"How did it look?"

"Peaceful," grinned the sergeant. "His worries are over. So are ours. Just another unsolved murder."

"Too bad," sighed Mannie. "Maybe the Coroner will think otherwise."

"The Chief is Coroner too—them jobs go together. The verdict will be suicide. Death by knife wound in the throat."

"Why not make it 'suicide by drowning'? Any witnesses to this crime—or whatever you call it?"

The sergeant shrugged. "How do I know? His daughter ain't been heard from since yesterday morning. She's a sort of modern *puella,* I guess. Works in Cicero's law office."

"Who told you that?"

"Search me. Might of been one of them acrobats from Pompey's Theater. They're all over the place."

Shouts of "Alley-oop!" came from the back yard.

"Mind my strolling around?" asked Mannie.

"Not if you don't take all day to do it."

Mannie began a careful survey of the *bungalorium.* It was of the regular type, parlor, bedroom, bath and sun-porch. Only, being truly Roman, the bath took up most of the space. The house differed from the ordinary in two respects. There was a bedroom on either end of the parlor. Entering the first, he found a little white bed, gracefully curved, little white chairs, a white bureau holding a silver mirror of Tyrian workmanship and dainty pots of rouge and perfume. A girl's room, too frivolous for a modern *puella.*

That it had been searched was evident, for the mattress had been turned over and the bureau rolled half across the room. Somehow ashamed of the profanation of a shrine, Mannie studied the marble bureau-top, then lifted it slowly; a tiny shred of papyrus fluttered to the floor. He picked it up and hid it in his tunic just as the sergeant came back, possibly to hurry him up.

"Who reported this case?" asked Mannie, covering his confusion.

"Tony did. Hey, Tony!" A smallish Neapolitan policeman approached, doffing his helmet. "Tony, tell him how you found the body."

Tony sheathed his sword, thus freeing both hands for gesturing.

"Dees-a way. One hour before sun-a rise, dass when I come on my beat—"

"He don't speak Latin very good," explained the sergeant, but Tony was pouring on:

"My beat go from corner of Euclid Avenue and Appian Way—"

"Cut that," said the sergeant, "and tell what you seen."

"Well. I com-a long by dees bongalo', and wot I hear? Beeg-a yell. Holy Cæsar, wot a yell! Den one beeg-a neeger he come ronnin' out—"

"Nigger?" asked Manlius coolly, taking notes.

"*Si.* Beeg-a neeger. He ronna down da street yellin', '*Mortuus est Romulus Comma!*' I know pretty dam quick wot dat mean. Somebody keeled. So I ron in da house—"

"Why didn't you run after the coon?" broke in the sergeant.

"I tell-a you," insisted Tony. "I ron in da house, and on sun-porch, by Saturnus, was a lot-a blod and Mist' Comma in it."

"Have you any idea who the colored man was?" asked Manlius.

But while the Italian shrugged the sergeant explained, "I went over the place later. The body was a-layin' right here." Pointing to a spot on the sun-porch. "There was a trail of blood from the parlor to here."

"Any marks on the body, except the knife wound?"

"Not a thing. Unless you count hair as a mark."

"Hair? Where was the hair?"

"In his right hand. A long hank of it. A woman's hair."

"What color?"

"Red."

Mannie was considering this point when Smithicus came forward with the question: "Might I be permitted to ask something, Sergeant?"

"Who ever told you a slave could speak to a policeman?" asked the sergeant. So the slave appealed to his master.

"I merely had a curiosity to know, my lord, if the police have kept the hair as evidence."

"What do you think we are, hair-dressers?" raged the sergeant, his pride touched. "We're not runnin' the force on any of your new-fangled, high-falutin' ideas. And now, sir, if you want to go on searching this house you can do it yourself."

The surly invitation was welcome to Manlius Scribo. His first act was to go on all fours, his eyes an inch from the tiles of the atrium from which, according the Neapolitan soldier, Comma's body had been dragged; he had mentioned a trail of blood from the atrium to the sun-porch. Now there was no blood. Only a long streak of dampness, such as a mop would make over a glazed surface.

"Who mopped up the blood?" asked Manlius.

"Me, meester," said Tony cheerfully.

"What for?"

"Gotta da orders."

"From whom?"

Tony answered with one of the shrugs born in the South of Italy, for evasive purposes. He raised his blunt Roman sword and pointed it toward the ceiling. A sign. The Man Higher Up.

Manlius remained on hands and knees, following every inch of the damp trail from atrium to sun-porch. Close to the sill of the solarium, near which the body had been found, his industry was rewarded; a microscopic tangle of red-gold showed in the afternoon light. Between thumb and fingers he picked up the important clue—three long auburn hairs. He rolled them up carefully, and was about to wrap them in the shred of papyrus he had found under the girl's bureau-top, when he saw that something was written on it.

"————t me at same pla————"

Just a fragment, but not too torn to destroy its Latin syntax. "Meet me at same place." Hm. A rendezvous, a murder, a missing girl.

Q. Romulus Comma's chamber was like a theatrical dressing-room, the wall covered with pictures of stage favorites and clever caricatures by Gallic artists. These aroused Manlius' admiration, and he was wondering how near crucifixion he would come, if he ran a thing called Capitol Hill Picture Gallery in Apex's new papyrus edition. Next to a mirror of polished bronze, over a grease-paint laden stand, he saw a small figurine of the goddess Thespis, enshrined in a niche; a bowl of incense still smouldered at her feet. Comma's resident deity, who hadn't helped him much. Mannie poked a profaning finger behind her terra cotta skirt, and a little silver disk came tinkling into his palm. A medallion, flat and plain on both sides and fastened with a clasp. It was hard to open, but the handy Smithicus, borrowing his master's dagger, sprung the clasp as easily as you'd open an oyster.

The right side of the locket showed a Medusa head; and on the left side, roughly engraved, were the words *Sic Semper Tyrannis.*

"Hm. I don't know what to say," mused P. Manlius Scribo.

" 'The plot thickens' would be an appropriate speech, sir," suggested Smithicus sadly.

Manlius tucked the locket in his toga and went on with his work. One end of Comma's bedroom was covered with pegs, hung with a number of wigs, beards, false noses, masks, sandals, tinsel crowns, brilliant robes. All the articles here were in perfect order, numbered, no doubt, to identify them with the parts they were to costume. Manlius examined each wig and beard minutely. There were white hairs, gray, gold, brown and black; not a sign of red in the orderly array, undisturbed by tragedy.

Rather baffling. Yet P. Manlius Scribo was far too cunning a technician to turn a hair, even in the presence of false beards. "Smithicus, my man," he drawled indolently, "this looks quite interesting." He was pointing to a collection of murderous weapons on the opposite wall; among them enough swords to depopulate a village.

"Quite," agreed Smithicus. But his tone was unconvincing as he took down the wickedest of the swords and handed it to his master. It was wood. One by one, and with growing impatience, Manlius weighed the weapons in his hands. All wood, the sort the chorus men flourish at the big finale in Act Two.

Through the window, which opened on a wide court, some hundred feet long, he saw a half-dozen nude athletes, curiously disporting. Three of them were playing medicine ball. A fourth, a dwarf, was picking up ivory eggs, tossing them in air, catching them in his mouth and, to all appearances, swallowing them. A fifth was balancing himself by his stomach on the end of a bamboo pole. The sixth was putting a dancing bear through his morning exercises.

"Come hither, fellow," commanded Manlius, leaning out of the window and beckoning to the dwarf, an ungainly pint-size person with large feet and hands. The midge waited to spit out a pailful of eggs, then came forward, bowing obsequiously.

"You are all actors in Pompey's Theater, I see, practising for tomorrow's performance," said Manlius in the kind tone he used with the lower classes.

"Nobleman, you've said it," replied the little man.

"All slaves, I suppose?"

"The same."

"Same what?"

"Slaves."

"Whose slaves are you?"

"No actor ever knows whose slave he is," chirped the dwarf. "But slaves we are and always will be."

He cocked an elfin eye at Mannie's press badge. "I suppose you're here about the murder."

"Something like that. What might your little name be?"

"Hercules," replied the midge.

"Hercules, how many of your brother actors live in this house?"

"Only one."

"Which one?"

"Me, mister. The others live around Pompey's Theater and just practise here where Comma can watch 'em." The dwarf stopped and gulped. "Excuse me. I meant to say where Comma *could* watch 'em. He was a beautiful character, was Comma. It'll be a long time before you'll find a man can step into his shoes."

"You're speaking in blank verse," said Manlius.

"Us vaudeville people get into the habit of it."

Manlius crawled out of the window and crouched like a giant over the little man.

"Did you sleep here last night?" he asked quietly.

"Sure. Same place I always do. Under the back steps. On a gunny-sack. It's quite comfortable, if—"

"Hercules, did you hear your master come home?"

"Sure I heard him. And I seen him too."

"Saw him?" Was the mystery to be unraveled so easily? Probably not.

"You bet I seen him. It was the second hour after midnight. Him coming up in a litter and sending the bearers back to town. A little tight he was, wabbling as he come up to the front porch."

"How did you know the hour?"

"The night watch went by a coupla minutes before. They ought to report him. He wakes up everybody in the block—"

"Are you sure Comma was quite alone?"

"Alone with his jag. He made such a noise, tripping over things, that I stuck my head in the door, thinking I'd help him to bed. But a big, fat fella like him—he'd a-squashed me flat. So I was going round the house, back to my gunny-sack, when I seen that other litter coming down the street, plain as day in the moonlight—"

"What other litter?" Manlius cracked out.

"Why, the one the vestal virgin came in."

"Vestal virgin?" The young Roman cowered at the sacrilege. "Boy, do you know what you're saying?"

"Sure I do, boss."

"But vestals never go out on the street, except in charge of a priestess—and in a theatrical man's apartment at night!"

"This is the first time she ever come here at night, that I know of. Usually it's the afternoon."

"How often have you seen her come here?"

"Two or three times. She never stays long, and comes and goes with her veil down. That's the vestal's racket—veil down and get away with murder."

"How long was she here?"

" 'Bout ten minutes, maybe. Ain't none of my business, what my boss does after work hours. So I went back to my gunny-sack again. Then I heard the front door slam, and when I peeked round the house the litter was going away."

"You didn't make any attempt to find out what had happened?"

"No, sir. I says to myself, What you don't know won't hurt you. But this morning, about sunrise, I heard Hambonius let out a yell. He's the African slave that comes in early in the morning to light the furnace for Comma's bath. He let out a yell like a sick elephant, so I run in the house—and there was my boss on the solarium floor, all covered with blood. Gosh, it was awful. He was drunk and a bum, maybe. But he was the best friend I ever had—"

The dwarf's funny chin puckered.

"And his daughter wasn't here last night?" asked Manlius inexorably.

"Search me, mister. I didn't hear a peep out of her."

"She was not home." It was a tall bear trainer who volunteered this. "It is my custom to guard the door for the first three hours after sunset. Up to that time she had not come home."

"Is she in the habit of staying away nights?"

"No," said the bear trainer. "Or—not often—"

"What's the girl's name?"

"Romula."

Naturally it would be, Mannie recalled, since daughters usually took their father's clan names.

"What does she look like?" asked the reporter.

"She's a sort of small young lady, mister."

"Tee-hee! *You* talkin' about small," jeered the bear trainer.

"I can lick you and your bear too," howled the mite, swinging his over-sized fists.

"Oh, key down," begged Manlius, "and tell me—what was her complexion?"

"Sort of lightish—but say, mister—"

"Color of hair?"

"Red." No hesitation about that.

"Small, red-headed girl named Romula, works in Cicero's office," Manlius noted down. The dwarf opened his mouth as if to speak, then closed it puckishly until the inquisitor went on:

"What became of Hambonius, the janitor?"

"What always becomes of a coon when there's trouble with the police? Search the Hesperides. Search the Styx. Hambonius is long gone."

"And Romula, daughter of Romulus, is long gone too," muttered the *Tiber* representative. "Why don't you want me to find her?"

"Because I don't know where she is. And don't you take away with you any notion that she's mixed up in it," said Hercules earnestly.

"Why not?" asked the bear trainer suddenly. "Comma ain't the man he used to be."

"I'll say he ain't," agreed Hercules, gazing balefully toward the spot where the corpse had lain.

"I mean," insisted the bear trainer, "he wasn't so good to Romula lately. Him, stewed to the gills half the time, pawning her clothes to pay the booze bills, threatening to put her on the stage—as if anybody would go on the stage unless he had to—"

"Shut up!" said the midget. He might have been six feet two, the way he said it. The tall trainer shrank back.

"Had he no enemies?"

This question gave Hercules a moment of pause. Then he was more eager than before, a man carried away by his convictions.

"Just one. His fool self. Do you think Romula was the kind of *puella* that would knife her old man just because he came home plastered? She knew, as well as I did, what made Comma that way. Troubles."

"What sort of troubles?"

Instead of giving a direct answer the dwarf doubled up his little forearm and stood like a toy gladiator.

"Here's the kind of guy Q. Romulus Comma was. Square. Many's the time he stood between me and the whip. Maybe I'm a slave, but I'm one of the family." The midge looked up, wild-eyed, furious. "And I'm telling you. Whoever got Romulus Comma has got to shoot it out with me before it evens up."

## III

"PLUCKY little chap, eh what? But a bit under weight," suggested Smithicus. It was nearing sunset, and Mannie's human steeds were bearing him at a sharp pace along the cluttered shipping of the Tiber wharves.

"Sure plucky," agreed the reporter absently. Like a good chess player Mannie was concentrating on the board before him. But something about Smithicus' gesture, as he ran along, caught the master's attention. The Briton was bringing out of his tunic what looked like torn fragments of a bearskin rug.

"What in Pluto's name have you got there?" asked Mannie.

"Wigs and beards, sir," said Smithicus brightly.

"Wigs and beards? But where—"

"I helped myself to them, sir, off the deceased theatrical gentleman's wall. It occurred to me that wigs and beards might come in quite handy for us, if we're going in seriously for murder cases."

This was all very well, but Manlius was not to be deflected from his mental chess-board, the significant moves in Comma's *bungalorium.* The dead man had clutched a handful of red hair, a woman's hair. A vestal virgin had driven the knife home—or else the dwarf was lying. Comma had been drinking, worrying, quarreling with his daughter. Red-headed Romula. The tell-tale red in the dead man's hand. Suppose, then, that Romula and the midget had hatched the plot?

Nonsense. Comma was a mountain of a fat man. The midge and the young girl, between them, couldn't have moved his body a foot, let alone dragging it to the sun-porch. Possibly they had employed Hambonius to do the actual killing. But the colored furnace man was never there at night . . . again, if Hercules was telling the truth.

Out of his tunic Manlius drew the little silver locket, opened it and read the words cut in the soft alloy. *Sic Semper Tyrannis.* So always with tyrants. The Gorgon's head, emblem of fury and destruction. The locket lay in the reporter's hand, an open book. It seemed easy to read. A tyrant was to be destroyed. And who was the tyrant of Rome? Cæsar, none other. Had Comma been plotting against his lord and master? Was that it? Had the Big Fella's mighty will directed the knife toward Comma's throat? Possible, but not probable. It was almost an axiom in Rome that much of Cæsar's power lay in the mutual loyalty between himself and his humbler dependents.

Or had someone, out of malice, put the silver token behind the statuette in Comma's chamber? The murderer, perhaps? Or even Chief Kellius, with his badly assumed indifference and his obvious anxiety to pigeon-hole the case? A vestal virgin with auburn hair. Hm. . . .

Mannie's eyes roved across the passing crowd, looking for red-headed girls. Funny how many there were in Rome. Slaves, middle-class *puellæ* out marketing, carrot-topped patricians going into the jewelers' shops. . . .

"Stop!" shouted Manlius. The bearers jerked to a halt. Oddly out of place among the rough sailors along the quays a small litter with pink curtains stood waiting for something, or nothing. One foot on the ground, Manlius hesitated until he saw the pink curtains part; a girl, holding her white wool cloak against the March cold, stepped out and slowly crossed toward a bench by the water-side. Her little green sandals went mincingly over the rough cobbles, her pert little head, tossing independently, gave forth a pale metallic glow, an exotic in murky sunlight. She was the girl with the silver wig.

"Smithicus," said Manlius, "step over to the young lady with the compliments of P. Manlius Scribo, of the equestrian order, and say that Scribo writes interviews for the *Evening Tiber.*"

Palpitatingly Mannie watched the Briton approach the bench where the *puella* sat; her violet eyes were so innocent as she looked up at the tall slave that Mannie was ashamed to have thought of her the things he had been thinking. Then Smithicus, with the air of a great ambassador came back and said: "The lady wishes to inquire, sir, 'What difference does that make?' "

Mannie wasted no time, but armed himself with tablet and stylus and went over to her. Again the wide, violet gaze under the fashionable wig of finespun silver wire.

"The gods favor me," he said, regaining his natural cheek as he poised and plied his stylus.

"In what way, please?" she asked. She knew how to take care of herself, this gal. But her look informed him that he had crashed into a pleasant garden.

"I've been spending my afternoon with a murder," he said, "and somehow or other you're a contrast."

"Thanks a lot." Dimples appeared in just the right places. Oh, joy, he was making her like him! But he should be rushing back to the office—there you go, Scribo, letting a *puella* cut into your time.

"Let me see what you've been writing about me," she demanded, reaching out like a kitten for a ball of yarn; her little hand looked so helpless as she read Mannie's words, imprinted in soft wax, *"Pulcherrimam puellam in tota Roma vidi."* " 'I saw the prettiest girl in all Rome.' " Her artful make-up could not hide the blush. "Oh," she giggled, "sounds like something out of the copy book."

"It's out of the date book," said he promptly; then, because she didn't seem to understand, "I'll fix it up so that it'll read fine when I get back to the office." He tucked his garments carefully and sat down beside her. He was gratified to feel that his white toga made him look like a patrician—which he really wasn't, exactly. Again he glanced at her hands, and this time without entire approval. Blood-red nails.

"You don't like them done this way?" she asked suddenly.

"They always remind me of a cat fight," he admitted.

"Thank you. Everybody's doing them that way this year."

"Maybe. Next year, probably, the gals'll be painting their toe nails."

"Don't be silly. And I'm sorry you don't like ruby nails when—"

"Well, they do look better than the black ones. And anything on you, nails or anything, gets sort of perfect. I suppose silver wigs are fashionable too. Funny about women. When Venus and Diana and all the rest of the goddesses do all they can to make them perfect, these women can't let well enough alone—I guess you think I'm awfully personal."

"Oh, no. Just fresh."

"You see, it's a habit. I run a personal column. In my professional capacity it's my duty to write up the brighter side of Rome. And you're it."

She giggled, somewhat too lightly, he thought. Her violet eyes had deepened; there was fear in them. But she mocked him: "Am I being interviewed?"

"Do you mind being interviewed?"

"Not in the least. Tell me about yourself."

"My life's an open book . . . Chapter One. Twenty-four years ago P. Manlius Scribo was born in the noble but hick town of Padua. Raised in the gutter, of an old patrician family, my dad made his fortune selling condemned army shoes back to the government. When Sulla was Dictator he made my old man a knight. Then the Civil War came along. Pa went blah. I worked my way through the University of Rhodes and went into the newspaper business."

"What's a newspaper?"

"A newspaper," said Mannie, "is the palladium of liberty. I quote no less an authority than Q. Bulbus Apex, my city editor."

"Really?" Starry eyed now. "But why do you call them that—papers?"

"Because, one of these days we're going to get the *Tiber* out on papyrus. Giant edition. Maybe a thousand copies!"

"But who wants to read a thousand papers?"

"You've got me there. Goddess, will you stop interviewing me for a minute and let me ask you a question?"

"When you get out so many papers do you sell them yourself?" Quite evidently she was stalling.

"What's your name?" he asked baldly.

"Because," she said, "if you have to write all those papers and sell them all yourself—"

"Look here, I've got to go in a minute."

"So have I." Her look became suddenly serious.

"Then let's make it brief. I'm the best reporter in Rome, if I must say so. What I'm out for I get. This time it's you—"

"Oh."

"I was awful the other day, trying to talk to you like that. But you knocked me dizzy. I've got you on my mind."

She didn't attempt to reply; her beautiful eyes were studying him. He felt that she wanted to talk, but somehow couldn't.

"And see here," he growled, irritated with himself, "you're not on my program. You haven't any right to get on my mind. I'm a serious worker, and when a *puella* starts messing up your life—"

But her voice was low and sweet when she answered, "That's all right, Manlius Scribo. I—I want you to be in love with me. But you mustn't—"

"Mustn't? Why not? When can I see you again?"

"Please don't try to. It's going to be all right, the way you feel—but—"

Iron-soled shoes pounded the cobbles behind them. Nervously the *puella* sprang to her feet as another litter, larger and gaudier than the one that brought her, came up. Two Numidian bearers, brilliantly uniformed, swung the red enameled pole from their shoulders and a massively built but sissified fellow stepped out. The girl ran toward him. Queer, her change of manner. She seemed to be seeking protection. Mannie winced. Like a true Roman, he hated this type of Greek lounge-lizard. His hair, black as night, was elaborately water-waved and fixed in the back with an amber comb; his beard, also black and water-waved, hung over a chest that clinked with necklaces. Yes, it was the same Greek pansy.

"Cake eater!" muttered Manlius Scribo, standing moodily. The Greek dude might have been deaf and dumb. Only his gestures, commanding but over graceful, showed her to a place beside him in the big litter. Before the curtains came together the girl's eyes sent forth a wild, somehow pathetic message. "Don't think I'm too horrid. Don't try to understand. Love me. And let me alone."

The bearers lifted the red poles and started away; and as if by signal the little pink litter followed down the street.

"Did you notice the fake whiskers on that Athenian violet?" asked Manlius of his faithful Smithicus. "What's the idea?"

"Perhaps there is none, sir," replied the Briton. "I find that people wear beards without any apparent motive."

Only on rare occasions did our sleuth-reporter accuse himself. But now he stood a moment, thinking of that new cuss-word imported from Athens.

*"Moron!"* he growled. For he'd certainly let the girl put it all over him. She said she liked him to be in love with her. Yeah. Probably she was saying that to the big Greek gigolo, right this minute. Possibly to every man she met. And she'd gotten away without telling her name.

By the water-side was a booth labeled "Information," and there Manlius found a funny little man in a funny little profession. His name was Bobulus and he was a public *nomenclator.* A *nomenclator,* as we doubtless all know, was a sort of walking Who's Who in Rome; his business was to whisper the names of important personages when his master went through the Forum. But this Bobulus, since the assassination of his owner, had set up business for himself.

"Now, Bobbie," said Manlius, dropping two denarii on the counter, "give me the works. Who is she?"

"You mean the one in the litter?" asked Bobulus, squinting.

"Sure. The one with the silver wig."

"Her name," said Bobulus, "is Romula. She is the daughter of J. Romulus Comma of the . . ."

"Ye gods and goddesses!" Mannie smote his forehead. Could it be possible that he, the *Tiber's* star, had let Comma's daughter slip through his fingers? And all because of that dinky silver wig! He'd let her dazzle him, steal away his brains.

"Cut out the rest," he said to Bobulus, who was still talking, "and tell me who's that Greek lizard with her?"

"Not listed," snapped Bobulus and turned to another customer.

## IV

Q. BULBUS APEX and P. Manlius Scribo sat alone in the office of the *Evening Tiber.* The home edition had been on the street a couple of hours, and with nothing more than a stick-long item to cover the Comma case. The copyist-slaves had retired to their dens, the big room was very empty, the city editor's dyspeptic little face was stingily illumined by two cheap stone lamps. As he talked he was nervously experimenting with a reed pen on a sheet of papyrus. Papyrus, papyrus, papyrus. Old Calamity's darling idea.

"Then you really think," he said absent-mindedly, "that this little stabbing might open up into something? You've been pretty busy this afternoon. I hope you haven't run your legs off for nothing. You say you went to the morgue and found they'd moved the body over to Cleopatra's house?"

"Yes. And I went to Pompey's Theater and tailed Hesiod all the way over to there. Just as he was going in he saw me—I guess he'd seen me all the time."

"Did he say anything?"

"Sure. You know that big, fine voice of his. 'Hail, O Manlius. You must be at the funeral tomorrow. My poor friend will have the ceremony of a patrician. It is the will of Cæsar.' Tie that!"

"Well, Cæsar's loyal to his gang, seems to me."

"Yes, but was Comma a member of his gang? I told you about that *Sic Semper Tyrannis* locket. That doesn't look as if Comma was so hot for the Big Fella. Sort of smells of conspiracy. Suppose Comma had tied himself up with the Brutus-Cassius mob?"

"Hey. Don't be fantastic. . . . Nothing serious is going to happen to Cæsar, worse luck. He's too smart. Next you know you'll be accusing Cæsar of the stabbing."

"In a murder case you've got to suspect everybody."

"Who told you that?"

"Plato."

"Huh. Do you suspect Cæsar?"

"He's only a possibility, the way Anthony and Cleopatra and the dwarf and Brutus and Cassius and Hambonius and Hesiod are."

"You suspect Hesiod?"

"I would, probably. But he was crazy about Comma. And, remember, he didn't get back from Naples until Comma had been cold twelve hours."

"Well, don't go following Anthony around, accusing him."

"That so?" asked our cheeky young reporter. "Since he came here this morning, offering that shipload of papyrus, I suppose you killed that hot editorial you were writing about Dictators—"

"Look here, kid. Nobody can bribe this paper. If I killed that editorial it was because I felt like it—personally, see?"

"Yeah. But you took the papyrus, didn't you? And you're that much in Bull Anthony's debt. Also, while I'm on the subject, why did Anthony offer me that easy political job, just to lay off the Comma case? What does he want? The same thing that Cæsar wants? Is Anthony really working for Cæsar, or is he in the big *Sic Semper Tyrannis* ring, waiting a chance to bump the Big Fella off?"

"If I had your imagination," said Q. Bulbus, "I wouldn't waste my time on a daily journal. I'd go in for detective fiction." The editor, who had just finished a jar of cheap wine, looked up speculatively, "Listen. How 'bout that vestal virgin?"

"I've been after her. I dropped in at the Temple of Vesta and talked with the High Priestess. Ain't that old maid the vinegar? When I asked her if any of the virgins had been missing lately she asked me how could they be missing and be virgins at the same time. Then she read me a lecture on purity that would curdle your blood. Once a vestal, she said, it's impossible for you to do murder or anything else that's interesting. The virgins hate men so that they go to the gladiatorial shows to see 'em killed. Eight-thirty's the bed hour at the Temple of Vesta, and no pillow fights. The High Priestess says she's got a checking system so that none of the girls ever get out of her sight. She sicced the watch-dog on me, practically, and went on feeding the Eternal Fire."

"What's your conclusion?"

"That some woman's been going round Rome, disguised as a vestal virgin. What she's after I don't know. It's up to us to find out. But I'll bet my shirt that the killing of Comma was only a step in her program."

"But motives, kid. Motives!" said Q. Bulbus impatiently.

"Motives don't fly up and hit you in the face," replied Mannie, flushing. "If you think this story's worth following up, it's going to take time."

"Stop seeing things, Mannie. The politicians in this town are tough enough, the gods know, without wishing an extra murder on them. Why not be satisfied with the simple solution. Comma's red-headed daughter, assisted by that fighting dwarf—"

"She's five feet three and he's three feet five. Comma weighed a ton. The body was dragged forty feet—"

"I don't say they didn't have an assistant—"

"Gals who bump their fathers off don't act the way Romula did this morning. Or I'm no judge of human nature. She had something on her mind, but it wasn't murder."

"See here, boy. Are you letting that jane get you?"

*"Nuxes!"* [1] snorted P. Manlius Scribo.

"But where's she gone?"

"That's what I'm going to find out. I was pretty dumb, letting her give me the slip. But she won't do it again."

"Huh. She'll wind you round her thumb and wear you the way Cleopatra wears that famous amethyst of hers."

"I'll bet you a month's salary she doesn't." The set of Mannie's jaw proclaimed the singleness of his purpose.

"Well, you're too valuable a man to waste on a lot of false trails," said Old Calamity. "But I'll admit that things look funny. Making a Chief out of that big punk, Kellius. And you say you saw a vestal signaling Brutus and Cassius as they were going through the Forum?"

"Yes, and they returned it. Vestals are the last people to go round signaling to men, you know."

Q. Bulbus smacked his dry lips. "That seems to hook the crime up with a conspiracy. Brutus, Cassius, Casca and that bunch have formed the Progressive bloc in the Senate, and they've been accusing Cæsar of trying to junk the Republic for a monarchy. Now how does this story sound? Comma had something Brutus and Cassius wanted. They bribed the *puella* to swipe a vestal robe from Comma's theater, carve

---

[1] Nerts.

the old gent, steal the fatal document and make a getaway. How's that?"

"Not so awfully good," said Mannie. "Remember that Kellius, Cæsar's kept policeman, has been trying to hush up the crime. Do you think the Big Fella would have tried to protect Brutus and Cassius, if they'd had anything to do with it? Don't make me laugh."

"All right. But you say you saw a queer vestal giving Brutus and Cassius the mystic wiggle. Don't that hook up somewhere? And why wasn't she, Romula, reporting that the stabbing was over?"

"*Nuxes!* I'll bet she didn't even know her dad was dead when I talked to her. Certainly she didn't act like a gal who'd put on vestal robes and sliced her old man."

"Huh. She had plenty of time to change her clothes and calm down. Old Comma was stabbed fourteen hours or more before you saw her. Women can change their faces with their shoes. Looks sort of suspicious to me."

"Well, I'll admit you might stretch it to look that way. The vestal I saw might very easily have been the gal who did the job. Brutus and Cassius and the rest of the Progressive Party certainly wouldn't kill a man just to please Cæsar. Especially a man like Comma, who seemed to be in their conspiracy."

"You feel pretty sure about this conspiracy, don't you?"

"Don't you?" asked Manlius sharply.

"Well, the time may come. This is still a republic, after all. And when they suspect a man of wanting to be king—*Qrrrrk*—knife in the back. And that guy's all swollen up like a toothache. Half the time he goes strutting 'round like an actor in imperial purple robes."

"Yeah," agreed Mannie. "And half the time he's just his old, sweet self, a dirty, bald-headed soldier. Sometimes it looks as if there were two Cæsars in Rome—the dirty one and the pretty one."

"Hm. Look at the way he's had the priests make a god out of him. See what he's let 'em name his new statue? Jupiter Julius!"

"Jupiter Julius!" echoed Mannie. "Anyhow, it makes a swell cuss-word. Some of these days, maybe, he'll make a big feature story to use up that shipload of papyrus."

Old Calamity stirred uneasily. After all the gift of paper had mitigated his anti-Cæsar policy.

"Hey, listen," he muttered. "Wouldn't this make a grand front-page spread—*TIBER* WARNS CÆSAR OF KILLER PLOT! We'll round up the conspirators, save Cæsar and knock 'em cold."

"Yeah. But suppose there isn't any conspiracy."

"You just said there was," said Q. Bulbus.

"I said I guessed there was. Of course, if we warn Cæsar—and can prove our case—it'll be a good story. But if they bump him off it'll be the biggest news sensation that's struck Rome since the Punic Wars. But don't let's spoil it, O Boss, by springing it half baked."

"Who's the baker here, you or I?" creaked Q. Bulbus. "Say, look here! You say the *puella* is a stenog in the office of Marcus Tullius Cicero. You describe her as a little chunk off the rosy dawn. Comma was Cæsar's pet. All right. Suppose Romula was Cicero's pet. All right again. You know how Cicero and Cæsar love each other—the way a gumboil loves dry toast."

"And Cicero bribed her to commit patricide just to annoy Cæsar," jeered Manlius. "Say, did you ever hear of that old puritan looking at a gal? Even if he wanted to, his wife wouldn't let him." He paused for words. "That *puella* strikes me as being purer than a sacrificial lamb at the Altar of Vesta."

"*Dixisti.*[2] Anyhow, I'll agree with you on one point. The thing is to find the gal. Get a statement out of her. And about Comma's funeral."

"Tomorrow morning at dawn. I'm going to look 'em over."

"What's the idea?"

"Several ideas. In the first place, if Romula's innocent she'll certainly be there. If she's guilty she might show up, on the principle that the murderer always visits the scene of the crime. Anyhow, it's significant, this funeral. Under Cæsar's personal management. With Hesiod, the Big Fella's employee, delivering the funeral oration. If nothing else, it'll be worthwhile giving the crowd the once over."

"You might dig out a human interest story, anyhow," said Q. Bulbus. "But I want you to do the Orphans' Fresh Air Fund Gladiatorial Show this afternoon. Might pick up something on the Comma case. There's a front row, you know, reserved for vestal virgins. All Rome'll be there."

---

[2] Says you.

Old Calamity put on his shabby toga and vanished toward a small chop house where he always dined alone, gorging himself with hot sausages and a cheap Sicilian wine; then later he'd stagger back to a little room over the office and go to bed with the only mistress he had ever known, the *Evening Tiber.*

That, at least, was the Q. Bulbus Apex whom Manlius had known before cross-currents began drifting him into the tide of the Eternal City.

## V

STANDING outside in the narrow street the young reporter was considering his next move. It had grown dark, and at night Rome looked like a continuous torch-light procession. It was hard to move unless one had a torch-bearer; otherwise one might stumble over dead horses, dead citizens, whatever happened to drop out of the city's busy and mysterious night life. Cæsar's traffic law, permitting chariots on the streets after sunset, caused the stones to thunder with iron-shod hoofs and wheels. There were occasional screams, whoops and curses as chariots collided with litters, spilling gilded youths and golden girls up and down the narrow thoroughfares.

Mannie Scribo adored late hours; but tonight there was purpose in his hesitation when Smithicus approached him with a heavy torch. The sleuth-reporter was carefully considering his next move. Should he go back to the police-guarded *bungalorium* in the forlorn hope that Romula might return there? Or should he search the places where lovers meet, in hopes of coming across Romula and her Greek?

Somebody touched his elbow; looking around he saw Egregius Rector, a smart Jewish leg-man who did real estate, politics, finance and lodge meetings for the *Evening Tiber.*

"Hello, Mannie," said Eggie, his round Semitic eyes beaming. "You look worried."

"That's just a pose. Listen, Eggie. You know most of the night clubs. I'm on that Comma case—"

"Yeah. So I've heard."

"Did you ever run across Comma's daughter? Girl named Romula?"

"I'll say so. She's a gal about town. There's a funny looking Greek giving her an awful rush. Saw them twice last week."

"Where?" asked Mannie.

"You know the Club Hibernicus. You've never seen them there?"

"Guess I got the wrong nights. Join me?"

"No thanks. Got a date. If they'll be anywhere they'll be there. But you don't think—"

"I'm not thinking tonight. So long."

The Club Hibernicus was going strong, full of music and onion-smells and broken pottery. Manlius looked over the dining room of imitation black marble with the Sports of the Sea Nymphs very realistically illustrated on the walls. A familiar scene. The usual crowd. Four little Egyptian girls were playing harps—one of Hibernicus' innovations—to accompany a hungry-eyed *lumenata,* or torch-singer, from Capri who wriggled among the tables, giving 'em all the latest hits. This time it was "Maid of Athens Ere We Part," and nobody was listening very attentively.

"Well, well, well!" It was Hibernicus himself, every freckle doing its duty. "Sure, and if it ain't the lad Mannie. And late it is tonight, me young spalpeen. Faith and begorra."

Faith and begorra, a phrase which Hibernicus had popularized in Rome, proclaimed him a naughty wag with a *sens humoris.*

"Hello, Irish," said Manlius jauntily. "Why don't they put a padlock on this dump and improve the moral tone of our fair city?"

"Prrrrotection, Mannie." Hibernicus—or Hibe, as the boys all called him—gave a sly and Celtic wink. "Prrrrrotection is nine points of the law, and sometimes ten."

"That goes for murder as well as wine-smuggling," said Manlius on a sudden thought. "Ye gods! Are *they* here again?" He glowered over at a corner where, at a three-sided table, nine quite young Romans lay on elbows, arguing importantly and picking at their food. They were crowned with laurel.

"Yes," said Hibe disparagingly, "them Young Intellectuals. I suppose they advertise the place. Young fella Mascenas is a-payin' for 'em, when he's wid the parrty. If it wasn't fer that I'd t'row 'em out on their ear, I would. When they're spendin' their own money they can talk more and order less food—"

True journalist that he was, Manlius hated the smell of a poet. These ones were starting a literary futuristic movement, which included the junking of good old fashioned Latin for a lot of Athenian bunk that annoyed the standard writers and gave old Cicero, as the *sermo vulgaris* hath it, a pain in the neck.

But in finding his table, Manlius was obliged to pass close to them. Whereupon a plump poet named Scabaius Torso, who had popularized himself by an epic about seven pages longer than *Anthony Adverse,* came to his feet. Last year he had bankrupted his patron, trying to choke a Greek comedy called *Lysistrata* down the Roman throat.

"Hail Manlius! But stay a minute. Meet our new member. Publius Virgilius Maro, shake hands with P. Manlius Scribo. Come on, Virgil—can't tell when you'll need a write-up."

A thin young man got awkwardly up, dropping his laurel crown.

"Pleased to meet you," he said in a provincial accent.

"This boy Virgil may not look so much just now," said the cheerful Torso. "But know what he's going to do? Write the history of Rome in blank verse."

"Uh," said Manlius cordially.

"He's going to begin at the beginning, the siege of Troy—and we Romans *are* Greeks, aren't we?—and cover everything. Even Hell. He's going to show a lot of places in Hell where famous Romans go—"

"I'm for it," said Manlius. "Put me down for a copy."

"He's only got the first two lines written," said Torso. "But they're probably the only absolutely perfect lines ever written by a Roman. Come on, Virgil, oblige."

"Oh, he's not interested," argued Virgil, trying to lie down again.

"Of course he is. It's just because he's a journalist. They never look what they feel. Now, Virgil, the lines."

The scrawny young poet braced himself against the table and quoted in rather a fine voice:

*"Arma virumque cano, Trojes qui primus ab oris."* Then he stopped and swallowed hard. "That's as far as I remember," he said.

"But, Mannie, isn't it perfect?" asked Torso.

"Sure," said Manlius.

"Tell you what I'll do. I'll bet you ten talents, twenty, any amount, that that line will be immortal."

"When you bet on immortality," said P. Manlius Scribo, "how are you going to collect?"

Then he crossed the room and found the table where the newspaper crowd usually ate, sitting upright like barbarians.

Two reporters from the *Tiber,* having finished dinner, were shooting a kind of knucklebone dice for the drinks. "Uh—*vent Suza-nula!"* [3] or *"Die lente, infans!"* [4] chimed with the rattle of the bones. Manlius, having handed his toga to Smithicus and ordered a good lamb stew for that hearty—to be served, of course, in the kitchen—found a seat next to a forlorn fellow named Cupidus, who did criminal news and politics for the *Daily Astra.* As the *Astra* came out about once a fortnight, and usually late at that, these rival reporters discussed their work with a sort of guarded candor. Cupidus, rather tight, was finishing a dessert of honey-cake and sour cream. A waiter brought in a second flagon of clear amber liquid labeled "CX Proof."

"Try a shot of that," commanded Cupidus. "It would grow hair on Cæsar's head, I bet."

Cupidus must have been pretty well gone to say a thing like that; the *Astra* was a damp, mildly pro-Cæsar publication. Manlius poured out two fingers of the stuff, strangled and reached for water.

*"Gemini!"* he coughed. "What do you call it? Canned lava?"

"It's a secret lost to the world," said Cupidus thickly but sadly. "Something we should-a discovered thousand years ago. Fire wine, boy—forty-fi per cent alcohol—whoopee! Invented by genius—make happy world, says he. But the secret's lost. Lost. Lost."

"That's the way it always happens," sobbed Manlius. "Find formula to make world happy—then some nut goes and loses it."

"Ain't that a mouthful? Spanish inventor found how to grind up corn, gemme, kid? Boil it till it turns to this magic juice. Neighbors said he was bewitched. Search me. Anyhow, the Proconsul of Spain had him drowned in last vat of this. Trust Hibe—pull like a mustard plaster. What you think he did? Sent to Spain and bought up the last vat—"

"With the Spaniard still in it?" asked Manlius.

"Sure. Try another."

After the second drink Manlius was all a-glow, as though loving kindness had been shot into him with a poison arrow. However, he was fortified with the knowledge that he was a

---

[3] Come on, little Suzie.
[4] Speak soft, baby.

great deal soberer than Cupidus when he asked casually, "Anything new on your beat today?"

"I'm a galley slave, if that's new. Covering the water-front and the Senate, all in the same day. Oh, my sore feet. Have to walk 'way over to that old barn the Senate's using as a Curia, then hoof it back to the Tiber Wharves to meet a ham actor."

"Been interviewing Hesiod?" Manlius tossed off carelessly.

"And how. O Mars! What a swell-in-the-head that guy's got. Came in on Cleopatra's own barge, mind you. Me there, promptly at noon. The Levantine Squaw's gilt boat got in half an hour late. You'd think that ham was doing me a favor, letting me hear about himself and how Naples ate out of his hand."

"He's the world's greatest mirror-kisser," agreed Manlius, helping himself to olives when the pork pie came on.

"Rather interview actors than senators," said Cupidus unsteadily. "And look at those Government jobs. Never get done. Capitol Building's developed a crack as wide as the Tiber. Big Fella's ordered the Senate over to that fire-trap on the Campus Martius, till repairs are done. Have another spot of this Spanish shampoo?"

"No, thanks. Has Senator Casca been braying some more?"

"Wow! There's a little group of wilful men up there ought to be put out of their misery. Knock Cæsar, that's the slogan."

"Huh. What's a Dictator for, if he can't have his say?"

"*O borax!* Let those yaps blow off steam. Didn't Cæsar pass his Centurion Bonus Bill over their heads? Even with a Senate that's a hold-over from the Democratic administration. Trust ole Mark Anthony to whip 'em into line."

"Yeah. And we're saddled with another half billion sesterces." Manlius tossed off another potion of the fire-wine, and began to like it. "Where we going to get the money, hey?"

"Gee Lucifer!" chortled Cupidus. "Where does Rome ever get the money? She grabs it. With the Soldiers' Bonus paid off, Cæsar has the army behind him. He's packed, practically, for that Parthian expedition. Parthia. That's the big money. Why, they say the Parthian ladies wear ruby buttons on their—"

"Yeah? Remember what happened to the big banker, Crassus, when he appointed himself field marshal and went up there to collect those buttons? The Parthians have a wicked habit of retreating and shooting over their horses' tails."

"Cæsar won't be any such target," said Cupidus. "He's thin as a straw."

"He's overworked. Dr. Hilarius says he has a gall bladder."

"Who hasn't?" asked Cupidus comfortably. "And remember, old boy, Cæsar's a god."

"Ain't that the truth," said Mannie. "He elected himself unanimously to that job. And, since gods are immortal—"

Just then a malignant echo behind Manlius seemed to be saying a fateful thing. A little drunk, he wasn't sure; he turned, but there was nobody there. *"Cæsar moriturus est."* Had the forty-five per cent drink played this trick on him? "Cæsar is going to die," the voice had said. Suddenly sobered, Manlius let his keen eyes travel across the room. The young man at the next table was quarreling with his girl. Other tables; men chucking dice, or throwing coins to the Egyptian string quartette, or passing notes to the torch-singer from Capri. Over in the poet's corner the big kid they called Virgil was beginning to cry, and Scabaius Torso, also unsteady in the legs, was leading him home.

Cupidus was gibbering foggily of the glories of the Administration, and Manlius wasn't paying much attention. That whisper about the death of Cæsar went further to justify his hunch, and he would have concentrated on his next move had not Cupidus' sudden remark brought him back to earth.

"Understand," said Cupidus, licking his numb lips, "that you covered that funny little Comma murder."

"You've said it," acknowledged Manlius. "Anything to it?"

"You ought to know." Cupidus tried to focus his eyes, gave up the attempt. His next speech was foggily revealing. "You can have that story, if you want it. The *Astra* ain't going to touch it."

"Why? Too insignificant?"

"Yeah. Too insignificant." Cupidus' crooked stare held a depth of meaning. "It was probably suicide—what?"

"Probably. Theatrical Man Cuts His Own Throat With Axe. Good headline, in a way."

"Undignified. Even if Brutus and Cassius furnished the axe, we wouldn't print it. Undignified still. Undig—un—"

Cupidus wasn't doing very well with long Latin words, and his mind went straying with unconsecutive thoughts. "Costs money to be a dictator—lots o' money—'specially when you gotta buy jewelry for an Egyptian sweetie—"

"He might simplify by letting Anthony take over her bills."

"Huh?" Cupidus wasn't listening. "Ever see that amethyst she wears on her thumb? Blue amethyst. Only one like it in the world. Just like human eye. Terrible. Cleopatra's third eye—hic—sees everything. . . ."

Cupidus laid his head on the marble top and went to sleep.

Meanwhile Mannie's eyes, a little fogged by the pleasantly biting CX Proof, went wandering over the crowd, in search of a silver wig, or a red-head, or a Greek dude with clanking jewelry. Wolfishly he gobbled his dinner, just remembering that he had had nothing substantial since early morning. He was thinking, "I'm wasting my time here. They won't show up. It's too public. I've got to be on my way."

He arose, a little unsteadily—that CX Proof had something in it, he felt. He found Hibernicus, overdoing the hearty host, moving among the tables. Seizing him, Mannie approached the subject directly. "Say, Hibe, what's the name of that Greek effect who brings Romula in here?"

"Greek? Romula?" Rather transparently Hibe was being confused. "Sure and bejabbers I don't remember such a combination."

In a flash, born of alcohol, Mannie spoke up. "Julius Cæsar has a controlling interest in this joint, eh what?"

"Ye're talkin' in figures of speech," said Hibe, pushing Mannie back toward his table. "Now set down and listen to our torch-singer. Her name's Doris—"

"She's great. I've heard her."

But Mannie went back and sat down. It was hard to concentrate. Too much noise. The voluptuous torch-singer was circling among the tables, wriggling and dispensing popular ditties. She came to his table; Egyptian harps whanged while she worked her knees and shoulders for Manlius, a hot favorite at Hibe's, and stridently sang:

"By the Nile-bank, soft and reedy,
What could a little girl do?

Cleo's life was not so speedy—
   What could a little girl do?
*Till* one day a Roman geezer
*With* the famous eagle beezer
Said, 'Hello, I'm Julius Cæsar!'
   What could the little girl do?

" 'Queen,' he said, 'you knock me silly.'
   What could the little girl do?
She replied, 'I'm not so chilly—
   But what can a little girl do?
*If* you feel you love no other
*Your* affections you must smother,
*For* I'm married to my brother—
   What can a little girl do?'

" 'Kid,' he said, 'your tale's tempestuous—'
   What can a pretty girl do?
'*But* it sounds a bit incestuous—'
   What can a pretty girl do?
Leave this small-town lotus thicket,
Come to Rome where we'll play cricket.
I am paying for the ticket.'
   What could the little girl do?

"Now the Lady of the Lotus—
   What does the little girl do?
Lives in style—but please don't quote us—
   What does the little girl do?
Cæsar, who should be in clover,
When he calls to pet his plover
Yells, 'Mark Anthony, move over!'
   What can a little girl,
   What can a pretty girl
      Do—
      Lilly—oo, doo—do?"

"Baby," said Manlius, during a pause between verses, "you've got a nerve, bawling out the Cæsar-Cleopatra-Anthony triangle like that."

"Oh, I just sing what's handed to me," she giggled.

"Well, look out that you don't get something hotter handed to you."

The girl leaned over for another kiss or two, and Manlius got the heavy shock of the evening, so far. Something which had been buried in the crease of her copious breasts fell out and swung on a chain from her neck. A plain silver locket.

"Baby," drawled Manlius, "you'd better keep your safe deposit box locked, or—" Deftly he reached out and took hold of the disk.

The girl snatched at it, but he had already snapped it open. Just as he thought. A Gorgon's head on one side, and on the other the familiar motto, *Sic Semper Tyrannis.* "Quite interestin'," he yawned, "quite amusin'."

"Fresh egg, ain't you?" said the girl from Capri.

"Funny," he said, "that a swell *puella* like you should be wearing something from the five-and-ten. It's not your type. You don't belong in the lower bracket, Doris. Why not amethysts?"

"Oh, yeah? Suppose you hang me with amethysts, big boy."

"Doris, tell you what. I'll fetch you something fancy, if you'll give me that piece of tin and tell me where you got it."

The girl sat beside him and fixed him with her china-blue eyes. "What's the ideer? Want to write me up?"

"Sure. I'll give you half a column, any time you say. How 'bout that toy dish pan?" Smilingly Manlius was concealing his inner excitement.

"A ge'l'man friend gave it to me."

"Who's the gentleman friend?"

"Malarius, that big German gladiator. Works for Senator Casca."

"Well, little girl, I don't think Malarius is going to come round very soon."

"Why not?"

"He got his in the arena day before yesterday."

"Really?" Doris lifted her plucked eyebrows. That was the way they took their gladiators in Rome. "Here today and there tomorrow," she said. "I never thought his uppercut was much."

"Punk," said Manlius. "So Malarius gave you that thing."

"Well, it was like this," she explained in her funny high voice. "One of Malarius' jobs was to help Senator Casca home when he was plastered. And one night, a couple weeks ago, when the Senator fell out of his litter, Malarius found this locket in the mud. Later on Malarius come around to get a drink in the back room, the way the police and the gladiators do, and he said to me, 'I'll probably drop it going home to training quarters. Would you take care of it until I can get it back to the Senator?' That was that, if you like to hear me waste my breath."

"Well," said Manlius, "since Malarius is practically finished, suppose I give it back to Senator Casca."

"I know you newspaper boys!" She cuddled and pulled his ear. "Nice ears. You wear 'em right. Close to your head, I mean. And I don't like earrings on men, the way them Greeks wear 'em."

"I'm looking for a Greek," said Manlius, taking advantage of her melting mood. "The one that's giving Comma's daughter such a rush."

"Oh, that feller named Homer. What's he done?"

"Nothing that I know of, except make himself scarce. Who is he? Where does he hang out?"

"Dunt esk," lisped Doris. "Here at Hibe's we don't know nothin' about anybody, so long as they pay up. And did he pay up? Spent with both hands and one foot. If I was Comma I'd get after that lad with a sharp javelin."

Apparently she hadn't heard of Comma's death; in spite of the *Tiber,* news traveled slowly in Rome; probably Doris didn't read very much.

"But if you want to find him," suggested Doris, "why don't you ask Romula?"

"Swell idea," said Manlius innocently. "I suppose she'll be 'round some of the night clubs."

"No, I guess she's home tonight, for once."

"Why?" Her suggestion had almost sobered him.

"An hour or so ago, just as I was comin' on for the night, I saw her in one o' them hired carts, drivin' out toward the Wall."

"Alone?"

"How can you be alone, foolish, when you have a hired driver? Oh, gosh. I gotta go on again."

The Egyptian string quartette piped up another new one entitled, "Give My Regards to the Appian Way," and Doris was on her feet again, wiggling and singing.

Manlius tottered toward the door, replying to Hibe's hearty protest, "Gotta sleep some time. Goo' ni'."

The Spanish elixir had affected his legs and tongue, but his mind went smoothly on. The possibility of finding Romula seemed to work, wheel in wheel, with the story Doris had told about Senator Casca's locket. Senator Casca, whom even Cicero had referred to as *asinus ferox,* or wild jackass, after the little Progressive Party's champion had put up a bray for public ownership and inflation. Senator Casca, all too chummy with the radicals, Brutus and Cassius. Hm. *Sic Semper Tyrannis,* sinister words, like a sign written across the Seven Hills.

Yes. But Romula. How close did she come to a deadly plot, which seemed to spread like an octopus over sleeping Rome? Was she the dove, pursued by hawks? Was she the hawk itself, disguised in dove feathers? Manlius, steadying his legs, pondered this.

It was Smithicus who took advantage of the pause to approach him.

"Sorry, sir," he said drearily, "but do you think that by any chance this might be of use to us in our detective work?"

Out of his lavish tunic he fished a flagon, half filled with a deep amber liquid. "Some of that corn-wine, sir," he explained. "I found it on the table in front of the lordly Cupidus, who seemed quite outdone with it. Quite. As a beverage it seems a bit hot. But as a sleeping potion it might come in handy, if properly applied."

"No sleep till morn," said Manlius. "Call a litter."

Once inside the litter Mannie lay back and sighed. "I'm a lone wolf," he reflected. It did seem unfair. A modern detective would have had at least two dozen assistants to shadow every shady corner in Rome. But you couldn't expect too much, back in 44 B.C.

So P. Manlius Scribo went to sleep.

## VI

"WE'RE here, sir," said the voice of Smithicus.

Mannie awoke and looked out. A ghostly moon, flooding over Hesperides Avenue, revealed a small moving van, hitched to a white mule, standing in front of Comma's house. The short sleep had sobered our reporter, so that everything was etched clearly, black on silver. And a faint streak of yellow light was coming through a downstairs window.

"Take the litter round the corner and wait," said Manlius softly to his bearers. "Here, Smithicus, take my sword."

"Quite," said the Briton, weighing the practical-looking hilt affectionately; slaves, even gladiators, were not permitted to go armed on the streets.

"Stand there against the wall," said the master. "Make yourself small as possible, and don't come unless I yell."

Mannie loosened the long straps around his ankles, took off his shoes and handed them to his slave. Barefoot he tiptoed around the house on a silent tour of inspection. The back yard, where acrobats practised by day, was bare and bald as Cæsar's head. Crawling on all fours, Manlius stared under the back porch. Moonlight, sifting in, showed nothing but tumbled sacks. The midget, then, was gone.

Now for the window with the light. Ashamed of peeping, but driven by the urge to know, he lifted himself to the sill, braced his toes in a convenient crack and looked inside. A wick flickered in a goose-necked lamp, bringing tender lights from the red gold of Romula's hair. She was in a simpler gown than he had seen her wear before; her face was very white, her eyes dreamily preoccupied as she knelt there, carefully taking small cylinders out of a big box, opening them at one end, taking out scrolls of papyrus, reading hastily. Some she would put back into the box, others she would drop into a little leather chest by her side.

Manlius clung like a lizard, watching. She looked so pitifully young and helpless, alone in the house of her murdered father, sorting out his possessions. The color of her lovely hair seemed to stain the room with Comma's blood. Then unexpectedly—possibly a pebble had dropped from the window sill—she looked up and saw him. Her mouth came open. She was trying to scream; but no sound came.

"Romula, don't be afraid. This is Manlius Scribo." Trying to make his voice steady.

"What do you want?" fluttered her scared treble.

"To help you, Romula—honest—to help—"

Without a word she closed the box and the leather chest, then crossed the room and shot back the bolt of the door. Crushing down his excitement, Mannie ran around to the front and saw her waiting for him in a yellow square of light. She bolted the door again when he came in. So there she stood, her hands behind her, her little head thrown back as wild eyes looked up at him.

"Why do you follow me?" she asked.

"Little girl," said Manlius, trying to keep impatience out of his tone, "do you realize that you're the central figure in a murder case?"

"Oh." Her voice was startled, worried. "You don't think I could possibly—that I could—"

"That's the trouble with the newspaper game, I'm afraid. We don't think. We find out."

"You have no right to meddle with my affairs like this."

The way she said it made him feel pretty small, and he said, "Romula, you're the last person in the world I want to find guilty. This afternoon I spoke out of turn, I guess."

"Then why—"

"I'm on this case, that's all. If you're innocent—and the gods know I want you to be—I'll bust my fool neck to clear you. If you'll help—"

"I—I can't help."

Gosh, it was a sin to bother her, standing there like a little statue of woe. Mannie could have swallowed his dagger.

"Look at the facts against you," he said, "Comma found cold, with red hair in his hand. You'd been quarreling. You stayed out that night. Some female, probably red-headed, comes back in vestal robe, spears Comma, escapes. How can you help being suspected?"

"Do you suspect me, Manlius Scribo?"

What could a gentleman in love say under the circumstances?

"No," said Mannie.

"But will you keep on—what do you call it?—investigating?"

"Sure will."

"Manlius." Her hands went up to his shoulders, an almost unconscious caress, and remarkably pleasant. "Manlius, don't go on with this. It won't do you any good. It may do me all sorts of harm."

"Can you beat that? How will it do you harm?"

"I can't tell you."

"Listen to me, kid." Somehow his arm had gone around her. "Comma was Cæsar's friend. Kellius has been acting awfully funny, I'll admit—but nothing can make me believe that he isn't trying to work this case out on his own. He's such a fat-head, Romula—"

"And you think he'll haul me in?"

"On the evidence, who can blame him?"

"I'm not afraid." She sprang away from him, a confident smile on her lips. Mannie wanted to slap her or hug her or something.

"All right—" he tried a new tack—"if you won't protect yourself, or help me, think of the duty you owe to the dead man. Don't you believe in ghosts? Well, Comma's is yelling for vengeance."

"Comma?" Her little face grew hard. "Comma? I hated him. He hated me."

"How can a Roman girl think those things of her father?" he scolded.

"But if I'd known—if they'd let me know—I'd have done my best to keep them from—doing that—" She gulped down the speech.

"Then tell me this." He tried being gentle. "Do you really know who killed Comma?"

"I can't tell you anything. Please go."

"Not until—"

"I'm not in danger, if that's what you think. But, Manlius, you are. Any minute they'll be coming."

"Who?"

"Never mind. But if they find you here you'll never get out alive. If you love me—at least go. I'll tell you some day. I'll—"

The sound of iron-shod wheels, bumping roughly on the cobbles outside. The girl's hand was on Mannie's sleeve, drawing him behind a tall, marble screen, protecting the entrance to Comma's bath. "Stay here," she whispered. And in that second he felt her lips brush his forehead.

There was an ornate grille cut through the marble, a convenient lookout. Here Manlius crouched, a hand on his dagger, prepared to spring to the girl's defense. But when Romula opened the door, responsive to three loud knocks, the highly decorative visitor was all deference. He was the bearded Greek they called Homer.

"Yes." His voice lacked the Athenian lisp and sounded very Roman. "I dismissed that slow cart outside. You see I've brought six mounted gladiators and a fast chariot. You should not have come here alone. I had arranged to bring you over."

Manlius' heart beat rapidly as he watched her look the Greek straight in the eye.

"I've not been annoyed," she said.

"Good. Are the papers all ready to go?"

"Almost." She went over to within a foot of where Manlius was hiding, opened the box and knelt beside it. The Greek followed and stood so close to the screen that the reporter clutched his dagger more tightly. Romula was searching, searching in the box.

"She'll be at the funeral," said Homer in a low voice. "Anybody else could do it. But she's temperamental. Likes the excitement—"

"Hush!" cautioned Romula, looking up from the box.

"Don't worry, child. Nobody can hear but the gladiators, and they're Germans. Hope that midget of yours isn't snooping around."

"No. He ran away somewhere." Romula still searched the box.

"She'll signal the right party. You know. Two jerks of the hand. He'll be needed this afternoon. Same old stunt." A short chuckle.

"I don't see why you need him for that. It's so foolish—"

"You won't think so—later. We'll tell you, when the time comes. Meanwhile, don't be afraid of him. He won't annoy you any more."

"You don't mean—" nervously.

"I don't mean anything."

"Then hush." She scrambled deeper into the box. "I can't find it. I must have left it at—"

"We mustn't stay here any longer," he cautioned. "Probably you'll remember tonight where you last saw it."

"I felt sure it was here—" But she closed the wooden box and pointed to the leather chest. "Will you carry it? It's light."

He picked it up, swung toward the door, Romula following. She stood there a moment, the lamp raised above her glowing head, her eyes turned almost beseechingly toward Mannie's hiding place. "Trust me," she seemed to be saying. Then she blew out the light. The closing door blotted the moon. Somewhere outside iron-shod wheels and iron-shod hoofs clattered away furiously, growing fainter.

Finally Manlius groped his way out and found Smithicus. Together they relighted the lamp and went searching every corner of the room. The box itself revealed nothing but a few old clothes. It was Mannie's trained eye which discerned a small object in a shadowy corner where, perhaps, it had fallen during the search. He picked it up in his hand, examined it quizzically. A little wax doll, such as peasant children played with. Its clothes were shabby, its face half melted away. Could this be what she had been searching for so feverishly? Possibly. At any rate, it was something of Romula's. He slipped it into the pocket of his toga.

## VII

MANLIUS awoke in his humble lodgings; the iron hand of his gladiator-valet rolled him over until he all but fell out of one of those queer beds on which Romans slept.

"Your tub, sir," said Smithicus, indicating a gigantic tin bowl which the Briton had got somewhere. What an insult to the cultured Roman, accustomed to princely baths and the soft hands of anointing slaves. But with a look of grim determination the Briton poured water out of a jug which, even at a distance, looked ice cold.

"If you'll permit me saying so, sir, I should suggest that you take it rather chilled. In Britain we find it quite bracing after a bit of a binge. And we should be pushing on soon, sir."

Plop! Holy Boreas! The frozen pain of it brought Manlius back to his senses, and in a quarter of an hour master and man were hurrying toward the Via Appia where important funerals were held.

Yesterday at dinner Mannie had about made up his mind to stay away from Comma's funeral, since it offered few prospects of drama. But after the Greek's muttered hints in the *bungalorium* last night the reporter's brief and troubled dreams had been throbbing with the question, Who's going to signal who, and what? On his way to the Via Appia he grew wider awake, and puzzled again over Romula's queer attitude. She was afraid. She didn't want help. She wouldn't tell anything. She hated Comma. She would have saved him, if she could. The Greek had a certain power over her. She had risked something to come back and get some papers. Papers in which she and the Greek, apparently, had a mutual interest. And she had mislaid a doll.

Dolefully he remembered the look she had given him, her lamp raised by the door. Castor and Pollux! Had the gods sent him out to destroy the girl?

In spite of Comma's inferior rank as a freedman and an actor, his cremation had something of senatorial dignity. True, it was not a first-class *columbarium* where they were about to lay his ashes away; but it was at least the resting place of some prosperous knights.

The funeral was well under way, and it had the look of something being staged at Pompey's Theater. A group of chorus men, clad as warriors, chanted an ode to Comma, written for the occasion. Like most chorus men, they chewed the words so that they didn't make sense. The funeral pyre, built like a log cabin, of Grade A sacred wood, showed the corpse on a cloth of scarlet. Priests, bearing a statue of Thespis, marched three times round, calling upon the dead; a signal for six pairs of imitation gladiators to pair off and fight with wooden swords. A silly kind of performance, thought the sports reporter, who hated to see a fight where nobody was killed.

Mannie Scribo, there ostensibly to write up the ceremony, really to scan the crowd and its behavior, muttered, "G. Pluto, who's paying for this funeral?" when four important-looking undertakers came in, burdened with a vast harp of pink roses with the astonishing motto in white immortelles, "Rest in Peace—from C.J.C." So that was it. Cæsar, himself, probably backing the whole show. Then, as a crowning sensation, Mark Anthony, as a prominent patron of Pompey's Theater, strode solemnly in, clad in the dirty brown robe of mourning. And on his arm, more astonishing still, little Senator Casca, leader of the anti-Cæsar bloc!

Now the actor-gladiators had finished their mumming and Hesiod, the actor, stalked majestically in front of the pyre. Hesiod, the wonder of the age; Mannie recalled how, last winter, he had mimicked Brutus, Cassius, Tamany of Athens, Cleopatra, all in one performance. Now, in the pose of the lordly Hector, his gilded armor flashed in the sun. Heroically he flourished his wooden sword, slanted his paper shield, then in his fine, round voice began the funeral oration:

"Romans, our Comma, whom Thespis has crowned with flowers and the muses with a starry diadem, is no more. . . ."

The same old hooey, reflected Manlius and turned impatiently; Mark Anthony too had turned and was gazing through the wide arch into the street outside. As though an invisible dagger had pricked him in the back, Mannie jumped around, followed Anthony's look. A veiled woman in white was leaning out of a chalk-white litter. A vestal virgin!

She lifted her hand, almost level with her forehead, then lowered it, lifted it again. There was the flash of an enormous blue stone, worn on the thumb! Then the curtains fell together. A frivolous pink ribbon fluttered on one of the litter poles.

All in the space of two heart beats. Instinctively Manlius looked around for Anthony; there was his large figure, vanishing under a small arch in the opposite direction. The vestal had signaled him! The same soft sign she had given Brutus and Cassius in the Forum yesterday. He must come. He would be needed. What was it the Greek had whispered to Romula last night?

Almost instantly Manlius was on the move, rushing into the street; but the vestal's litter had two hundred yards the start of him, the Nubians trotting at a fast clip. However, the reporter was gaining on it inch by inch and might have run it down had not a half-dozen gladiators, plodding drunkenly along in their iron-soled shoes, lurched in his way and knocked him sprawling across the cobbles.

"Take that and that and that!" It was Smithicus, swatting manfully right and left. The men of blood, unused to the British fist, fell like so many ninepins and lay neatly stretched out in a row.

"Well played, Smithicus," said Manlius. "You couldn't have done better with a cestus."

"I never cared much for those iron boxing gloves, sir," said Smithicus.

The largest of the gladiators was finally able to sit up and murmur, "What did you hit me with? A tombstone?"

But Manlius was in no mood to bandy tombstones.

"Who told you gorillas to block me?" he asked harshly.

The gladiator's thumb made a hitch-hike motion toward the litter, now disappearing through an alley.

"Well, what's her name? Who is she?"

"All vestal virgins look alike to me, boss," said the gladiator. "She just slipped us the price of a drink and told us what to do. So we done it."

"Did she mention me in particular?"

"No. She just said she didn't want to be follered. And if she was, she said, we'd know what to do."

So the four gladiators, being by necessity an insensitive lot, scrambled to their feet and rolled merrily away toward the nearest saloon. Too late now, Manlius hurried back to the *columbarium.* The funeral was over; and Senator Casca was not among the crowd filing out.

Experienced detectives favor three methods of tracing down a crime; induction, deduction and seduction. Sometimes they will choose one way, sometimes another, sometimes all three at once. Inductively Manlius Scribo took it for granted that a crime had been committed; deductively he realized that a great many queer things had happened; seductively he had to admit that *cherchez la femme* had been, thus far, considerable of a flop.

But events, pressing around him, seemed to be carrying him on toward some sensational conclusion. It was like one of the new-fangled Greek plays which Virgil's gang were always trying to choke down the Roman throat—everything looked like a puzzle, then all of a sudden, you woke up and guessed what it was all about. Twice, in as many days, he had seen the guilty vestal—Brutus, Cassius and Anthony, all concerned in the same plot. It gave the reporter some consolation to know that Romula was, quite evidently, not the white-robed virgin who had driven the knife into Comma's throat. But that comfort was dulled by a memory of what she must have known last night, whispering to the Greek. And what were those papers she had taken such a risk to carry away? Try as he would to white-wash Romula, his common sense told him that she knew too well the import of the vestal's wig-wagging hand. Yes, and the great blue amethyst, flashing on her thumb. Cleo . . . impossible. But was anything impossible nowadays in Rome?

Back to Mannie's inner ear came an echo of a drunken voice, caught out of the crowd at Hibe's Cafe last night. "Cæsar is going to die."

How? By the same quick hand that had laid Comma low in his humble *bungalorium?*

Manlius was gobbling a dish of beans at a quick lunch place on the edge of the Campus Martius when in came Egregius Rector, the *Evening Tiber's* routine man. As Mannie Scribo's chief admirer, Eggie was always ready to do anything for him, within reason, and since the star reporter had dashed off a brilliant account of the funeral—omitting, of course, its most dramatic point—he found a way of making Eggie useful.

"I've sent my slave over to the office with the story," he said, "and now I've got to cover the Fresh Air Fund Gladiatorial Show. Partly business, partly pleasure. I'm going there to watch both the fighters and the vestal virgins. The vestals never miss it."

"Yeah. There must be some connection between purity and bloodthirstiness," agreed Eggie, his round Semitic eyes snapping. Manlius had told him briefly of the Comma plot and its more important possibilities. You couldn't keep anything from Eggie, and he was as safe as he was willing to help.

"Old Calamity's sending over Pulvius Sex to do the society end," said Eggie.

"What have you got on the fire this afternoon?" asked Mannie.

"My story's in," said Eggie. "I'm looking up some real estate transfers, but they can hold till tomorrow. What can I do for you?"

"Get after Senator Casca. Tail him. See where he goes, what he's doing with his time, where he's been at night lately." Manlius brought out one of the lockets, showed the motto inside and gave it to his confrere. "Go to all the pawnshops handy and see if they've got others like it. But keep your eye on Casca."

"What has Senator Casca got to do with a theatrical murder?"

"That's what I'm trying to find out."

"Well," said Eggie, "Old Calamity says he don't think the vestal did it. It don't look natural."

"What does in Rome nowadays?" asked Manlius Scribo, tossing a sesterce to the waiter and reaching for a toothpick. Then he wended his way toward the Fresh Air Fund gladiatorial combat, which was to be for the benefit of the Hippocrates Hospital for Orphans.

He had reported so many of these combats that they were beginning to get tiresome to him. But people liked his vicious, biting style of doing a sports column. Today there was the added excitement of mystery in the air, of a spiritual something snapping electrically over the Eternal City. The day was bright, but trouble seemed to cover the arena like a threatening cloud.

The usual mob, only a trifle politer than at the big popular butcheries. In Section A, reserved for senators, nearly a hundred old gentlemen, looking for all the world like so many statues, sat in their white draperies. There were many recognizable faces in the grandstand, among them Clodia and Fulvia and Mucia, merry widows, both grass and sod, their lipsticked mouths and penciled eyebrows, under enormous wigs, trying to stare Time out of countenance. These old girls had swung a mean love-light in their day. In actual years, they ranged between forty and fifty—very old in ancient Rome. All of their stories wove around Cæsar, in one way or another. Mucia, for instance, had amused him all too well when Pompey was away at war. Fulvia was still Mark Anthony's legal wife—and look how Mark was behaving with Cæsar's own Cleopatra. And Clodia, naughty sister of naughty Clodius. . . .

Hello! Speaking of Clodius, see who's here now; that pretty, plump, comfortable matron, mincing her way to her seat. Pompeia herself, by the mirror of Venus! Clodia's brother was the cause of it all. Pompeia was Cæsar's second try at matrimony; about fifteen years ago the Big Fella had been in Spain or somewhere, pacifying the country with a battering ram. One night he came home without any advance notice. Just unlocked the front door in time to find Clodius jumping out of a bathroom window. Sly old bird, Cæsar. Did he call in the cops, as some would have done, and have Clodius fried? Not Cæsar. He gave Pompeia the most respectable divorce in history—and elevated Clodius to a major generalship!

Manlius, watching, studied Cæsar's ex-wife as she took her reserved seat, not so far from the Dictator's golden chair. Sedately she took a vanity case from her handmaiden and powdered her nose. Another one of your die-hards was Pompeia; she might still stage a good scandal. . . . Fulvia sat two seats beyond her, pretending not to notice. There was a secret rivalry between these two ladies, Pompeia planning to win back the Conqueror she had lost, Fulvia crazy to drop her Anthony and grab Cæsar before some other wishful matron got there first. Yeah. But what about Cleopatra? In spite of everything, she had Cæsar around her thumb, like that famous amethyst. . . . Heigho! These women. . . .

And now the vestals came filing in, a long, white line of purity, led by the high priestess. They took their seats, as was their ancient custom, on the tier nearest the arena. On a purple dais above their heads a golden curile chair, awaiting Cæsar, hinted at the imperial gesture, growing rapidly more pronounced in the Big Fella. Across the way, in the open bleachers, the mob raised its lusty *vox populi.*[5]

Manlius in the press box, surrounded by the subservient journalists who gathered news from Cæsar's free billboards, gazed narrowly at the white vestal row. There were twenty-six seats reserved for them; rapidly Manlius counted the pale line, filing in. Three, five, nine, fourteen, twenty-one, twenty-four, twenty-five, twenty-six—and twenty-seven! Again he counted, as they were seating themselves. Twenty-seven. An extra vestal. One on the end was left standing. But only for a second. Deftly a slave slipped a chair under her, and the white line sat compacted into an unbroken formation.

Then the braying of the Legionaries' short field trumpets. The crowd came to its feet, right hands raised, roar after roar saluting the man-god who, not so long ago, marched into Rome on a bet and financed his own dictatorship by looting the bullion from the Temple of Saturn. C. Julius Cæsar, the train of his purple robe dragging far behind him, a wreath of bays sitting on his bald head like parsley on a hard-boiled egg, his right hand clasping a jeweled marshal's baton which, from the press box, looked mighty like a scepter, advanced with measured tread, graciously bowing as he came toward the chair of state, which from the press box looked mighty like a throne. Centurions with drawn swords guarded him right and left; a swanking general in a uniform with a slightly Egyptian touch—Mark Anthony himself—bowed the Dictator to the seat of honor.

The citizens of a free republic roared salvo upon salvo to their successful tyrant. The press box alone kept its head. P. Manlius Scribo was especially calm. He had seen Cæsar, maybe fifty times, on public occasions and at work in the Senate. He had interviewed him twice. But today the *Tiber's* keen representative made a mental note: The Big Fella's getting self-conscious. He's not the hard-boiled old cam-

---

[5] These open air spectacles were usually arranged for spring and fall, when the weather was mild. But the year 44 B.C. enjoyed an especially mild winter.

paigner, a little bored with public appearances, a little stiff in the elbows. Every move's a picture. Oh, violets! The old fool is getting graceful, like a professional orator. Or an actor. It's lucky he's going to start that war with Parthia. He'll be on the job again, in a dirty tunic, bossing a battering ram crew personally. This life is too soft for him. He's getting to be a damned Persian. Yes, Cæsar had changed a lot, even since last Wednesday when Manlius saw him in the Senate.

The gladiatorial show was in full swing. There had been two draws, three kills and one bad fizzle when Cæsar, as Editor of the Games, had risen and rather too dramatically requested that the fighters be sent back to their quarters to learn their business. Now and then he would call Mark Anthony to his side, go into a huddle, pat him on the back; it was as though he wanted all Rome to see the pretty group they made.

But Manlius was under instructions to roast the show. His sports column had become famous for its cynical tone, and today he was outdoing himself. Bitingly his stylus ripped across the wax:

> Well, folks, maybe your humble scribe doesn't know a sword from a shoe-lace; but who was it, a few weeks ago, that prophesied that the gladiatorial racket would hitch its way into the Society Column and stay there until somebody booted it out to where it belongs?
>
> The Fresh Air Fund Benefit has about proved the case. And I'll tell you why. There were ladies present. O Gemini, what a lot of ladies. They didn't used to let 'em in—not the respectable ones, at least. Yet, if you'll look across the arena while the big palookas are pretending to fight, you'll see most of the female Social Register admiring the sword-sticking fraternity, looking wise and betting on some wind-bag from Helvetia, merely because he looks cute across the chest.
>
> As far as the combat—if you can call it such—was concerned, it was a pretty dull fake. Of course the presence of our Divine Julius gave it a certain tone. But as sport it was all wet. Possibly the customers liked it—the magnates of the Murder Industry have confused the customers to that extent. Now look, for instance, at

the so-called combat between those two muscle-bound wonders—Carnufex, all armored up as a *lecutor,* wearing the latest thing in sheet-iron pyjamas; and Horribilius, stripped to the buff as a *retarius* and waving the regulation nine foot fishing net. It used to be good fun, *retarius* vs. *secutor.* Them was rough, happy days. But what now?

Carnufex had been dining last night, I suspect. Anyhow, he tripped over his own big feet and went down like a cartload of kitchen stoves. Just to make it look pretty, Horribilius looped the net over the fallen chump of chumps, held him down with the three-pronged spear and turned to the audience. Did the thumbs go down? They did not. The Junior League gals began fluttering pink handkerchiefs and chirping feverishly, "Please don't hurt Sweetie!"

Tie that, if you're a good knotter. And it goes to show just what I've said. The arena game has grown into a big come-on, and since they've let the gals in. . . .

Manlius paused for a figure of speech, his eyes traveling dully over the foot-trodden sand. The two gladiators, whom he had just scorified, were dog-trotting toward quarters. A new batch, booked for a battle royal, marched ceremoniously around the Altar of Pluto. But the reporter's eyes had wandered back to the white row where the twenty-seventh vestal sat, just behind the press box.

His familiar spirit might have nudged him, for Manlius turned at the psychological moment; a household slave had just come down the aisle and lingered casually at the end of Vestal Row. His movements were plain from where Manlius sat; looking the other way, the slave had slipped a note into the hand of the twenty-seventh vestal. The veiled girl hardly moved. The audience was roaring at the battle royal in the arena; but the slave leaned down while the vestal whispered. . . .

Then the man stole upward to the section reserved for Cæsar's guests. For a while he was invisible. The crowd roared again. Something had happened in the arena. Another killing. Assistants were dragging away the fallen. Slaves with buckets were sprinkling sand on the smear. But Manlius held his gaze, first on the vestal, then on the spot where the message-bearer had disappeared.

The vestal sat perfectly still, her face invisible under the thick white veil. Out of his obscurity the slave stole forth and sought the place where the curly-haired Mark Anthony sat apart. Another secret, quickly whispered. Down in Vestal Row the one on the end concealed a guilty hand inside a sleeve, but not soon enough to hide the flash of a precious stone, possibly on her thumb.

From that moment Manlius' mind was not on his work—or his routine job, at least. Once in a while his eye would stray over the doings in the arena and his stylus would jot down the flippant cynicisms he signed. But every half minute he would turn and study the mysterious comedy in Section A. The vestal was growing restless; occasionally her veiled eyes would travel up toward the spot where lusty Anthony sat talking politics with this one and that. In the royal chair the Big Fella looked a little bored; today he was in one of his remote moods. Aloft on his dais, he seemed to be keeping the Senators at a distance. He was making himself unapproachable; this was Cæsar's way when he appeared in those gaudy royal robes. Yes, he might have been a statue of the real Cæsar; a stilted, moving statue, decked out in purple. . . . Now and then he spoke to Anthony, and gestured, too much, his eye on the public. . . .

In the senatorial section the fat fellow Cassius, who always seemed to have a finger in every pie, and had prated so much lately about restoring Rome to the Common People, sat beside his friend Trebonius, who had done so well by himself when he looted Asia. Near them sat General Decimus Brutus and his hysterical little cousin, Junius Brutus.

A good picture of politics, reflected Mannie. Cæsar never was so hot for these blood-letting contests, but he knows how it peps up the voters. He won't let the senators, who've been calling him names, come within a hundred feet of his golden chair. He's showing Rome who's boss. Being Dictator's a good life, if you don't weaken. . . .

Another roar from the crowd. Another gladiator was down. Mannie was studying his form chart when a nudge from his familiar spirit caused him to turn again toward Vestal Row.

Suddenly, with a muttered curse, he rose and handed his tablets to the society columnist. "Finish it," he growled, "and tell Boss Apex I'm on that other assignment."

For the vestal on the end had risen and was making her way toward the nearest exit.

## VIII

THIS TIME he wasn't going to lose her. In defiance of custom he sprang up the middle aisle; when a lictor attempted to stop him he showed his press badge and elbowed on. Perhaps he knocked down a few Romans, for he heard cross voices behind him inquiring, "What's your hurry?" Throngs were going home early; among them, moving decorously, he saw the white snood of the vestal bobbing toward the main entrance. An arm's length behind, he followed her outside to the parking place where the patricians kept their family litters.

"If you don't mind, sir—" It was Smithicus, coming out from behind a post—"I've ordered you a litter with a pair of rather fast Cappadocian runners. I mean to say, sir—"

Good old Smithicus, the ever handy bonehead! The litter was standing beside him. "Get in," said Manlius to Smithicus, "and tell your marathoners to keep right behind that little white litter with the pink bow on the handle-bars."

The way was crooked, as about everything was in Rome in those days. Peeping through the curtains, Manlius saw the white litter winding its way through snake-tail streets and angleworm alleys, turning now and then, obviously to double on its tracks. It started up Quirinal Hill, then changed its mind and went through the dirty, smelly Subura below. Then it dodged through town—the litter bearers ahead were fast runners for Nubians—and turned at last into the handsome, if somewhat dubious, section of the Janiculum.

Now the white litter was winding between stuccoed walls, shaded by ilex trees. The bearers were slowing down as they approached a small door, indented in the wall. Here Manlius, afraid of discovery in this remote spot, dismounted and crept along among the vines. He felt the breath of good Smithicus on his shoulder.

Manlius' heart was beating like a trip-hammer, for the biggest story on earth was opening up before his eyes. The white litter came to a dead stop. A handy slave jumped out of somewhere and divided the curtains; one red shoe—this time encrusted with rubies—came slowly down to earth, then a vestal virgin, swathed in filmy white, marched sedately toward the door.

Now was Mannie Scribo's one and only chance. Like a wounded lion at the Circus Maximus he leaped forward. "Madam," he roared, "one minute, please."

The door, of iron-bound oak, clanged mightily in his face. Outdone, Manlius rushed it, beat upon it with his fist. Nothing but echoes came along the neat, ilex-trimmed lane. Then a sound of iron-shod feet on the cobbles. Two brute-faced gladiators, of the type the best families hired as killers, hove into view, filled the alley. The biggest one, with an ogre's smile, spread his vast legs and asked, "Hey, fella. Know whose house you're breakin' into?"

Despite the ban on weapons for slaves, the gladiator drew a sword; Mannie was quicker on the draw. The small dagger he always carried under the left fold of his toga, was out like a flash and pressed uncomfortably against the fellow's fairly unconditioned stomach. "I've got the drop on you," he said, knowing the proper formula. "Put 'em up. I'll take that sword, thank you. And while you're about it, you might hand me your helmet."

Disdainfully he threw sword and helmet over the wall and turned to see the second bravo sprawling about ten feet away, where Smithicus had knocked him with a short one on the chin.

"Just tell the lady that we called, will you?" requested P. Manlius Scribo, and departed.

But, as usual, things weren't so easy at the office. When Manlius faced Q. Bulbus Apex the little man gave him his best sour-raisin look.

"Boss, I've found the vestal virgin," said the reporter.

"Well? Where is she?"

"Remember how Cæsar queered himself with the Pontifical College by building that six million sesterces love-nest on the Janiculum? Remember who he built it for, and who's living there?"

"Ought to. It's Cleopatra."

"I suppose you read that report I sent in, about what happened in the *bungalorium* last night? How some She was going to signal some Him at Comma's funeral? Well, there at the funeral was the vestal, signaling with Cleopatra's ring. And there at the Charity Fund Fight was the same vestal, swapping notes with Mark Anthony. Same amethyst ring, too. I shadowed her as far as Cleopatra's gate—then her gladiators jumped me."

"What's the connection?" asked Q. Bulbus, strangely uninterested.

"Aw, nothing. Except that she's probably Comma's murderer—or the active agent in the crime."

"You're guessing."

"Yes, and you're stalling." Manlius was growing irritable.

"Talk about stalling," said Q. Bulbus with a hard cackle, "why didn't you rope in that Romula gal while you had a chance?"

"Because I think she's innocent."

"Ah. Are you a police judge?"

"No. But I'm the only man on this paper who's giving a dog's notice to this case. And I tell you, Boss, this isn't just murder. It's world politics. Cleopatra giving the mystic high-sign to Brutus and Cassius. Kill-the-Tyrant mottoes sneaking all over Rome. And Anthony in on it, somehow, up to his neck. Probably to please Cleopatra—"

"Listen, son." One of Apex's knotty hands went up. "If there's an Anthony and Cleopatra story going round, better lay off it."

"What do you mean, lay off it?"

"Just that."

"Castor and Pollux!" swore Mannie. "Isn't this an anti-Cæsar paper? Haven't we been lacing it to Bull Anthony and the Isis cult and the Egyptians generally, especially—"

"No more."

P. Manlius Scribo, at the slight risk of dismissal, straightened up and was very Roman again.

"I'm on this story," he said, "and I demand an explanation of your sudden change of front."

Q. Bulbus Apex sat a minute, considering. Silence reigned in the city room, broken only by the dripping of the *clepsydra,* the old water-clock that was never quite on time. Then dustily the Boss cleared his throat.

"I'll tell you why," he said. "Late last night Mark Anthony came over here and bought the *Evening Tiber* for a hundred talents, cash down. I remain the executive head. But from now on this is an Anthony publication."

"Gosh, what a price! A hundred grand!" Manlius clung to the city desk, but his wild eyes roved over to his British slave. "Smithicus," he asked brokenly, "is there anything left of that bottle of fire-wine you took off Cupidus last night?"

## IX

P. MANLIUS SCRIBO, in all his career as a journalist, was no nearer to resigning than at that moment, and Q. Bulbus Apex, perhaps, no closer to accepting that resignation. However, our enterprising reporter saved the situation, temporarily, by turning on his heel. On the stairs, going down, he ran into Egregius Rector; his round black eyes were snapping so that they seemed to illuminate the dark.

"Hold up your toga, Mannie," he whispered, and when Manlius had lifted the front of his dignified robe Rector poured into it full half a pound of round, silver disks that rattled as they fell. Lockets, exactly like the ones Mannie had found in Comma's room.

*"Sic Semper Tyrannis,"* said Eggie excitedly. "Got these in pawnshops. If I'd had the time and the money I guess I could have collected a hundred. *Sic Semper Tyrannis."*

"Yes," mused Manlius Scribo. "But what does it mean?"

"So always with tyrants—"

"Shut up. I can read easy Latin. I mean, but why so many, all alike, all over town?"

"Maybe it's some sort of campaign button," suggested Eggie. "You know, when you're running for something you always call the other fellow names—"

"Have you been tailing Senator Casca?"

"Nothing but. Followed him from the temporary Capitol to lunch, and from lunch to the Fresh Air Fund fight—"

"Where did he lunch?"

"With General Decimus Brutus. The same bunch."

"What same bunch?"

"Oh, Mealy Mouth Brutus and Metellus Cimber and Trebonius and Fatty Cassius, the thinking machine. Everything close harmony. I snuck up to Casca's house and handed a lot of sex stuff to Casca's secretary, female. It seems those boys have been dining together about every night for the past month. I asked the gal about that *Sic Semper* locket and she got sore—you know—admission of guilt stuff."

"Do you think those babies are trying to start something?" asked Manlius.

"Do you think water's wet?" asked Egregius Rector. "When five Romans meet together five consecutive times they always start something. Now the question before the house is: What izzit? By the way, did you surround that vestal virgin you were looking for?"

"No. Old Calamity's killed the story."

"Good Juno, why?"

"Mark Anthony now runs the paper," said Manlius. "He bought it last night, and from now on we're going to be very, very vestal."

"I won't stand for it," snarled Egregius Rector. Which would have been noble of him, if he had meant what he said.

P. Manlius Scribo shuffled toward his humble lodgings, following his husky torch-bearer. Was he down-hearted? Not exactly. But sore to the gizzard. Old Calamity had sold out. Oh, well, most Romans did that little thing, first or last; selling out was one of the principal industries of the fast growing Empire.

Just the same, Mannie was disappointed in his Boss. Q. B. Apex had been, in the beginning, the whole show. He *was* the *Tiber.* He had owned a majority of the stock, and had managed to remain independent. But selling out to Mark Anthony!

Mannie Scribo stopped in his tired tracks. Just what did Mark Anthony want with a newspaper? Certainly he didn't need advertising; his big, overblown figure never showed in the Forum but what he drew a crowd. He was fed up with publicity. Unless—

Unless what? Was he after something new, fresh and delightful? Could it possibly be the golden crown which once, in a well staged show, he had offered Cæsar thrice, only to be thrice refused?

*"Bolonia!"* muttered the weary reporter, shuffling along. But what did Anthony want with a paper? If not to advertise, then to suppress. Yes, that was it. To keep something vital out of the news.

P. Manlius Scribo was dead to the world. He didn't want any dinner. He hadn't had a real bath for two days, and he was too fagged out even to dread the horrible cold plunge Smithicus would throw him into in the morning. But when he crawled to his simple couch and Smithicus, a fresh air fiend, had opened a window on him, Manlius lay wakeful, summing up the case, as every detective must do at frequent intervals, so that he won't get too mixed up in his own theories.

In the silent watches of the night he catalogued his observations as follows:

MOTIVES

I. Somebody wanted to get Comma out of the way.
II. Somebody killed him in a fit of jealousy.
III. Common racketeers attacked him with intent to rob, or intimidate, or extort.

Suspicion No. III Manlius eliminated almost at once. Valuable costumes, jewels of some worth, lay carelessly all over the *bungalorium* when Manlius had called to inspect the crime. Professional crooks, composing about a quarter of Rome's population, did things more neatly than that. No, the robbery theory was out.

Jealousy? Possibly. There always was, and always will be, plenty of back-stabbing in the theatrical profession. But under the sheltering wing of Cæsar, Comma had had no apparent rivals. They were thinking, in fact, of closing Pompey's Theater for the lack of a practical man to carry on.

There remained, then, the sparkling possibilities of Motive No. I—somebody wanted to get Comma out of the way.

Ah, there lay the land of juicy conjecture! From the very first Mannie had felt that a big Higher Up story was about to break out of the muddle of this seemingly inferior crime, and his investigations had led him further and further into the ramifications of *weltpolitik.* From this the sleepless reporter-detective drew up a mental diagram entitled:

LIST OF SUSPECTS

I. Romula. Red-headed. Disappeared night of murder. Hated Comma. Much in company of suspicious, unknown Greek, who helped steal papers out of Comma's house. Some mystery about the mislaid wax doll. In whispered conversation with her the Greek had hinted that prearranged signals were to be given by some woman, very probably—

II. Cleopatra in vestal disguise. If she had grown tired of Cæsar she would go to any length to get him out of the way. Comma might have had something she wanted, or have known of her plot against Cæsar. But Certainly she had been caught flagging Cæsar's arch-enemies—

III. Brutus and Cassius. A pair of sore-heads. Started that whispering campaign against Cæsar; accusing him of ambitions to become Emperor and ruin the Republic. Again, as was possible in the case of Cleopatra, they might have killed Comma as some part of their anti-Cæsar policy. Probably they had invented the *Sic Semper Tyrannis* slogan. And one of the slogans had been dropped by their great friend—

IV. Senator Casca. *Asinus ferox,* or wild jackass. Taken to drink, and midnight meetings with Left Wing Republicans. Hated Cæsar because C.J.C. exiled his brother. Certainly one of Casca's pet lockets was found in Comma's room. Possibly he quarreled with Comma over some detail in the plot against Cæsar. For no particular reason Casca had showed up at Comma's funeral in company with—

V. Mark Anthony! Cæsar's boy-friend, that's true. But what is friendship among politicians? Bought a paper to hush the news. Maybe the Comma murder. A whisper in the murder-house had sent Manlius to the spot where the vestal had signaled—

Yes, but then what? Wheels within wheels, cogs within cogs. The heavy-handed cutting of Comma's throat and the dragging of his body was not the work of any weak woman. Anthony and Cleopatra were in it somehow, up to the neck, as were Brutus, Cassius and Casca. Yet who again could put a finger on a motive—save for the sensitive feelers of the sixth sense, the detective instinct, which again warned Mannie Scribo of many daggers, pointing toward the strong man who owned Rome, body, soul and breeches.

Therefore Manlius fell asleep on one of those solid oak beds which made every Roman wish that somebody had enough get-up-and-get to invent springs.

## X

IT WAS THE DAY before the Ides of March. Mannie Scribo, again tormented by Smithicus' frigid bathtub, went forth in a state of extreme irritation. Q. Bulbus Apex had summoned him by messenger earlier than was his wont, and met him in the office, wearing a new toga and a chesty, plutocratic air. Dictatorially, as though he were C.J.C. himself, Old Calamity ordered his star reporter to lay off sports and politics for a while and write a society column.

When Manlius walked away with a hidden sneer he had half a mind to sic Smithicus on the little man and pull his lopsided head off. Society indeed! What did the Boss think he was, a Greek? To be mincing around with a lot of painted mommas and pansies, squeaking out compliments and raising their little fingers when they drank? Ye gods and goddesses! Manlius had a notion to quit without notice and walk over to the *Astra* offices, where they'd be lucky enough to get a real reporter. Only the *Astra* was dead from the neck up, and Anthony or no Anthony, Manlius was out for a life of action.

And another thing. Society fluff was pretty easy pickings; there was the Junior League Fair, out in the Circus Maximus. Roman dames, mostly of the fast set, were going to be there selling dingbats. Cæsar himself was to be patron. That, of course, was the story. Funny that the Big Fella, with all his troubles, packing up to conquer Parthia and everything, had time to fool with this pink-wine-stuff. Well, politics is politics. *Politico sunt politico,* meaning pigs is pigs.

Manlius comforted himself with the thought that this fluffing through Rome would give him the best possible opportunity to hunt down Romula and the vestal mystery. For in his heart he was a stubborn cuss, true descendant of the wolf-bred Remus.

Passing the Capitol, Manlius noted that the stately new building still bore the sign "Closed for Repairs," but a brilliant annex with elaborate Doric columns was plainly labeled "Police Department." In a sarcastic mood Manlius lingered in a gilded anteroom outside the Chief's office and sent in his card. Clients, professional bondsmen, and the usual rats who practise small criminal law, stood in a throng. After a long wait a sculptured bronze door swung open and Johannus, the office boy, ushered Manlius in to the presence.

Kellius, who had laid aside his uniform for a smartly cut patrician toga, held out a limp hand, adorned with three or four enormous seal rings. Kellius, the cop, had changed even more rapidly than Apex, the editor. His accent was so affected you'd have thought he had studied four years in Athens.

"I hear the *Tiber* has changed hands," he commented busily. "Things are moving about, aren't they? What can I do for you?"

"Nothin'," said Manlius in *sermo vulgaris.* "Just dropped in to see what you've made out of that Comma case."

"Comma case?" The Chief fussily consulted the tablets in front of him. "Comma case? Oh, yes. I remember it now. Quite so. We don't follow up suicides, you know."

"You still believe that?"

"I believed it from the very first." Kellius was showing signs of irritability. "I know, you yellow journalists always want to drum up a murder. But no chance there."

"All right. What have you found out about Romula?"

"Our Department of Missing Persons has gone into that. They have drawn up a table to show plainly how 9½ per cent of the middle class working girls in Rome disappear every twelve months."

"Where do they go?"

"Where do the flies go in the winter time? Good Jove, my boy, I'm not the Delphic Oracle. I'm Chief of Police. The new traffic regulations are driving me crazy, we're trying to round up the olive oil racketeers, and on top of that—" He broke off.

"On top of that," prompted Manlius coolly.

"Nothing of importance." Kellius' shifting glance gave the lie to his negation. Then he began to smile, rather unhappily. "I'm sure," he said suddenly, "that the *Tiber,* under its dignified new management, isn't going to fritter away its time with bagatelles."

"Like the Comma case, for instance?"

"Well, yes—poof!"

"Two poofs to you," grinned Manlius, and left the presence.

Kellius wasn't very smart, and he had let out more than he intended. Pretending he didn't know where Romula was! Plainly big news impended somewhere, and Kellius was there to sit on the lid.

Outside Manlius found Egregius Rector, he of the comic oriental eyes, waiting beside Smithicus and swapping detective story plots. "I'm on my way to tease the Senate," he said excitedly, "and I was wondering—is there anything I could fetch you—unofficially, I mean?"

"If you've got time," said Manlius, "would you mind dropping into Cicero's law office and finding out all you can about that gal Romula?"

"Sure," said Rector. "But listen. Everybody in that dump knows I'm a reporter. They just won't talk."

Now it was the ingenious Smithicus who came to the rescue. Reaching into his slave's tunic he brought out a disheveled bunch of hair. "A wig and a false beard, sir," he suggested, "comes in very handy, by way of disguise."

"You've said it, slave," cried Egregius Rector, putting on the wig and beard. "What am I?" he asked.

"A Hebrew prophet," cried Manlius.

"Or anything," said Rector through the mat. "I'll walk in there selling life insurance, and if there's any information worth getting, I'll get it."

On the way over Mannie stopped at the great Temple of Jupiter Capitolinus and slipped a denarius to a dirty little priest who, when he wasn't too far gone in drugs, furnished gossip.

"What's the dirt?" asked Mannie.

"Going to the Junior League Fair? Well—tee-hee—so are Fulvia and Pompeia. You know what that means."

"That Cæsar's going to drop in on the girls?"

"Yes. It's said that Cæsar favors Pompeia this week. But when he comes he won't be among the girls, exactly. He'll be surrounded by his boyfriends."

"Boy-friends?"

"See for yourself! Sometimes it's nice to keep your boy-friends close around you—so that you can watch them. Tee-hee."

"You speak in parables."

"Priests of Jupiter usually do. But you're a reporter. You must know that our Divine Julius is in a ver-y in-ter-esting position."

A bell sounded. The messy priest hobbled behind a shrine.

The Junior League Fair spraddled all over the northwest end of the Circus Maximus, as far as possible from the smelly dens where they kept the animals. In this naturally masculine edifice, built for racing and violent deaths, everything was now so feminine that it gave Manlius quite a pain. Silk canopies spread over the arena, pink tablecloths over every marble surface, and a hundred dinky little booths, selling articles of a remarkably worthless character. One young lady, for instance, was offering hand embroidered dagger-holders, the kind no he-man would be caught dead with; another was raffling off a very wide black female who tweaked a red bandanna turban and protested, "Laws, honey, what yo' Maw gwine say when she fine out you done sole ole Diana down de River?"

The usual Charity Bazaar hooey. Society flappers with shadow-blue make-up on their eyelids and a coat of kiss-proof on their lips were busily extorting money from the mushy old bankers and fatuous retired generals who ambled from flower to flower.

The high-bred *puellæ* here were so-so; put alongside of Romula they'd look like a lot of second-hand sandals, Mannie thought. That smallish dark one over there, the one in red, might pass in a crowd. So would the straw-colored blonde impersonating a Helvetian and barking loudly for a side-show. . . . "Well, folks, it's only two sesterces, and it's wonderful—wonnn-ddderful! They eat glass, they swallow fire, they walk on swords—every performer a star from Pompey's Theater—"

All from Pompey's Theater! Manlius, who had been listening without animation up to then, perked up his ears. Some of the performers, he suspected, would be from the little troupe he had seen practising in Comma's back yard the day after the tragedy. He showed the amateur ticket seller his press badge and sauntered through the wicket. This show was popular, he could see at a glance. Stately patricians were jammed together, laughing like the great big boys they were, while an Ethiopian in pink tights swallowed a cake of soap and blew a flock of green balloons. Yes, and there was the bear trainer, doing a *tango vulgaris* with his hairy pet.

When these stunts were finished the crowd moved to a far corner to watch a dwarf in devil-blue walk a tightrope and balance three knives, end for end, on the tip of his nose. Mannie Scribe's heart played a queer tattoo—for the pint-sized man up there was Hercules, the nearest living witness to Comma's murder. Craftily the reporter edged himself over to one of the poles supporting the tightrope, and when the act was over Hercules, as luck would have it, slid down that very pole, right into Mannie's arms.

"Hey, what's the idea?" squeaked the dwarf, kicking and dropping knives in all directions.

"You know me," whispered Manlius. "I'm the reporter from the *Tiber.* The one who believes Comma's daughter is innocent."

"Sure. I know you now, nobleman." The midge had braced his feet on a tub, and stood with his mouth almost level with Mannie's chin. "And you're dead right about Romula."

"Do you know she's been back to the *bungalorium?"*

"No. But she didn't kill her father."

"Do you know who did?"

The elfin eyes were round as buttons. "Yes, I do. I saw it all through a crack in the door."

"Then why did you lie to me?"

"Nobleman, I was scared. I thought you was one of them secret service dicks. But now I know different."

"Then who killed Comma?"

"I'll tell you, mister. Listen—"

But Hercules cringed away; for a brute-faced assistant stage manager came rushing up, swinging one of those Roman cat-o'-nine-tails with a string of bone buttons on every tail.

"Hey, what you think this is, a petting party? All you slaves get to hell back into your dens. The act's over." He took little Hercules by the slack of his tunic and was swinging him for a forward pass when Manlius beckoned quietly to Smithicus.

"Give him a short one, Smiddy," he suggested. A jaw cracked and Hercules' persecutor lay sleeping on the sand. The crowd, taking this all as a part of the show, applauded, although some averred that it wasn't sporting to use the bare fist when Roman ring-rules called for a boxing glove stuffed with nails.

It was all good fun, but it failed to interest Manlius any more; for the midget had disappeared with some piece of information which might have solved the whole puzzle.

Outside, among the catchpenny booths, was a gaudy affair marked MYSTIC EAST, and behind a red, white and blue counter lolled two fortune-tellers who, despite their fanciful Egyptian costumes, were easily recognizable as those belated rivals for Cæsar's affection, Fulvia and Pompeia. By measurement of years they were a little past the dangerous age; but what couldn't the facial artists do in these progressive times? Pompeia, the more quietly dressed of the two, wore an immense peruke of greenish hair, woven into the shape of a peach basket. With it all she maintained a plump queenly dignity. Because she *had* been the Dictator's wife, and that was something, wasn't it?

However, the Mystic East wasn't doing so well as some other shows. The gilded youth—usually broke—buzzed around the two experienced man-snatchers, and did everything but spend money. The bankers and contractors and senators preferred such booths as the one where a deb was raffling off her mother's cook and another running up the price on those silly embroidered dagger-holders. But the porky Tamany of Athens, Rome's richest building contractor, came waddling up to the amateur fortune-tellers and gave his lard-white palm to Pompeia while Fulvia pretended to be busy with her nails. Miaow, miaow. . . .

Then everything was stricken into silence by the centurions' short field trumpets, braying fiercely.

Ta-ra, ta-ra! Caius Julius Cæsar, the Living Jupiter, Conqueror of the World, Grandson of Divine Æneas, Dictator of the Republic and Administrator of Farm Relief was now approaching the Junior League Charity Fair. The cream of Roman girlhood stood stiffly at attention; yea, and the sour cream of Roman matronhood stood likewise. Lictors with their axe-crowned fasces came forward, posted themselves here and there, giving a forbidding touch to the frivolous occasion. Then the brawny centurions, their brass-bound kilt-straps flashing below crimson tunics. Then a flock of white-robed statesmen, marching afoot around a litter so adorned with heroic paintings and golden studs and hand carved poles and crimson curtains that you could well believe that the passenger inside was no mortal, but a god.

"The Fusion Administration sure can put up a show when it tries to," was Manlius Scribo's unspoken comment.

Eight coal-black Nubians, perfectly matched, set down the litter. The officers of the guard divided the curtains while a third spread a crimson carpet.

Cæsar, who, in spite of a dictator's purple border around his toga, looked plain and businesslike, stepped out and returned a tired smile to the usual acclaim of "Ave!" Manlius, a professional observer of public characters, preferred the unadorned Cæsar of today to the fancy, theatrical one he had seen at the gladiatorial show. The Big Fella wore nothing to cover his baldness, and his sharp face, like that of a pink hawk, seemed to take in every detail of the Fair.

Yes, here was the sensible old field marshal, having a good time among the girls; the real Cæsar, the one who ought to go down to history, instead of the strutting doll in purple robes.

Mannie studied the statesmen who followed Cæsar as he walked along on the arm of Mark Anthony. The oddly matched pretors, Brutus and Cassius; Senators Casca and Cimber. What had the priest said about them? "You surround yourself with your boy-friends when you want to watch them." Yeah, they'd bear watching. And Mark Anthony too.

So Cæsar strolled along, ordering his secretary to drop a small bag of gold on the counter when he bought a half dozen dinky dagger-holders. He took twenty tickets on the colored cook, remarking to the debutante who was selling her, "The fellow who gets black Diana better send her home, or there'll be trouble in the Tullius family."

Manlius, true to instinct, kept himself within listening distance of the Dictator's entourage; but as they rounded the bend and started back among the booths on the right side, the reporter took his station near the fortune-teller's booth. The priest's hints about Fulvia, and more especially Pompeia, renewed the journalist's curiosity. As the great man approached the rival mystics became horribly unconscious; Fulvia toyed with her blood-red nails again, Pompeia with her crystal ball. Both were pretending to look the other way when Julius Cæsar, his senators following at a respectful distance, stopped and chose a booth. Pompeia's.

"Well, kitten, still tempting the Fates, I see," he chuckled.

Pompeia looked up, feigning great surprise; her handsome eyes were very young as she said, "Julius! I didn't see you come in. This *is* a treat. But I don't suppose there's any use trying to tell *your* fortune, now that you're a god."

"We gods don't know much," he grinned, like the old atheist that he was. "We're only human, you know, when it comes to youth and beauty."

Came a clatter from the next booth; Fulvia dropping her nail polish.

"I think I know your palm," said Pompeia sweetly.

"Oh, but it has gone through a great deal, my dear Pompeia, since last you studied it," said Cæsar coyly.

"The hand that rules the world," admitted Pompeia, "is bound to show the strain." She giggled and examined the base of his thumb. "A great many small affairs there. They don't count, really. But what a silly boy you were—"

"When?" Rather fondly. Jealous Fulvia in the next booth was now openly listening.

"You know when, innocence. Imagining all those horrid things about me. Let's see your heart line—"

"Just a minute," commanded the Dictator genially, and turned to beckon toward his retinue. "Hey, senators, listen in on this. A lot of you fellows want to know what your Cæsar's like," he smiled. "Here's the inside mystic story. Pompeia, has the *haruspex* given you a license to practise soothsaying?"

"Indeed he has," said Pompeia, still holding the hand of her much desired ex-husband. Something like a psychic flutter seemed to pass through the attendant politicians as they gathered closely around.

"She's a licensed practitioner of divination and prophecy," explained Cæsar. "What she says is written in the Book of Fate. Jupiter himself can't change it."

Brutus and Cassius crossed their fingers; their faces paled with superstitious dread. "Here, Cassius, you fat rogue," said the Dictator, "and you too, Casca and Cimber, listen well. Now Pompeia, my dear, what about my heart line?"

"It's broken fairly early—a disappointment in love. Then it runs along, deep and straight, until it gets another bump—about your middle age. But it's mended and becomes very, very beautiful."

Something in Cæsar's eagle eye indicated that his ex-wife was chiseling a bit on her own account. Calling the Cleopatra affair "another bump." But the Dictator raised the large, gruff voice that had commanded legions and almost shouted: "Never mind my heart. It can take care of itself. How 'bout my lifeline?"

"It's different. Yours *would* be." She squinted at his palm. "In one way it looks like a long, long life. But there's a queer arrowhead right here. It means great, great danger."

"Danger's my dish," smiled Cæsar. "Comforting, isn't it, boys?" giving Cassius' fat shoulders a hearty slap. "I always wanted to die in battle, boots on. But to pine away by inches, having to go down to the senate every day and listen to you fellows—yo-hum. I guess I need a rest more than a hand-reading. When's this big danger going to crop up, Pompeia?"

Impressively Pompeia brought out a crystal ball, the kind the wizards of Cathay blessed with magic. Her eyes seemed to sink into it. A dull thump—Brutus and Cassius knocking their heads together.

"It is written," repeated Pompeia slowly.

"What's written?" asked Julius Cæsar. "Come closer, boys, and hear what's written."

Pompeia's gaze was still on the crystal; her voice came hollow and far away.

"Beware the Ides of March!"

Cæsar leaned over the counter, still smiling. "You'll have to speak a little louder, dear. What am I to avoid?"

"The Ides of March!" Quite shrilly. "And that's tomorrow."

"Ha-ha!" Cæsar broke into one of his pleasant laughs. "Pompeia, I'm afraid you got your license from the wrong *haruspex.* The Fifteenth of March happens to be my lucky day. The high priest of the Temple of Jupiter—that happens to be my temple, gentlemen—read my auspices this morning. He's quite infallible."

"I'm sorry you don't like my reading," pouted Pompeia.

"Oh, it's splendid, for an amateur. But you can't expect, can you, dear, to compete with the high priest of Jupiter?"

"Well, what did he say about the Ides of March?" asked Pompeia.

"My day to accomplish things. My day for work. The sort of day I enjoy. Gentlemen—" turning to his followers—

"expect me down to the Senate at ten A.M. on the Ides of March. I'm afraid I'll give you a pretty busy session."

He motioned to his secretary to toss an extra large bag of gold on the counter and almost giggled, "Beware the Ides of March! What a splendid slogan for a Third Party movement."

"Isn't it!" tittered Brutus and Cassius nervously.

"Well, let's toddle!" commanded the Dictator. "Pompeia, if you want to take a course in soothsaying, just charge it to my account. Pretty head of hair you've got on today, my dear. And thanks for the prophecy."

The party moved on.

But Manlius, his ears standing up like those of a listening rabbit, lingered by the booths of the Egyptian Mystics. Had Pompeia, right in public, been trying to warn Cæsar of a real danger? Or was she just being sensational, as so many Roman matrons were in those degenerate times? The latter, most likely. Anything to catch the attention of the man she desired to recapture. Whatever her motive, she had all too obviously failed in the attempt. She should have known that Cæsar's pet organization was the Temple of Jupiter. Every word the priests there said to him Cæsar incorporated into his active life. Pompeia certainly had her nerve, naming the Ides of March as Cæsar's dangerous day. But what did she know? Was she really spilling a date, for her ex-husband's best good?

Mannie Scribo sidled up to Pompeia's booth, where she was polishing her nails, in silent competition with Fulvia.

"Would you mind reading my palm?" he asked.

"No more readings today," she replied haughtily.

Sore as a crab, reflected Manlius.

"Wonderful about you soothsayers," he persisted. "The way you can see a date in a crystal and know something's going to happen—"

"If you're a reporter," she snapped, "I'm not giving out any interviews, if you don't mind."

One of Mannie's rules was never to outstay his welcome. But, after Pompeia had withdrawn to an anteroom, he found a more receptive person in Fulvia. That lady, still beautiful, but growing rather fox-like in her thinness, smiled a smile of quiet satisfaction.

"I think they steered the Big Fella wrong," began Mannie with a light laugh. "He was aiming at your booth, but he got all tangled up in senators."

"Tangled up in senators is about right," said Fulvia pleasantly. "Maybe that's why he's going to war. To get rid of senators."

"I guess Pompeia was speaking out of her turn when she made up that Ides of March prophecy."

"She's fifty if she's a day," said Fulvia, "but she's never learned to keep her mouth shut."

"But does she know something—"

"Pompeia? She never did know enough to come in when it rains. But there, I'm being uncharitable. But why should she be so childish, trying to worry Julius?"

"Or maybe to warn him honestly?" in Mannie's most careless tone.

"Does a foolish old woman like Pompeia know enough to warn anybody? She's heard a lot of gossip. I don't say it's without foundation. But she's not the person to consult on dates."

"Who is?" Trying to keep excitement out of his voice.

A hard malice came into Fulvia's olive green eyes.

"I doubt very much if even a reporter can get near *her.*"

"You mean Cleopatra?" It was one of Mannie's keen guesses.

"Well, since you mention it—"

Rome's arch-grafter, Tamany of Athens, came up and presented his suet-like hand. Manlius lingered awhile, but other statesmen crowded around Fulvia's booth. Now that Pompeia had quit, she reigned alone. Manlius circled the Fair, in hopes of finding Hercules again. And when he came back to her Fulvia had knocked off for the day.

So he found a table and wrote his story. It might have glittered and burned with one of the world's most fateful warnings. Instead it ran like this:

> . . . and the Committee was greatly pleased by the Dictator's gracious, unofficial visit to the Fair, accompanied by many prominent Senators and Cabinet Members, including C. Cassius Longinus, Marcus Junius Brutus, General Decimus Brutus, Senators Casca and Cimber. The Imperator, as he is now good-humoredly called, was especially amused by the psychic demonstrations of

Rome's most popular hostess, Pompeia, who wittily predicted health and happiness for our Republic's Chief Executive.

Pompeia, in the costume of an Egyptian mystic, was lovely in an over-mantle of rose voile, bordered with pearls and . . .

## XI

MANNIE'S highly perfumed account of the Fair seemed to please Q. Bulbus Apex far more than a really serious murder story would have done. The copy was in in time for the home edition.

"We'll run more of that sort of thing after this," he beamed sourly, approving.

"What you turning the *Tiber* into—a woman's magazine?"

"Another crack out of you and you're fired," said the chronic city editor.

"That wasn't a crack. I'm just asking for information. When Mark Anthony—"

"Shush! Haven't you even learned to shut your mouth when you get a piece of inside information?"

"Oh. That was what it was? I thought, the way you acted last night, that you were telling the cockeyed world that Mark had gone into publishing in a big way."

"Well, Mark's publishing ain't for publication—yet. Understand? How did the Big Fella look today?"

"A darned sight more natural than he did at the games yesterday. He's getting moody, or something. He changes so from day to day. And I suppose, since this is an Anthony sheet, you wouldn't want to mention what that Pompeia woman said to him."

Briefly Manlius repeated Pompeia's Ides of March speech, taken from the crystal. Q. Bulbus Apex rubbed his hairless chin.

"How did the Big Fella take it?"

"With three loud guffaws," said the reporter.

"Funny thing for her to say, before that gang. Was she sober?"

"Seemed to be. But you can't tell about these Roman matrons nowadays. It takes a sledge hammer to knock 'em out. Cæsar was cool as a cucumber, but a lot of those statesmen, especially Cassius, sort of swallowed hard. I thought maybe he'd drop another *Sic Semper Tyrannis* badge, he was so rattled."

"Boy," said Old Calamity, "I think you're just theorizing about Cassius."

"All right. I theorize on my own time, anyhow. And I'll tell you what. It's my theory that the little murder out on Hesperides Avenue the other night comes so close to Cæsar that he could kick a sandal across it, if he wanted to. But he don't want to."

"Go take a bath," Q. Bulbus grinned like a puckered apple. "You don't smell like a society reporter."

On his way to the baths, hurrying this time, for fear Smithicus would grab him again and dump him into the dismal tin tub, Manlius caught up with his friend Egregius Rector.

"Well, Eggie," said Mannie, hooking arms with the enterprising Rector, "how did the false whiskers go in Cicero's office?"

"Oh, I've been looking all over for you," said Eggie. "I thought you'd be on the usual bench at Hibe's."

"No, I prefer a bath to a drink."

"Some do," admitted Egregius Rector.

"Well, how about it? What happened to the grass-grown chin in the office of Rome's Peerless Orator?"

"It was like this. I walked in behind the hair and found one of his copyists, a gal named Clara who's crazy 'bout Jewish salesmen. I gave her the old S.A. And did she fall for it! Told me all she knew, which wasn't much. You know how gals are, especially in offices. Clara said she thought Romula had been stepping out lately. She came in late and went home early. She had an outfit of fancy clothes in the washroom—"

"Was there a vestal's robe among them?"

"No. I asked about that. Nothing so dove-like. But Romula put on her night-club outfit the afternoon before Comma was murdered. She was trying to sneak out by a side entrance when Clara, accidentally on purpose, bumped into her. And Romula said a queer thing."

"What did she say?"

"She said, 'Clara, just forget you saw me in these clothes, will you?' Clara watched her go out into the street and step into a pink litter, one of the kind poor working girls don't ride in."

"Hm," said Manlius, for lack of a suitable Latin expression.

"Then," said Eggie Rector, "I interviewed Cicero."

"No!"

"Yes!"

"But nobody ever sees that old ice bag. Since he started writing essays on 'Life Begins at Sixty' he's been twice as hard to get at as C.J.C. himself."

"Just the same," said Eggie, "I got him. I happen to know that he's crazy about fancy paper for his books, and I had in my pocket a couple of sheets of the sample papyrus Q. Bulbus Apex has been fussing with lately. I slipped five sesterces to the office boy and introduced myself as a representative of C. Numbius, his publisher. This got me in. There sat Cicero, looking like a marble bust, cut for the benefit of posterity. I showed him my samples, and he bit. 'This is Grade A,' he said, "I'll order a thousand sheets.' Does that amuse you?"

"Intensely," said Manlius breathlessly. "What did you say then?"

"I fished around, then thought of something. 'We were going to publish Comma's "Twenty Years Behind the Footlights" on this stock. Too bad he went so suddenly.' 'Did you happen to know his daughter?' asked Cicero, snapping out of his scholarly trance. 'I've only met her,' says I, 'but she seemed a nice *puella.*' 'Yeah,' says Cicero, 'but take this from an old criminal lawyer. A nice girl can swing a mean knife. But there never was a murder without a motive. What motive could Romula have had?' 'Did Comma leave a will?' I asked, thinking of the old dodge. 'He did, and we drew it up.' Cicero rang a bell, a boy showed up. 'Bring in the will of the late J. Romulus Comma.' "

Eggie Rector paused, maybe for effect. Manlius caught him by the arm. "The will, the will!" he all but shrieked.

"The boy brought it in," said Eggie, "and it was about five lines long. Cicero read it aloud. 'To my beloved Romula all my possessions, e.g., the mortgage on my *bungalorium,* the mortgage on my faithful janitor Hambonius, my accumulated bills and my stage jewelry, mostly glass. To her also I bequeath my apologies with affectionate hopes that, as an old time actor, I have done a father's part.' "

"You wouldn't murder your father for that," said Manlius, "except on general principles."

"I said as much to Cicero," explained Eggie. "He looked sort of queer and said, 'When you seek for motives in Rome, you usually go to Capitoline Hill.' I asked him why, but he just tinkled his bell and said to the boy, 'Show the gentleman out.' "

Manlius stood at the door of Hibe's night club, rapidly analyzing these new developments. Cicero had a right to be sore at Cæsar, who had practically engineered his banishment once, then stuck him off as governor of a hick province from which Cicero had come back penniless and with a lot of reform ideas. Cicero had his eye on the Administration. He had put his finger on Comma's murder as a political crime. He was probably right. Queer things were going on in Rome this week.

"That's all I got," said Eggie, licking his dry lips as he turned toward Hibe's door.

"It's enough," said Manlius, "to hang half the Senate. You'd better lay off this case, kid, or you'll steal all my stuff. And I'm supposed to be central character in this story."

Bathing in Rome was no longer in its infancy. Long gone was the day when the rugged Conscript Fathers pulled out the old wash boiler on Saturday night, filled it from the tea kettle and got in with a chariot-sponge and a piece of laundry soap. On the banks of the yellow Tiber the bath, as such, had begun to increase with the growth of public dishonesty.

Bathing had passed its childhood stage and grown to adolescence. True, it had not attained the pompous lather-and-scrub dignity of Caracalla's day. But the larger racketeers of the Eternal City were beginning to experiment along that line. Tamany of Athens, having failed to account for half the appropriations used in the Appian Way Improvement, had made a large patriotic gesture and evaded a super-tax when he gave the Baths of Tamany to the Republic.

In this munificent gift Tamany of Athens remained true to character; the concrete was porous, the marble cracked, the water pipes from a lot that had been condemned in the Alexandrian sewer scandal. But from this Tamany gained great merit, and he was lucky because the thing didn't begin to fall down until a week after he was poisoned by one of his Persian concubines.

Today Manlius Scribo chose the Baths of Tamany in preference to the cheaper wash-houses, for the very good reason that the place was frequented by gentlemen of the equestrian and patrician order, and among these, as it were, the dirt was dished. Under the pillared arches and mosaic walls of the dressing-room, where his outer garments were removed by Smithicus, he enjoyed a glimpse of great men in the nude. Lucky, he thought, that Romans wear togas. So many of 'em are bow-legged or knock-kneed; and you can fold one of those table-cloth effects in such a way that a bay window can be made to look like a sphinx.

But to P. Manlius Scribo the undraped aristocracy was no treat, and today he had come as much to listen as to bathe. In spite of what was on his mind he couldn't help laughing at Tamany of Athens, that very pompous crook, strutting around like one of the three little pigs trying to impersonate Apollo Belvedere. And in the exercise room, leading into the *tepidarium,* it gave the sports reporter a kick to watch seven slaves turning a hose on the places where seven bankers had swollen the fastest. "A little deflation this morning, gentlemen?" giggled Manlius as he passed the tormented row. For this he got merely seven glares from seven bankers.

As all Rome was struggling to get thin without giving anything up, except their dinners now and then in the exquisitely decorated *vomitoria* outside their gorgeous dining halls, the exercise room bristled with various kinds of reducing apparatus. The jolliest of these was a spanking-machine, tuned up to deliver CCCXLVI strokes to the minute. While the heaviest eaters in Rome howled for mercy a number of brawny slaves cranked the mechanism, working with rare gusto; for of all the elaborate torture chambers of Rome, here at least was one where the slaves could beat up their masters.

But Manlius wandered on and plunged into the lukewarm pool of the *tepidarium.* Even as he stretched out for a good crawl stroke he was mulling over Fulvia's tip about seeing Cleopatra. Fulvia, of course, was jealous in two directions. Jealous of Pompeia, because of Cæsar; jealous of Cleopatra, because of her errant husband, Mark Anthony. But jealous people, like other drunkards, spit out the truth. By nothing less than a stroke of genius Cleopatra could be approached. Dangerous as an asp, she guarded herself and, if necessary, killed at sight.

The star reporter was working this out on his imaginary chess board when his quick ear caught the murmur of voices. Who were those two, seated on the tiles above him, their heads together, muttering? Brutus and Cassius! Softly Manlius dived under and came up against a side of the tank just below the whispering pair. He shook the water out of his ears. Mumble-mumble went the sly dialogue. Words began to grow distinct, to take on form.

"Listen, boy," said Fatty Cassius, to the slightly effeminate Brutus, "when the lady said, 'The Ides of March beware' he didn't listen."

"Yes, I noticed that," jittered Brutus.

"But he might have listened, if I hadn't fixed that high priest to tell him that March Fifteenth was his lucky day. You heard Cæsar say, 'Business as usual.' That's settled."

"But Cæsar—"

"Didn't he say distinctly that he'd be down at ten o'clock?"

"Let's move into the hot room," trembled Brutus. "I feel a cold draft on my feet."

They moved away.

The hot room, into which Manlius' lynx-like tread had followed them, would have offered good literary material for Virgil's forthcoming description of Hell. Tormented beings, running back and forth, swathed in steam; vague figures, the color of rare roast beef, moving about in infernal vapors. And over there, their close-locked heads above a medium-sized cloud, were Brutus and Cassius again. Manlius snuggled behind a handy bunch of steam, unlimbered his ears and listened.

"Never trust a woman," said Brutus.

"Cleopatra's not a woman," said Cassius. "She's the daughter of a hot goddess and a bull snake."

"Anyhow," said Brutus, "she's overdoing it. If she passes too many of those things around town he's sure to get wise."

"Forget that. Like a lot of great men, he's pretty dumb. Just keep your mind on the Ides of March, and leave the rest to me. . . ."

"How will Comrade X get to her without causing suspicion?"

"The oriental way—roll of carpet—coming tonight—"

Manlius sneezed, an unfortunate habit of his when his pores were suddenly opened. The two heads jumped apart.

And when their personal cloud lifted Brutus and Cassius were no longer there. Nothing remained but a roomful of poor boiled souls, passing through steam, grunting miserably.

## XII

CHERCHEZ LA FEMME, as the Gauls would have said, maybe. At the risk of a bad cold Manlius ordered Smithicus to dress him, and they got out of the Baths of Tamany as fast as circumstances would permit. Sneezing petulantly, Manlius roamed the streets of Rome, devising an immediate assault upon the guarded house of Cleopatra.

"Smithicus," he said, coming out of his dream, "how long will it take you to collect me twelve reliable gladiators?"

"Half an hour, sir. There are quite a number of unemployed fellows in Castor's School, where you bought me."

"Get 'em." Out of a bag he dumped the major portion of his week's salary. "Use this and take 'em up to the Janiculum. You remember Cleopatra's house where we tried to get in the other day? Grab those strong arms at the gate; you needn't kill 'em. Just gag 'em and tuck 'em away. Then hang around till I come."

"Very good, sir." Clothed in his intense British respectability, Smithicus departed on his desperate errand.

Mannie's restless mind had been working like this: Rugs. 'Way back in Alexandria the Serpent of the Nile had rolled herself in a rug and been carried into the presence of an unapproachable Cæsar. Good. What was sauce for the gander was sauce for the goose. Mannie Scribo, in his intensive study of Rome, happened to know the rug market very well. A fashionable rug dealer, F. Jonas Pinkus by name, catered to Cleopatra's passion for oriental carpets. For the past two months he had been sending daily consignments to the Janiculum love-nest.

In the wait for further developments Mannie Scribo considered the scrap of conversation which had sent him flying from the baths. Comrade X. Cleopatra was expecting Comrade X, some go-between, sent by the conspirators. Before this person arrived Mannie must go into the presence of the dangerous queen and filch the truth from her lying lips; for now he knew her for the very heart and center of the conspiracy.

But how to get at her? Piecing together the whispers from Brutus and Cassius, he concluded that Comrade X would be carried to her, oriental fashion, rolled in a rug. That could be worked; but how to identify himself, once he got inside? Ha, a letter of introduction! Rapidly Manlius plied his stylus and wrote the prettiest letter he knew how.

Then he strolled over to the Public Markets where the less fortunate business men, with no time to waste in voluptuous bathing, loafed in front of their shops, hoping for casual customers. Trade languished among the idol-sellers, perfumers and jewelers. So at last he stopped in front of Pinkus Brothers Rug Emporium. F. Jonas Pinkus, the popular Jewish rug merchant, was standing in the door, his smile set toward invisible customers.

"Hello, Pink," said Manlius, "how's the rug racket?"

"Can't complain," said Pink. "With such a stock exchange we got now, up comes a fella, rich over night. First thing he wants a woman. Then some wine. Then some rugs. But you gotta ask cash down in this business. Sometimes people go bust before we can deliver the rugs. But old family trade don't go back on you."

"Like the Julian clan, for instance?"

"Sure. Cæsar gets his rugs on contract, now he's the Administration. Who sends Cleopatra rugs? Dunt esk."

"Lots of rugs for Cleopatra?" insisted Manlius, seeing a fading light in Pink's eye.

"You said it." Mysteriously. "Right now this minute such an order you never saw goes up to her house on the Janiculum."

Manlius stood trying to think up some jaunty pun about cozy as a rug in a bug, or rug and the world rugs with you, sweep and you sweep alone—but ideas wouldn't come. For he had just seen a pair of slaves, carrying a long roll of carpet on their brawny shoulders, pass through a side door and down the street. Hurling a light farewell after F. Jonas Pinkus, Manlius followed in the wake of the slaves and caught up with them just around the corner.

Two small orientals, struggling on, had a six-foot roll on a long bamboo pole between them. The young reporter tagged along, his new formed idea growing, throbbing like a song inside his head. Tit for tat, tat for tit . . . into the great big house up yander, what's sauce for the goose is sauce for the gander. . . .

Again he recalled the story of Cleopatra's introduction to Cæsar. Just get inside a rug and let them unroll her at the conqueror's feet. How we get acquainted in Egypt. Of course, all jokes involve the risk of a violent death. Every humorist appreciates that. But Manlius also appreciated his own personal pulchritude, and how a really live serpent like Cleopatra might greet a good influence, suddenly introduced into her poisoned environment.

These speculations brought the panting Manlius, closely following the rug-bearing slaves, under the ilex shades of Janiculum Hill. It warmed his nervous heart to see Smithicus, backed by a dozen barbarous fellows, loitering around Cleopatra's gate. The two men from Pinkus' Emporium lingered at the door in the wall, knocked timidly, looked at the gladiators, waited.

Now was the time for decisive action. Manlius had merely to signal his Briton. In a moment Smithicus had put a strangle hold on the rearmost slave, gagged him with his own tunic and tossed him over the opposite wall. The other bearer, being Chinese, beat a remarkably able Chinese retreat. So far so good.

"Knock again. Make it loud," said Manlius to Smithicus. "When the gate opens, gag the man."

Smithicus pounded until the oak door shook on its hinges. In less than a minute it opened cautiously. The Briton's great arm went inside, pulled out a smallish *ostiarius,* wound him in his tunic, set him aside in a convenient cranny.

Manlius looked over his gladiators, a murderous, seamy lot.

"I don't want any rough stuff," he said, "unless I give the signal. You're here as gaggers, not stabbers," noting the disappointed look on their big faces. "When Smithicus carries me inside I want you to follow—all but two." Pointing out the largest pair. "You two stick outside the gate and grab anybody that comes up; hog-tie 'em, but make it quiet. The rest of you come inside the gardens and hide yourselves as near the doors and windows as you can. For heaven's sake, don't start anything. But if I holler, bust in the house and get me out of there."

"I shall see to it, sir," said Smithicus, as mildly as though his master had asked him to iron his shirt.

"All right, Smiddy," said Manlius. "Now here's what I want you to do. Roll me in those rugs, carry me up to Cleopatra and unroll me."

"Yes, sir. Quite right, sir."

Smithicus was a rapid worker, once he got the idea. In another minute his master was encased in a solid cylinder of hand-woven Bokhara; and if any one of us has ever sought romance in this fashion he will recall the tonic effect of several rugs, wrapped tightly around the face. Journalist to the finger-tips, Manlius, as he felt himself being picked up and moved forward, went over the vital statistics for the past ten years, dealing with the ratio of suffocation to every thousand rug-rollers. II.OIV out of every M survived, as he remembered the figures.

Jolt, jolt, jolt went the march toward Cleopatra. Through nine or ten thicknesses of rug, Manlius thought he smelled a subtle incense. Then he felt himself being lowered to the floor. Another wait, very grateful, because the rugs had sagged and let in a little air. Then Manlius felt himself being kicked gently, and his head spinning round and round as the rug unrolled.

Lights burst around him, mostly pink. He was staggering to his feet. He clutched at his toga, and found that it was wrapped around his neck. The great, gaudy room, of gold and ivory and tortoise shell, reeled like the main saloon of a ship at sea. Gradually the scene quieted, and he was aware of a slim ivory couch, and upon it a slim ivory woman, the Queen of Egypt, leaning delicately forward, a cobra-headed crown upon her small, auburn head.

In situations like this you have to make quick decisions. Manlius decided to sink on one knee and compose a speech beginning with, "O Majesty of the East—"

"How very foolish you look!" laughed Cleopatra; and her laugh had in it the ring of an elbow hitting an iron gate. Her eyes were a heart-breaking, wicked blue; and as she raised a hand to her chin, a huge amethyst ring, worn on her thumb, gave the illusion of three soul-draining eyes, looking straight into the victim's heart. "Suppose you get up and straighten your toga. It's a charming view, but people might talk, you know, seeing you like that."

One seldom makes one's toilet in the presence of royalty, but it's really not so bad as it sounds. The very act of patting down his draperies managed to put him at his ease, although the glare of that living stone on Cleopatra's thumb seemed to pierce into his every thought. Now he was arranged, and she was saying in her throaty, slow Greco-Egyptian accent:

"Brutus and Cassius are very romantic fellows. If they had sent their messenger to my door in the ordinary way I would have received him. But they must do everything in a roundabout way. Oh, well, I'm an oriental, and I understand why they love intrigue. Did they think to send credentials?"

"Here, O Queen." Promptly Mannie Scribo whipped out of his toga his self-written letter of introduction; Cleopatra leaned languidly over the tablet and read aloud:

> "To the Queen of Egypt greetings—*Sic Semper Tyrannis.* Comrade X is one of us. Make use of him as you wish.
>
> "BRUTUS."

"You have a nice face, Comrade X," crooned Cleopatra, her three eyes—two in her head and one on her thumb—glowing over him. "Too bad that you may be killed."

"Striking at a tyrant is always dangerous, Madam," he said on a bold guess.

"Isn't it?" she agreed sweetly. "But this one must fall. I have gone to so much trouble, I should hate to see anything slip up now."

Mannie's heart beat triumphantly. The beautiful serpent-woman was revealing the whole conspiracy against Julius Cæsar!

"Madam, permit me to congratulate you on all you have done. The removal of Comma, although it was of lesser importance, was a master stroke in itself."

"Comma?" Three eyes blazed incredulously. "Why should I have wanted to remove that little fellow?"

Mentally our reporter kicked himself. He had been barking up the wrong clue. But he regained his poise immediately and said:

"He was, as you say, nothing."

"As buyer of the lockets he was useful. But he has done his part. Tomorrow tells the story." She put her hands behind her head, and the light of her amethyst disappeared. The flesh under her transparent robe seemed to glow with its own light. The eyes which nature gave her—if there was any nature in the woman—smouldered sleepily upon Mannie Scribo. He wished she wouldn't do that. She was trying to get control over him, and he resented that, even in women he liked.

"Roman," she said, "do you know you have rather fine eyebrows? And I adore the lay of your ears."

"Women do," he admitted rather tersely. But that didn't discourage her. Nervously he felt the need of haste, lest he be caught in this dangerous game. But she went on:

"Comrade X, do you understand all women, of every kind?"

"All but vestal virgins, madam."

"Naughty of me, wasn't it, putting on the vestal's robes? But someone had to distribute the lockets, after Comma collected them for me. He got them for us from a special jeweler, you know. It was really great fun, going about disguised as a virgin—don't you love it? It was nice and dangerous, too, passing the medallions out to the conspirators. And signaling, when there was another meeting on. I really enjoyed it. Heigho!" She yawned, showing a curve of pearls around a ruby tongue. "Heigho! Women are so weak. So very, very weak!"

"Madam, let me congratulate you on the perfection of your—"

"Perfection of my what, pretty boy?" She was leaning several degrees farther back into the cushions.

"Perfection of your plot, lady," said Manlius in haste.

"Oh." Sleepily. She seemed to be waiting for something more.

"Women are so much smarter at plots than men are," insisted the sleuth-reporter, trying to remain impersonal.

"We are not clever," she sighed. "What are we but playthings?"

Mannie couldn't answer that, offhand. But her eyes and her amethyst drew at his heartstrings; her body languished among the cobweb weaves of Ind and Cathay. For a swooning second he forgot the questions that had been bursting to be answered. Then like a slack-wire performer he straightened himself and said:

"My share in the conspiracy is a humble one. I have come to be instructed."

"Sweet lad." She seemed almost asleep. "You have come to the right place."

But Mannie tensed his muscles and stood like a soldier, saying grimly, "If this plot is dangerous, O Queen, I'm for it."

"Comrade X, you have too beautiful eyes to be dimmed in death," she crooned. "It must be thrilling to be so brave in a desperate adventure. Now let me tell you. Cæsar comes down to the Senate at the third hour—" That would be about ten o'clock, Eastern Standard Time—"and you will post yourself at his private gate, to warn the conspirators of his approach. You remember, pretty boy? Tomorrow at the third hour."

"The fatal Ides of March."

"Yes, handsome." Still sleepily. "Knives are so coarse, aren't they? It is better to die by poison, I think. Much more amusing—and civilized. But Cassius prefers knives."

"They're more to the point," agreed Manlius.

"You have a neat way of saying things." She inched over on the couch and patted the cushions beside her. "Can't you come a little closer, pretty Roman? You look so formal, standing there."

He glanced around him nervously, the eye of his imagination seeing the garden outside, posted with his gladiators, waiting to do violence at the drop of a sandal. In the room there was no living thing but himself and the enchantress. The useful Smithicus had disappeared. But look. Slyly edging toward him from under a couch, a long, slim hunting-leopard with a workmanlike concentration, regarded the calf of Mannie's leg.

"Why hesitate, noble Roman?" cooed Cleopatra. "Don't you like cats?"

"Well, as a matter of fact, I rather prefer dogs. I'm not a very subtle person, I'll admit."

The leopard had crawled an inch closer.

"Why do you prefer dogs?" trilled the lovely queen.

"It's this way, the way I figure it. When you call a dog he comes just to *you.* But when you call a cat he comes half to you and half to himself."

The Serpent of the Nile developed a remarkably kissable pout and spoke to the leopard: "Go back, Peaches. Naughty man doesn't like 'oo."

Peaches, opening its mouth to show a perfect set of teeth, retreated under the couch and set up a purring that sounded like a witch's cauldron boiling some irresistible hell's broth.

"Am I like a cat?" she half whispered, her eyes and her thumb-ring now turned on him full blast. Manlius felt his knees.

"I didn't mean to imply anything like that, Cleo—I mean, O Queen."

"You may call me Cleo," she said faintly, and turned on the incense in a huge jade brazier by her side. The room swam with aromatic smoke. Manlius' resistance was weakening, but still he held ground. Her voice had changed to an alluring whinny.

"Psychologists tell us," she said, "that the cat-dread is merely a phobia."

"A phobia's what I prefer to dodge," he insisted. "But I'll catch one sure, if Peaches ever takes a nibble out of my—"

"In Egypt," she drawled, "the cat is held sacred."

"Old time religion's good enough for me." He drew farther away.

"Silly boy!" she gurgled. "Do I look like a queen?"

"Every inch." He should have known, because her gown was several ounces less than nebulous.

"I'm so glad, so glad you think so." She lay back, as one about to faint. What's she driving at? Mannie was asking himself. Is she trying to kill time; or trying to kill me?

"Roman—" her drawl was half a whisper—"are you a coward? If so, you are ill chosen for tomorrow's enterprise. And if not, why do you shrink away from a weak little woman?"

Now Manlius knew that he should act up to the difficult part he had chosen for himself.

"Who's afraid?" he asked, and seated himself boldly beside her.

"That's better," she said. One of her arms, white as a water-snake, went over his shoulder. She moved her lips toward his, and he felt her cobra crown tickle his hair. No, he wasn't exactly afraid. The touch of her was curiously pleasant; he began to realize how she had gone at it to twist Cæsar around her thumb, and to make a traitor out of Mark Anthony. He wished that the soft incense in that brazier would stop going up his nose; she had set him next to it.

"Cleo," he said with difficulty, "get me right. I'm a man of action."

"How wonderful!" Her voice had grown so far away.

"I mean that I'm here under instructions from Brutus. For the good of the conspiracy I must report to him at once—"

Suddenly Cleopatra sat up and listened. Manlius sat up too. Somewhere from the garden outside came the sounds of battle. The clash of blade on blade; dull curses in Latin, German, Gælic. Good gods, those hired palookas of his had funked the job, let themselves be discovered!

"What do you think that is?" asked the queen, but not nervously.

"Possibly a brawl among your servants," he said in his best offhand manner. "Shall I go out and quiet them?"

"No, dear boy. You have danger enough ahead of you without that. Stay where you are."

She reached up and sounded a crystal gong. Ping! its tenor note screamed through the palace. Almost immediately an obese eunuch waddled in and spoke to her in Egyptian. With a careless smile Cleopatra waved him away; he disappeared into the dim, drugged silence.

"It is nothing," she sighed, and again her snake-white arm went over Mannie's shoulder. "A quarrel among my kitchen slaves."

Queer, this heaviness that had come over him. Mannie seemed to be telling someone else to use his wits, or to cut his way out of there before it was too late. But it was already too late. Something in that horrible incense pot was stealing away his brain, his muscle, everything. He was like another person, feeling her arms, and the aromatic smoke, closing around him. His hands and feet were numb, his body unable to move. Her perfume penetrated his pores. Half drugged though he was, he was glad he'd taken that bath this afternoon. . . .

He was sinking away, away. He tried to talk, to accuse her of committing one murder and conspiring the greatest assassination in history. But he only laughed emptily. Delusions of grandeur tickled his empty brain. He could feel Cleopatra's hand, alive with the magic seeing-stone, creep across his face, into his hair. Through a fog he saw her head thrown back, her cobra crown rumpling the pillows; and vaguely he heard her voice:

"Manlius Scribo, my palace spy has found out your name and signaled it to me. Your gladiators have all been killed.

So you are alone with me, Manlius Scribo. And do you know, this is the first time I have ever been alone with a man?"

And then the lights went out . . .

His ears, not dead like the rest of him, heard her slide away like a snake through dry grass. His empty arms tried drunkenly to reach out for her; almost simultaneously a slight pain in the leg informed him that Peaches, the leopard, had reached out for him. It didn't hurt much, because Manlius was almost under. Weakly he fumbled for his dagger, but couldn't locate the handy pocket he had had sewed in for a quick draw. He didn't care. He didn't care about anything. But he revived slightly at the sound of Cleopatra's voice in the distance, now harshly efficient:

"Sam, throw on a little more hasheesh. Give him the trap door, Charley."

Vaguely he felt the floor give way under him and his half-conscious body sliding helplessly down a greased chute.

Then oblivion.

## XIII

A DEEP, dank dungeon, a futurist's paradise of musty arcades and pillars which seemed to lean every way but the right way. Trying to follow the diagram made Mannie's headache worse. He swooned comfortably for a while, then revived to study his situation. Faint light filtered in through slits in the wall. Distantly the amateur detective saw a row of enormous ovals, their contours so balling up the design of crooked pillars and jumbled arcades that he became temporarily seasick, and felt better.

The true Roman spirit came to his rescue, and he tottered to his feet, guided by a familiar smell. Things began to shape themselves, and now he could see what the line of ovals truly meant. They were so many enormous wine casks, each one plainly labeled with its brand, and below the telltale markings, "C.J.C. Roma."

"The aroma of Rome," thought Manlius, and wished he had an audience to appreciate the pun. And how his dry throat longed for one reviving swig from these uncounted gallons, stored by the great Cæsar in his private cellars. Mannie's tongue grated like sand against the roof of his mouth; but his quick, objective mind began to revive slowly. After his adventure with Cleopatra he had been dropped into Cleopatra's cellar. True, the big casks bore Cæsar's stamp—birthday presents to the Levantine Squaw, no doubt—but the smaller ones, daintily hooped with polished brass, were labeled, "H.R.M. Cleopatra, Not to Be Opened Until 43 B.C." Liquor, liquor everywhere, and not a drop to drink. Now realizing that he had been drugged and dragged, as the *sermo vulgaris* hath it, Manlius closed his fist and pounded upon the great oak barrelheads. The sound produced was like that of a quartette at the Bass Drummers' Annual Clambake. A hollow advertisement.

And not without effect. A ghostly form materialized into Smithicus, the perfect valet-gladiator. His tunic sat as well on his shoulders as though he had just finished pressing it. His hair and his walrus moustache were humbly but neatly combed, and he stood holding his master's thick woolen raincoat.

"It's a bit damp down here, sir," he suggested. "It might do no harm to slip this on. It's a dreadful season for liver chills."

The extra garment made Manlius feel two or three degrees better, although he was still so far below the normal that Depression looked mighty like Prosperity to him.

"How'd you get here?" asked Manlius thickly.

"Wotan—he's rather a top-hole god with the barbarians—only knows. Those oriental perfumes, sir, are in rather poor form. Far too heavy. I was waiting in the anteroom when that eunuch chap perfumed me, and I fear I lost possession of my senses."

"Is it true that our gladiators were all killed?"

"Only three quarters true, sir. Some of them escaped. I had time to finish four of Cleopatra's fellows when I thought of you, sir, and went to the anteroom."

Reason, flooding back to Mannie's brain, revealed the seriousness of his position. Ingeniously he had forced his way into the very heart of the conspiracy against Julius Cæsar. Cunningly he had wheedled from Cleopatra's wicked lips enough of the truth to assure him of the very hour when the Dictator would meet his doom; the very spot where he was marked to fall. Other questions, which had plagued him for days, faded into insignificance. Comma, as Cleopatra had said, was just a "little fellow." Even Pompeia's warning, shouted at the Junior League Fair, made no great difference now.

The main point was that Cleopatra knew and the conspirators knew that Cæsar would walk up to the shambles on schedule time. Indeed, had he not said so, in no uncertain voice, smiling into the traitor eyes of Brutus and Cassius as they fawned upon him at the Fair? The high priest of Jupiter had decreed that Cæsar should fall into the trap. Hm. And the high priest himself was on Cassius' payroll—or still more likely, Mark Anthony's.

Under the shadow of a greater tragedy ahead, Manlius tried to minimize his own peril. Cleopatra had caught him cold-handed; and she had but one way of dealing with cold-handed people. In Mannie's death she had everything to gain; a dead Roman was a good Roman, as Cicero might have said. And she could not afford to let Mannie Scribo, knowing what he did, wander at large in Rome on the day of Cæsar's assassination.

"What time do you think it is, Smiddy?"

"Four hours after midnight, sir."

How the British wonder knew that didn't concern Mannie. All he was thinking of was: It's already the Ides of March. The greatest news story in the universe will break in six hours. And I'm here. But if I can get there on time, will I stand by and let Cæsar be nicked to pieces by a lot of amateur patriots? It's not sporting, and I'm a sports writer. Suppose I jumped in and stopped the show at the dramatic moment—Castor and Pollux, what a story there! Cæsar saved exclusively by the *Evening Tiber. . . .* But the *Evening Tiber's* now an Anthony paper. Hell and Pluto, what a mix-up. . . .

"If that German gladiator hadn't dropped his sword in a garbage can," Smithicus was saying, "we should never have been discovered. You seem to have quite a nasty wound, sir. Fortunately I still carry a spot of that fire-wine."

"Gimme," said Manlius.

But the handy Briton shook his head. "It would be better to rub it on your leg, sir," he said, "where Her Majesty's leopard bit you. If you don't mind being burned, I mean to say—"

*"Holy Remus!!!"*

Manlius went dancing among the dim pillars, for his slave had sprinkled a thimbleful of CX Proof on the sore spot. Up and down the cellar our hero executed a bacchanal, discovering new steps and swearing at all the gods and goddesses he could remember. At last, the smart subsiding somewhat, he reached out for the bottle with another harsh "Gimme!" Into a leather cup, which Smithicus had concealed in his obliging tunic, the slave poured a stiff drink of the Spanish elixir. Manlius tossed it off, revived magically, felt his oats, felt his hay, his spinach and his corn.

"The walls here," he said valiantly, "are only five feet thick. It's all so simple. We'll bust through 'em."

"A minute, sir," suggested the tame gladiator. "I have investigated, and I find that behind the wine casks there is quite a long corridor. It leads somewhere, I fancy."

"Yeah. Corridors usually do."

"I dare say, sir." Rather incredulously. "And if you'll forgive my saying so, I have found at the end of it—"

But that was all, because oaken doors opened somewhere with a dreadful clang. Suddenly the wine-cellar was bathed in a diabolic light. Tramp-tramp-tramp came iron-shod feet, and the red flicker revealed a company of leather-aproned executioners, carrying charcoal braziers and an elaborate collection of instruments. Not a pretty sight for a lone spy, caught in the mazes of Cleopatra's villa.

Businesslike, scientific persons, these Roman executioners. Some of them, after years of brilliant practice, received doctor's degrees; the heads of the profession affected operating room manners.

Already the head executioner was fussing about, putting on rubber gloves and assuming all the swank of a really fashionable practitioner. Three or four orderlies were heating instruments to the proper temperature, others were wheeling in a cast-iron operating table.

"What's the case, doctor?" asked a square built assistant, sidling up to the head executioner.

"Exploratory operation, doctor," replied the chief, pulling a pair of medium-sized pincers out of a brazier and testing them.

A female slave in a white cap walked up to where Manlius stood very close to Smithicus. "Please state name, age, religious convictions if any, residence, where born and nearest living relative," she intoned, holding up a little silver stylus.

"What for?" asked Manlius sternly.

"Merely a matter of form," said the female.

"Well, suppose I won't tell you." He reached for his dagger, only to find it gone.

"Then I'm afraid we can't torture you until you do," said she with a severe smile.

"Oh, yes, we can," broke in the head executioner. "This is an emergency case, and we'll waive formalities. Would you mind removing your toga, tunic and under-tunic, and stepping over to the table?"

"I don't happen to want to," said Manlius, sizing up the armed guard and an assistant moving closer with a hot brazier.

"Dear, dear," said the head executioner, "this is very irregular. But if you refuse to cooperate, I'm afraid we'll have to—Nemo!" snapping his fingers at an enormous black slave, "remove the gentleman's clothing . . . *ouch!*"

This last remark, uncharacteristic of the scientist's cool behavior, was caused by the strategy of Smithicus, who had slyly picked up the distinguished man and set him down in a burning brazier. After this, of course, the scene was tremendously confused; red hot pokers were flying through the air, Manlius plying them with fine effect on the heads of swart tormentors, closing in on him. Meanwhile Smithicus had picked up the cast-iron table and was mowing down everything within ten feet of him.

The fight was going well for a while, and the two captives might have come out victors, even as they battled, with ten to one against them, had not the black Nemo, demonstrating an ancient jiu-jitsu trick, laid his knee gently against the small of Mannie's back and sent him sprawling. After that the tired hero was just a mass of torturers, gladiators and others. The head executioner, after putting out the fire in the seat of his tunic, quite lost his operating room manner.

"Tie him to a post!" he snarled, "and let me have a crack at him."

It is not a pleasant sensation, being tied to a post; especially when the post is the focal center of large iron kettles, containing hot coals. Mannie Scribo, had he been of weaker clay, might have prayed to the shades of his ancestors. Instead he began to swear.

"Listen, you goddess-damned son of a butcher, if you dare to touch me with that cheap curling iron the *Evening Tiber* will roast you so that you'll want to go to hell and get cool."

But the head executioner, selecting a mean looking pair of tongs, plunged them into the fire and stirred thoughtfully. Smithicus, who had been lashed to a rival post, gazed upon the operation with disapproving British eyes. But this grim comedy could not go on forever. At last the scientist, having tested the hot-points of his tongs, and finding them the indicated temperature, slowly approached Manlius, the instrument pointed toward his unprotected stomach. Closer and closer came the heat, the victim cringing involuntarily. Then—

*"Ow!"*

It was not Manlius who made the noise. But under a dark arcade a wildcat scream fairly shook the wine-casks, causing the tormentors to drop their tools and fall back in something like a panic. Toward them, out of the darkness, shot a little figure in a pink robe. A red-headed girl, full of the fury that comes with that kind of hair.

Romula!

"You ought to be ashamed of yourselves. You brutes. You—you regular—devils. Can't you fight like men—you—you yellow—"

Manlius, unclothed and helpless, experienced some of the embarrassment of a freshman nudist. But Romula did not turn a hair of her lovely auburn head as she stood in front of him, bullying the executioners.

"If you dare—even dare—to touch either of these gentlemen—I'll—I'll tell Anthony—I'll tell Cæsar—I'll have you all crucified—"

"But, madam," the head executioner was curiously humble and deferential, "we are not doing this out of malice. We are under orders to—"

"I don't care what you're under. If you burn him, you devil, you've got to burn me."

Still unconscious of his nudity, she threw her arms around Mannie, clung to him, sobbing and panting.

"Drag her away," commanded the head executioner irritably.

The hands of Nemo went around her waist. "Y-e-e-e!" she howled, kicking his shins with her sharp heels. "Let go of me, you black—"

Then suddenly the room was ablaze with torches and the brilliance of centurion tunics. A big, curly-headed man in a general's uniform stood in the midst of the horrid circle, folded his arms and smiled the smile that made him Rome's popular hero.

"Well, Manlius Scribo, they're giving you a warm welcome, I see," said Mark Anthony.

"As a representative of your paper, sir, I thank you," replied Mannie, not to be outdone.

But the big man's face grew stern, his voice a bullish bellow as he turned to the head executioner and asked:

"Whose orders are these?"

"Her Majesty's, Excellency," replied the quaking scientist.

"What does she mean by interfering with the policy of my paper?" he thundered. "Untie this gentleman. Untie his slave. Next time you're sent on a job like this, consult me."

Quick hands loosened Mannie's bonds; and it was characteristic of Smithicus that, the instant he was untied, he leaped to the rescue with his master's remarkably dirty tunic and toga. With almost nervous haste he draped the Scribonian shoulders and whispered confidentially, "You're a bit more tidy now, sir." Then hastily he reached for his own garments and slipped them on. Whatever happened, British decorum must be observed.

"Here gathering news, I suppose?" remarked Anthony, his handsome face quizzical as he watched the performance.

"Yes, sir, in a way," said Manlius. "You see, I'm investigating a murder case."

"I'm only an amateur journalist," smiled Anthony. "But might I hint that this is a poor week to investigate murders?"

Romula stood there, twitching nervously; Anthony patted her arm in a way that annoyed Manlius out of his thought of more important things. But Anthony was going smoothly on:

"I approve of your enterprise, young man. But enterprise sometimes carries us a little too far. You've broken into the wrong house this time, my boy."

"I apologize," said the reporter, not without wickedness. "I was under the impression that this house belonged to the Dictator."

The temper which Manlius had seen before flashed in Anthony's prominent eyes; possibly he would summon the torturers back to go on with their work. But his good natured smile returned.

"I've always enjoyed your sports column," said Anthony. "And I think you're better at that than at criminal and political news. In the meantime, I shall be delighted to make you our guest here until tomorrow. Sorry the accommodations are so poor. But you'll not be annoyed again, I assure you."

"I'm supposed to report to my city editor in the morning," said Manlius, holding on to himself.

"I'll arrange that with him. Put your mind at rest on that score. Well, we must be toddling."

Without another word he took Romula by the hand and led her away. Fury got the better of P. Manlius Scribo, and he would have plunged after her, accusing her of every crime under Apollo's sun, but eight centurions with drawn swords blocked his path.

"Romula!" he shouted desperately. "Romula!"

And there she was, dodging under the elbows of the soldiers and throwing herself into his arms.

"Don't think the worst of me!" she was pleading. "Don't—Manlius, didn't I save your life?"

"Yes, you did." But he was stubbornly unbending. "But does that account for your being here in this nest of killers? Does that explain the company you keep, the way you're doing nothing but block my way when—"

"Hush!" Her little hand went over his mouth. "I can't say anything—now. I'll tell you when I can. Everything's all right. But I must go—Manlius, don't—"

"Romula!" It was Anthony's big voice, commanding in the distance. She wriggled out of her lover's arms, ducked again under the swords of the centurions and vanished into the dimness.

An hour, perhaps more, had gone by. Manlius sat on an empty crate, nursing his tired head. Romula loved him; no girl that isn't crazy about a man would throw herself in front of a pair of red-hot tongs in order to save him. But she couldn't do anything to square herself. Voluntarily she had gone into the biggest nest of crooks in all Rome. Romula was out, as far as he was concerned.

Q. Bulbus, editor of the *Evening Tiber,* was out too. Anthony would fix it with Q. Bulbus. Yeah. Old Calamity was backing the assassination, that was plain. And what did Manlius owe Q. Bulbus, after all? Loyalty? The ancient rascal had a favorite motto, "Every reporter should be loyal to his papyrus." But it went pretty far, being loyal, when you found your paper backing a cold-blooded political murder. But just the same—here the reporter in Manlius came to the fore again—it would be swell to be on hand at that assassination. An exclusive story. Wow!

Presently Smithicus came back, rather damp after his tour of inspection.

"What did you find?" asked Mannie, hoping against hope.

"That corridor behind the casks, sir, extends into a tunnel, which must go under the Tiber. At the extreme end, sir, there is a water-tight box which, by an arrangement of pulleys, can be raised up a shaft through the river."

"Oh. An elevator?" asked Manlius, who had seen one in the house of Saleratus the banker.

"No, sir. A lift."

"Lift or fall," said the reporter, who had suspected some such ingenious arrangement, "let's go." But again he hesitated. "How about the guards?"

"I gave them each a spot of the fire-wine, sir. They're now quite unconscious, strewn about the corridors."

Without hesitation, following his slave, Manlius plunged between the wine casks, found the great black hole, leading nowhere, began groping his way through darkness. How he stumbled, how he barked his elbows against jutting stones, only slightly concerns this chronicle. Smithicus had him by the hand, helping him along. His eyes were becoming accustomed to darkness when, in the far distance, he saw a tiny, twinkling light. It was a little lamp, set by an oak door.

"This is the lift, sir," was Smithicus' unnecessary explanation.

"Must be used a lot, to have a lamp by it," mused Manlius. "Wonder who it's for? Cæsar, or Anthony?"

"Both, no doubt," said the Briton. He opened the door and showed a box-like contrivance full of pulleys and gadgets.

"I think we'd better take the lamp with us," decided Manlius. "We won't be long in this, unless—"

Smithicus closed the door, pulled a rope. There was a melancholy creaking, a horrid rush of waters and the box-thing bounded up with such force as to slump them both on the floor. Five seconds, maybe, or an hour—then *boom*. Timbers crashed, all the dirty muck of yellow Tiber came flooding in on them. Manlius closed his lungs, his teeth, his nose and found himself swimming on the surface of the river, under one of the docks of the Tiber wharves. "Something must have gone wrong with the mechanism," suggested Smithicus, bobbing up beside him.

The sun was up when the wet adventurers found a landing stage and dragged themselves on the wharf. Drippingly Manlius computed the distance between himself and his humble lodgings. Plenty of time to get there, rest, change togas and get over to warn Cæsar, as he had decided now to do.

It would have been simpler, perhaps, to have gone directly to the Dictator's house with the sinister truth. But there would be no news in that. And once again Mannie Scribo saw the glorious headline, "*Evening Tiber* Hero Saves Dictator from Killers."

Soon Manlius was back in his economical bedroom—about three dollars a week at the present rate of foreign exchange, soap and towels included. He lay on his solid oak bed, dreamily watching Smithicus ironing the second best toga for another public appearance. This finished, the dutiful Briton tensed his muscles to give his master a vigorous rub-down. Vigorous was the word; horny hands made welts in the patient's flesh, but restored young blood to the boiling point.

"Why don't you take my skin off and dry clean it while you're about it?" he growled appreciatively.

"That wouldn't be quite decent, would it, sir?" asked the Briton, still rubbing holes in his master.

"All right," said Mannie Scribo. "I'm polished to the limit. Hand me those."

Smithicus presented the *brevis vestis democraticus,* or B.V.D., and reached for the other raiment proper to a gentleman of culture. Bathed, shaved, breakfasted and freshly pipe-clayed, Manlius made his handsome way to the door.

"And now, my slave," he said, "we'll trot over to the scene of the assassination. Perhaps we can add another chapter to Cicero's book on *Why We Behave Like Romans."*

## XIV

DUE TO repair-work on the Capitol, the Senate was meeting nowadays in an old barn of a Hall of Records out on the Campus Martius. To get there sooner, Manlius should have hired a public litter; but he had lost his last denarius in his watery escape from Cleopatra's house. He was disturbed, in passing a jeweler's shop, to see that the water clock marked two hours after sunrise, about 9:15 Eastern Standard Time. These water clocks were usually wrong, but just the same a little speeding up wouldn't do any harm.

The natural vigor of a healthy and athletic youth—Manlius had twice been runner-up in the annual Marathon at the University of Rhodes—quickened his pace. He stretched his stride to a fast cross-country dog-trot, moving so swiftly that he could hear the heavy Smithicus puffing at his shoulder.

In spite of a leopard bite in the leg, a twelve foot drop into a cellar, a thorough drugging and an experiment in drowning that would have killed the ordinary man, Manlius was himself again. The morning air, the wholesome exercise brought his nerves up to concert pitch.

He was just gaining his second wind, and was perhaps a quarter mile from the old Hall of Records, across the street from Pompey's Theater, when he passed a heavy bronze litter, the kind that fat men use, escorted by some fifty soldiers in a dainty pink uniform. This, then, would be Tamany of Athens and his personal bodyguard. As Manlius and his slave went scooting by the litter's golden curtains parted and Tamany's broad face, pale and pig-eyed, was revealed.

"Hey, young fella!" he shouted. Despite his haste Manlius paused. "Are you going to the Senate?" asked the nervous voice.

"If nobody else stops me," responded Manlius, on his toes for another spurt.

"As friend or foe?" asked Tamany.

"Friend, sort of."

"Friend of Cæsar?"

"Sort of."

"Then, listen. Ten golden talents for you, if you hold the conspirators away from Cæsar until my army comes to his defense."

"It's bad as that, is it?"

"Worse. The stabbing's booked for ten o'clock. Make it snappy, kid. I'll raise it to fifteen grand if—"

"What's your cut in this murder, anyhow?" Manlius stopped to ask, in spite of his hurry.

"Cut?" piped Tamany. "I can't afford to lose a customer like Cæsar. Not today. Do you realize that, on his personal account, he owes me two thousand talents, gold, and not a word on paper? Just a gentleman's agreement? If he's bumped I'm ruined. Hurry, boy—in the name of Mercury, god of thieves—"

Manlius plunged on. He could see Tamany's predicament. With his heavy litter and his soldiers armed with boiler plate from head to foot, they could only plod, and would be late for the tragedy. But old Tamany's confession thrilled Manlius to the core. And what journalist is not thrilled to know that his predictions are coming true? *Cæsar moriturus est.* The Big Fella is about to die!

And Manlius, with the aid of his trusty gladiator, would be there in time to prevent it.

## XV

AT a gateway in the temporary forum, outside the Hall of Records, Manlius saw Chief Kellius, loitering under an arcade with two or three professional crooks, hanging around for their morning's instructions. In 44 B.C. the alliance between the Police Department and the underworld was so well recognized that only by his uniform could the hunter be distinguished from the hunted.

"You seem to be in a hurry, young man," sang out Kellius.

"I *was* in a hurry," admitted Manlius, pausing. "But since the Force is on the job, law and order will reign, I suppose."

"You've said it, lad," smiled Kellius. Then he lost interest and, turning to the big Italian at his side, went on explaining how the poultry racket was all right, if only you changed the license on your chariot often enough.

Inside the forum Manlius faced one of the galling little anticlimaxes which bother even the modern detective. People were going about, doing business as usual, opening the branch stock exchange, putting in advance bids for blondes from the Circassian market; several hundred of the courtroom bums we always have with us were loafing at the foot of the Rostra, waiting for the judge to come in and review the morning's cases. Here Junius Brutus as pretor was supposed to hold court. The reporter's breath caught sharply as he saw Brutus himself, with his cousin Decimus and Senator Casca, come strolling by, looking all too carefree and jolly. They stopped at the foot of the Rostra; the face of Brutus was drawn to a fixed smile as he glanced at his confederates, then mounted the platform.

This, then, was a part of the show. Cæsar hadn't arrived on schedule, and Pretor Brutus would have to put up a bluff of going on with the day's work. Stiffly, like a moving corpse, he began fumbling with legal scrolls, scolding the attorneys. . . .

But no Cæsar.

Manlius wandered into the Senate Chamber and saw a suspiciously large attendance of solons, standing in groups, stroking their bald heads. The usual scene, a lot of confused lawmakers, trying to make up their minds. Valuable clue;

there were too many of them. Possibly it was merely because the Committee on Finance had been working out a 15 per cent income tax raise to float the coming Parthian war. Casca, as usual, had been with the opposition. But snappy little Casca wasn't there to whip 'em into line.

And no Cæsar.

Out in the forum Casca was still shuffling around, self-consciously innocent, eyes furtively studying the water clock. Cousin Decimus had joined Senator Cimber. Just for a second. Their eyes were worried. Cassius came along, wearing a liar's smile.

But no Cæsar.

It was getting on Mannie's nerves, and the conspirators', no doubt. Finally Casca nudged Cousin Decimus; Decimus significantly disappeared. But Brutus, in his capacity as pretor, sat up on the Rostra and began, a little shrilly, to outline his rulings in the case of The People vs. Squintus Simplex. The suit involved ten sesterces, or about forty cents, but Brutus was several degrees too serious for the size of the trial.

"Might I suggest, sir," asked Smithicus, sidling up to Manlius, "that you put on a bit of disguise? A gentleman of your prominence, sir, might be recognized, as I once said to the Duke of Axminster—"

In Rome it was always easy to hide, because the town averaged ten statues to the block. In a narrow street between the Curia and Pompey's Theater the two found a statue of Cupid and Psyche and crept behind it while Smithicus, from his ever ready tunic, brought out a large gray moustache with eyebrows and hair to match. "Now they'll never guess, milord, that you're a reporter from the *Tiber,* and if you wish to address Cæsar—at your own risk, I fear—you may do so without the slightest suspicion of your identity."

"Funny," said Manlius, "that Tamany and his soldiers don't come up."

"I'm afraid they won't, sir," sighed Smithicus. "One of the Senate page-boys just informed me that a hundred mysterious gladiators popped out from behind a building and butchered Tamany's soldiers properly. Lord Tamany, I understand, is in retreat. The fortunes of politics, I am afraid—"

"What's making Cæsar so late this morning? He's usually such a crank about being on time."

"The senate page, sir, informed me that His Lordship the Dictator is suffering from a touch of ptomaine."

"Cleopatra?" gasped Manlius.

"No, sir. Oysters."

"Practically the same thing." Manlius stroked his long moustache, vaguely wondering what excuse he'd make for this queer get-up when the time came to jump between Cæsar and the knife. Then his keen intelligence came to the rescue. Too bad that he was short-handed in assistant sleuths.

"Smithicus," said Manlius solemnly, "how loyal are you?"

"I'd lay down my life for you, sir, in a manner of speaking."

"Fair enough. Truly British. Now listen. Major General Decimus Brutus has just left the forum. It's likely that he's been sent to bring the Dictator down to the Curia. Chase over there, as fast as your big legs will carry you. When Cæsar comes out run back and tell me. How well are you heeled?"

From his tunic Smithicus brought the sword which Manlius, in defiance of the law, had lent him.

"Good," said Manlius. "Use it, in case of. If you're in trouble trust in the *Evening Tiber to* fetch you out."

"And you, sir?"

With one flip of the wrist Manlius produced his personally designed .xxxii dagger from the special breast pocket in his toga.

"Quite impressive, sir," said Smithicus. "Shall I go to Cæsar's official palace on the Palatine, or to Cleopatra's residence?"

"Try the official residence," said the master.

Smithicus stalked away, while Manlius turned his toga inside out—it was lined with red flannel—and in this disguise sauntered back to the forum, stroking his long gray moustache as he sauntered.

Eleven forty-eight by the water clock. The nervous excitement which had been passing quietly through the forum, like a cold draft, had somewhat subsided. Brutus was still on the Rostra, mumbling legal idiocies, a man talking against time; now and then he looked wistfully into the crowd below.

Inside the Curia the Senate had gone into session, in charge of a president *pro tem.* Mannie's wild disguise was hardly noticed; so many freaks came to Rome nowadays. He edged closer to a knot of senators who had abandoned their senatorial tasks inside the building. Casca, Cassius and Cimber, hypocritically clapping hands at the cheap oration of a cheap lawyer; their anxious eyes roving toward the Alley of Statues, watching no doubt for Cæsar's entrance. . . .

Manlius jumped. It was Smithicus nudging his elbow.

"We played the wrong horse, sir," whispered the slave. "He was at the house of Cleopatra, after all. I hurried over there, but he had just left with Mark Anthony."

"Then Anthony *is* the stool pigeon, huh?"

"I dare say so, sir."

"Where are they now?"

"Just outside Cæsar's gate, sir. His Lordship the Dictator has paused by the Altar of Justice to wash his hands. In a minute, I should say, they'll be coming down the Alley of Statues."

A hint was sufficient, and there was no time to lose; seizing his Briton by the wrist, Manlius sneaked along the marbled shadows and cuddled again behind the heroic version of Cupid and Psyche. A terrible silence, broken by loud applause and ribald laughter from Pompey's Theater, right behind him; Hesiod, the comedian, had no doubt offered another of his antic ribaldries to the brainless populace. Peering round the statue's polished base, the anxious reporter could count five conspirators, drawn tightly together under an arcade; Cassius, Casca, a lawyer named Pansa, Cimber and Cousin Decimus. Then the sixth stole up, belatedly. Brutus.

From every toga the broad handle of a twelve inch dagger obtruded. The conspirators were pushing each other further forward.

Every nerve taut, Manlius realized that he held the strategic position; it would be impossible for Cæsar to reach the spot on which he was being put without passing his intended rescuer's hiding place. Long time did Manlius linger there, holding his heart, his breath, his dagger. Down the line, in the conspirators' huddle, someone was giving Brutus a push; as if to say, "You take the first whack."

At the end of the alley was the big iron gate, through which the Dictator must come—for he had chosen it as his own gate and crowned it with an eagle. A few yards from it, across the street, the Statue of Pompey frowned, its back to the main ticket window of Pompey's Theater. This was no more than twenty feet from where Manlius and his slave were hiding; beyond them, far too near for comfort, the waiting assassins crouched, fondling their guilty knives.

Stage settings in detective stories are frequently a little confused, at first glance; but we hope our reader will get this situation clearly, because it is of great importance in the world-shaking drama which followed. Let's rehearse it rapidly again before we proceed with our murder.

Face Cæsar's gate (the one with the eagle on it), and the first building to your right is Pompey's Theater. Pay no attention to the other statues lining the alley—Rome's so full of statues you'll go crazy if you notice them all—but keep your mind on Pompey's statue. Then diagonally, across the street, there's Cupid and Psyche, given to the city by an amorous old pretor who—but never mind that. There's Cupid and Psyche, concealing Manlius and Smithicus. Then, six or eight feet beyond them, on the same side of the street, coming this way, is the arcade, practically filled with knife-wielders, thirsting for Cæsar's blood.

Is that plain now? Then we'll proceed.

From where he hid in a convenient jog in the pedestal Manlius could hear the low voice of Cassius, brain of the conspiracy. "Junius Brutus," he was saying, "you will strike the first blow."

"But, listen, Cassius—" Brutus was beginning, when the strong man broke in, "Shut up, and do as I say. You've balled things up enough already. Now this is what you're supposed to do. Wait till he's just inside the lobby, then stick him and yell the slogan. You remember it?"

*"Sic Semper Tyrannis,"* repeated Brutus faintly.

"Don't say it in that sick-cat voice," demanded Cassius. "Remember you're freeing Rome from a tyrant. And the object of this is to gather the Senate around us and start the Big Parade."

Mumble-mumble went the voices while Mannie tensed his muscles for the high spot in his professional career. Then a hideous silence. A young Italian, maybe Comrade X, sauntered across the alley and gently raised his hand.

Something rang like a great bell. It was the lifting of a latch on Cæsar's gate. Smithicus began to wheeze and was silenced by a poke in the ribs.

A moment of tremendous thrill; positively the last appearance of Julius Cæsar on any stage!

Quite unconscious of danger, apparently, and somewhat affected and too awfully imperial as he had been the other day at the gladiatorial show, Cæsar, on the arm of his unworthy friend, Mark Anthony, came slowly through the gate. They were discussing vegetable gardens.

"No, my boy," insisted Cæsar, "I don't think a carrot over four inches long is fit to eat. I had a cook poisoned once for feeding me old carrots. It was a case of me or her, so I let 'er die."

"But sometimes an old carrot done, you know—sort of braised in beef gravy, with a couple of large onions—"

"You talk like a German," laughed Cæsar in a strangely affected voice. "Coming into the Senate?"

"Pretty soon," said Mark. "I'm dropping into Pompey's Theater for a minute to look over that sword swallowing act."

"Wish I could join you," simpered the Big Fella. "But duty is duty. So long."

With a high-handed Roman salute Anthony disappeared in the theater door. Was it a signal for the conspirators to fly forward and begin their dirty work? Possibly, for suddenly they were all on their toes, every dagger drawn. But their quarry was whimsical. Something written on a small tablet seemed to amuse him, and he took out his stylus to jot down a few notes.

Then he moved slowly on toward his doom. One, two, three steps forward; a threatening move among the conspirators—Manlius, deciding that his opportunity had come, touched up his false moustache and doubled his knees to spring to the defense. But the decision came too late.

*For Julius Casar, walking quite alone, fully a dozen feet beyond the reach of any assassin's arm, suddenly threw his stylus in air and fell forward on his face!*

*A deadly knife, coming out of nowhere, had pierced him straight through the back and stood quivering in his bleeding and lifeless body!*

This was confusing as well as ghastly, both to Manlius and his slave; but to the conspirators it was intensely embarrassing.

"Who in Helvetia did that?" cried Decimus Brutus in a rough soldier's voice.

"I didn't," quavered Junius Brutus. "I was going to, but—"

"None of us did!" muttered the others.

"What are we expected to do now?" asked Casca petulantly. "We came here to kill Cæsar, and he's done the job himself."

*"Bolonia!"* snarled Cassius, "a man can't stab himself in the back, even if he is a politician."

For an instant they stood irresolute, not knowing where to turn. But it was Cassius, as usual, who kept his head.

"Grab the credit for it, boys! That's the main thing. Brutus, turn him over, take that hog-knife out of his back and stick your own dagger in his chest. Atta patriot. Now, boys, give the yell—one, two, three—"

"*Sic Semper Tyrannis*—rah-rah—Liberty, Liberty—Ti-ger!!!" roared the Six Savage Senators, appropriately dipping their swords in blood as they waved them aloft. The effect was instantaneous. Rome began to howl, the loudest, longest howl within the memory of its oldest inhabitant. Senators, their togas immodestly lifted so that they could run faster, boiled out of the Curia, blinking confusedly and repeating, "Well, well, well!" over and over.

"And who is responsible for this?" asked an old senator, speaking for the first time in twenty-five years.

"The Author of Freedom! Author! Author!" cried the fat Cassius, laying down his knife to clasp the hand of Junius Brutus, who modestly stepped forward, his schoolgirl complexion deepening to a maiden blush.

"My friends," he began falteringly, "I have no great experience at public speaking—and I feel sure—er—that for our little success more credit is due to my talented company than to its principal performer—myself—"

Howling Rome drowned out the rest. The mob, always waiting for a little fun of any kind, seemed to boil out of the ground, ecstatically yelling for both sides. A moment later a hundred heavyweight gladiators, completely encased in iron, marched single file out of Pompey's Theater. On their backs were large painted placards, "Down With Tyrants!"

"Down With Taxes!" "We Want Wine!" "Give Us Another New Deal!!!" Twice around the forum they marched, the people shouting, not because they knew what it was about, but because they always shouted at public pageants. The two largest gladiators picked up Junius Brutus and put him on their shoulders.

"Our hero!" "He's a bum!" "He saved Rome!" "Crown him with roses!" "Crown him with a brick!" Mingled cries of the populace. Somewhere a band struck up, "Hail, hail, the gang's all here." [6] Then a scattered few of Tamany's soldiers broke in and started mixing it with a little bit of everybody. By this time, of course, nobody remembered what it was all about; just gloried in the perfect Roman sport of Mayhem vs. Manslaughter.

Only P. Manlius Scribo stood aside, pondering as he leaned weakly on the arm of his Smithicus. Who killed Cæsar? Certainly not Brutus, carried aloft there, dodging brickbats and bouquets as he took all the credit. Certainly not Cassius and his cowardly crew. Certainly not Mark Anthony, for Anthony had disappeared into Pompey's Theater a full minute before Cæsar, standing beyond stabbing distance of anybody, had fallen with a knife between his shoulder blades.

For a split second Manlius felt what all detectives feel sooner or later, a questioning regret: "Why did I ever take up this sort of work?" Mystery problems can become so involved. The young detective felt his moustache slipping; impatiently he let it slide.

"You're out of disguise, sir," said Smithicus, dolefully.

"What of it?" snapped his master.

"Nothing at all, sir. I thought you might like to know."

Manlius took off his toga and put it on properly. Meanwhile the historic scene continued in the grand old forum. The frantic mob milled around Junius Brutus, either kissing him or killing him—a matter of indifference to Manlius—and a Jewish profiteer passed among them, selling liberty caps for two sesterces each.

Suddenly to the *Tiber* representative came the sharp question: What happened to the knife Brutus pulled out of

---

[6] *Ave, ave! Omnes hic sumus!*

Cæsar's back when he planted his own blade in the place where it would show to more advantage?

Regaining strength, Manlius ran over to the foot of Pompey's statue, and was scarcely surprised when he found that the body was no longer there. A trail of blood led across the paving stones from the statue's base to a concrete trap door at one corner of the Senate building. Two of Kellius' policemen, with drawn swords, were guarding the spot. In spite of them, Manlius seized hold of the big iron ring which should have lifted the heavy lid; it was locked on the inside.

"Move on," said a brawny cop, laying the flat of his sword on the reporter's shoulder.

"By Kellius' orders, I suppose," ventured Mannie, glaring at them and wondering if it would pay to turn Smithicus on them.

"Move on," repeated the big man, turning the edge of his sword toward Mannie's neck.

"Let's go," said Mannie disgustedly to his slave.

"Possibly the corpse walked away, sir, and made good his escape," suggested Smithicus.

"Yeah," grunted Mannie. "The trap door was down when Cæsar came this way. Certainly a man of fifty-six with two stabs in him couldn't lift a ton and slide under it. Use your head, Smiddy."

"I shall endeavor to do so, sir."

"The police, as usual, are trying to suppress the news. But I guess we've got quite a story, in spite of 'em. Quite a story. Let's scoot over to the office as soon as the gods'll let us."

Under a gate beyond the forum they came upon Kellius, comfortably chatting with a crook.

"Hey, there, Chief," sang out Mannie in passing, "you have the body, I see. Another case of *habeas corpus."*

"I'll have your body one of these days, young fella," snorted Kellius, "if you don't keep your nose out of the Police Department."

## XVI

NOW MANLIUS SCRIBO and his slave were panting on toward the offices of the *Evening Tiber,* Manlius absorbed in his own problems. The killing of Cæsar was one of the stinkingest public murders he had seen in his three years of experience. Why, if a mere gladiator pulled anything as raw as that he'd be ruled out of the arena. Taking credit for a murder you haven't even done—it revolted Mannie Scribo's every sporting instinct.

But his heart rebounded with the glee of a born journalist. Old Calamity, who'd been pretty queer lately, was waiting to spring a big story. Did he have a story? Wow! And with P. Manlius Scribo, the star reporter of all Rome, to write it, was the *Tiber* in luck? Glowing with the artist's urge, he forgot the differences which had arisen lately between himself and the temperamental Q. Bulbus. Be loyal to your papyrus. That was the idea. Give 'em the best you've got. Here was the story of the week, the month, the century. With columns and columns of follow-up mystery stuff which Manlius alone could handle, because he had been the only reporter on the scene. . . .

*"Hi yah! Even' Tibe, all ablah hooly-hooly wow. Hi yah!"*

The yell caused Manlius to stop in his tracks at a street corner, not many blocks from the *Tiber* office. An unformed suspicion shook his nerves as he viewed a perfect cloud of small boys, running every which way, waving folded sheets of papyrus with an added bawl that sounded like *"Huxtray, huxtray!"* What was this? Rome's latest novelty in mob-scenes?

But passing citizens were pressing around the boys, reaching feverishly out for the squares of papyrus, shelling out money regardless. A new and larger suspicion rose suddenly and shot a poison arrow through and through Mannie's pumping heart. Savagely he elbowed his way into the throng, reached over many struggling shoulders and snatched a papyrus from an outstretched hand.

"My gods!" he muttered, gazing stupidly at the sheet which swam before his eyes . . . *Evening Tiber* . . . and the enormous banner headline across the front page:

TYRANT CÆSAR ASSASSINATED!!!!!!

It couldn't be true. It was just a nightmare. Maybe that leopard bite had started infecting and gone to his head. You couldn't get out a Roman paper in less than eight hours, work your ink-driving slaves as you would. Cæsar had been murdered, say, half an hour ago. Way over on the Campus Martius. Manlius had run like a scared pup to bring in the first news. Yet here it was, fully printed and trimmed up, out on the street!

Groggily Manlius read on. If he had been surprised before, now he was perfectly astonished:

> ". . . Tyrant Cæsar entered the Senate Chamber and took the president's chair exactly at ten o'clock. . . ."

But Cæsar hadn't shown up until nearly noon, and the murder had been committed out in the alley.

> ". . . then at a given signal, the patriots came boldly forward . . ."

They had been hiding behind a post when the blow was struck.

> ". . . and Senator Cimber, chairman of the Committee on Ways and Means, spoke briefly on the unjust banishment of his brother, J.L. Cimber. The Tyrant, whose unfriendly attitude toward the Progressives has threatened a revolt among the Democrats, made some sneering reply. Whereupon, according to eye-witnesses, Senator Cimber seized hold of the Tyrant's purple robe, possibly in supplication. But the well known Cæsar temper seemed to have been aroused, for he made a violent gesture, and the garment was torn away from his shoulders. . . ."

Whew!

> ". . . Hon. M. Junius Brutus, Farmer Laborite, was first on the scene with a drawn dagger which he planted just above the Tyrant's lower rib, slightly to the left. Ex-

tracting the gory blade he raised it above his head and shouted, *'Sic Semper Tyrannis'!* amidst wild applause. . . ."

That last line was only three-quarters wrong, anyhow.

". . . Those standing near the Tyrant as he fell, allege that they heard him cry, *'Et tu, Brute!'* But in the ensuing confusion, and the necessity of calling a special session to consider ways and means of reorganizing the Government, this death speech was. . . .'

A copy of the *Tiber's* first papyrus edition crumpled in his hand, Manlius steamed up the stairs and burst into the city room. Q. Bulbus Apex wasn't at his usual place on the platform; but his assistant sat there, busily dictating newer and wilder news to the rows of sweating copyists. Even in his rage Manlius couldn't help notice how the force had increased. There must have been a hundred of these slaves, working like slaves too, with reed pens on so many sheets of papyrus.

"Hey! Where's the Boss?" thundered Manlius.

"Where'd you think he is?" asked the assistant, mildly looking up from the last paragraph. "He's in the back room getting lit up like a basilica." Then with a wide grin, "Some story, eh what?"

"Yar!" snarled Manlius, and lion-like he bounded into the little back room.

In there it was a sight for sore, tired eyes. Q. Bulbus Apex sat alone at the chipped marble table. Alone with his liquor. There was a flask in front of him and the usual two glasses, one of which he held unsteadily under his tweezy little nose.

"Well, Manlius, my playboy of the Appian Way, my dish—dishappearing star!" he maundered, "Home at last! Come and kiss me."

"I'll come and kick you for a plugged denarius," muttered his aroused employee.

"Have a care, young man! Have a care! Know whom you're addressing? The greatest journalist of this or any other age. Behold the climax of Apex. The high spot in his dishtinguished career. Aspiring youth, drink to my success."

"I don't drink," said Manlius, drawing a little closer. "Who's responsible for getting out a report of Cæsar's murder hours before it happened?"

"Say, who's running thish paper?" asked Q. Bulbus, trying to draw himself up to his full height.

"That's what I'd like to know. No, I wouldn't. I don't care. I've resigned. But as a student of abnormal psychology, I ask you this. How in hell did your papyrus edition get out that way?"

"Glorious, glorious!" shouted Old Calamity in ecstasy. Like a mad votary of Bacchus he bounded to his feet and began to dance; torn fragments of papyrus whirled about him like autumn leaves. "Happy days are here again, I've won!" he chanted. "Didn't I tell you I'd get out two thousand copies—hurray!—two thousand copies—when the big story broke? Did you see the newsboys? Did you hear 'em?"

He paused to pant and take another drink. His voice grew magnificently sober as he held up a sly forefinger.

"Now watch the advertising come in, young fella. Watch the new Tiber Building rise in its majesty behind the Temple of Venus Genetrix. One big scoop like the Cæsar murder—"

"Oh, glue it down, glue it down!" roared the enraged Manlius. "Your big scoop was about as much like the Cæsar murder as I'm like a fried eel. You couldn't have gotten the story so wrong if you'd hired a Chinese idiot with a hare lip to tell it backwards."

"On what do you base this preposterous mess of tripe you're hurling at me?" asked Q. Bulbus, holding himself up with dignity.

"On the testimony of eye-witnesses."

"Meaning which?"

"Myself, for instance. And your owner, Mark Anthony, quite likely."

"Quite likely." Even in his cups Q. Bulbus must have felt that he had admitted too much, for he stopped suddenly and bit a small hole in one of his thin lips.

"I saw Cæsar knifed," insisted Manlius coldly. "I was the only reporter present, and I wasn't much further from him than I am from you."

The city editor moved back two or three feet before he thought of a good reply. "Well," he said, "why didn't you hustle your story in in time for—"

"Hokum! What do you think this is, the Magic City? Can reporters talk over wires and get the news in the minute after it happens? Don't be silly. And you know darned well that you wouldn't have used my story, even if it *had* come in on the dot."

"It *would* have been a little late!" tittered Old Calamity. "You see we had the whole Papyrus Edition finished and ready for distribution day before yesterday. Ha-ha. Tee-hee. High pressure journalism, my boy."

"Who tipped you off, so far ahead, on the murder of Cæsar?"

"That, my son, is none of your goddess-blasted business."

Manlius squared his chin and his knuckles as he asked, "Was it Mark Anthony?"

"Why drag in Mark?" nervously.

"He bought the paper, all of a sudden. Ever since then you've been putting a husher on him and Cleopatra. Yes, and who was the handy man around the Senate this morning? The one that obligingly led Cæsar up to the pig-stickers? Anthony." Manlius paused for effect, then went on, "Yeah, and they'd have got Cæsar too, if—"

"Holy Mercury!" broke in Q. Bulbus, now quite pallid. *"You don't mean to say Casar wasn't killed at all!"*

"He was killed all right. Don't worry about that." Old Calamity's sigh of relief was touching as Manlius went on. "But he wasn't even touched by the so-called patriots you've been playing up. That's just one of the twenty points you got wrong in your story. By the way, who wrote it—Anthony?"

"None of your—" Q. Bulbus paused on the insult, catching at a thought. "If they didn't kill him, who did?"

"Parties unknown. He just walked out and got a knife in his back. You know. The way you get a cold in your head. Listen, Boss, I'll give you the story—the right story—complete. And I'll write the right story right, as nobody else can do it. If,"—here Manlius paused and soothed his cracked throat with a spot of the rejected wine—"if you promise me you'll run my stuff tomorrow as a denial of the tripe you published today."

"I thought you'd say that," sneered Q. Bulbus, taking the flask away from Manlius and hiding it behind a sink. "Haven't you worked on this paper long enough to know that a fact isn't a fact, really, until it's appeared in the *Tiber?* Don't you know our slogan, even?" Shaking with wrath, Bulbus picked a front page from the floor and pointed to a prominent line at the top:

IF YOU SEE IT IN THE TIBER IT'S SO

"And now," said Old Calamity, "I'll suggest your going elsewhere, if you wish to criticize the policy of this papyrus."

"You've named the very place I'm going," responded Manlius.

"If that means you're going to peddle your story over to the *Astra,"* gibbered Q. Bulbus furiously, "a fat lot of good that'll do you. Mark Anthony bought the *Astra* too, late last night."

Unable to retort, P. Manlius Scribo walked dizzily away, realizing for the first time in his young life, how it feels to be utterly foiled. Foiled more by Cæsar's friends than by his enemies. And somehow the behavior of Captain Kellius and his cops irritated the reporter more deeply than Mark Anthony's hellish treason.

## XVII

AND that was that. Manlius took the thought with him to Hibernicus' night club. He took it thence to other night clubs, to practically all the night clubs in town. He wanted to forget, but the more he drank the clearer his mind became.

Wonderful liquor they had in those days.

The second time he came round to Hibe's he said, "Hibe, I'm sober."

"That's all right, me bye," said Hibe, "ye'd better go home and sleep it off."

"Hibe," said Mannie, "I'm out of the newspaper game from now on."

"Nayther reporters or gladiators ever quit until they're kilt entirely," said Hibe. "Once ye're in there it's fight to a finish."

"Hibe, I wish you'd think up some new cracks," sighed Mannie, and melted away in the throng. Smithicus, of course, melted with him. It was getting so that Manlius could neither melt nor congeal without the help of that handy Briton!

The crowd was moving, moving, and Manlius with it, his ideas keeping pace with his uneven steps. Girl gone, job gone, faith in human nature gone blah. The big story a wash-out, Q. Bulbus printing some sort of boiler-plate tripe that had been handed to him by Mark Anthony—and before the murder! A joke. Ha-ha. Not so damned funny, after all. And that big palooka, Mark Anthony, what was he grabbing at? Getting a bunch of bush-league knife-pullers to bump off the Big Fella so that Anthony could corner the prize plum. Cæsar dead, hail the Emperor. Long live Anthony I, Emperor of Rome. . . .

Give him the raspberry!

And the crowd moved on.

"Smithicus, where are you?"

"Here, sir," said Smithicus, who had had his arm around Mannie for several blocks, trying to steady him in the traffic jam.

"Oh, so you are, my slave. Slave. That's a joke too. I'll bet your father was a prince, or something."

"No, sir," responded Smithicus modestly. "He is the Earl of Essex."

"Hotcha!" said Manlius. "First time I set eyes on you I knew you ranked something higher than a policeman. These Romans, too many of 'em, are just cops trying to impersonate the nobility. Look at Kellius. You'd think he was running Cæsar's murder."

"The police service here, might I suggest, is rather poor."

"Poor? It's reeking. That's the trouble with a cop, Smithicus; when he tries to make society he reeks."

The streets now were like a type scene on Armistice Day. All Rome linking arms, blowing horns, popping bags of flour over this one and that. All in good fun—getting ready for more bloodshed, of course. Soldiers, sailors and civilians climbed balconies and pitched laughing girls down into the arms of their admirers. Sometimes the balconies came down too, but who cared? A few good-natured murders were committed, but nothing serious. As it grew darker everybody lit a torch, setting fire to an occasional building, and making brave show of the holiday spirit.

"Smithicus," asked Manlius as they rambled along, "where did you say we were going?"

"To a funeral, sir."

"Of course. How careless of me. Cæsar's funeral. Kind of prompt, this one, eh what?"

"In this comparatively mild climate, sir—"

"I get you, Smiddy. Nothing keeps long here. Not even the virgins. Cæsar's funeral. They weren't so prompt about burying Comma, though. Well, well, *tempus fugit,* isn't that the truth? Here today, there tomorrow—"

"We'll have to hurry a bit faster, sir, if we wish to make it." Smithicus was pulling his master rapidly forward toward the Forum where a thousand torches threw a nimbus to the sky as though to greet the heaven-borne soul of Divine Julius. A good bit of local color, thought the reviving Manlius; something fine to work into the story if he were writing any more. Which he wasn't.

Everything now was a seething mass, people pushing, shoving, gouging and biting to get a look at the splendid blaze the late Dictator would make when they set fire to his funeral pile.

"All I can see is the backs of their necks," complained the retired journalist. Then he was aware of something lifting him higher and higher, and looked down to see good Smithicus' stalwart chest below him.

"If you don't mind perching here, sir," apologized the perfect slave, "we'll find something better for you in a jiffy."

Thus traveling aloft, pushed steadily forward, Manlius at last reached out for the pediment of a convenient statue and drew himself up, with the aid of powerful shoves from behind. "Swell!" he grinned, coming momentarily out of his depression. Before him lay the marbled wonders of the Forum, flickering in torchlight; the buildings of ambitious gods and more ambitious mortals, pillar on pillar, portico on portico, trooping down from the height where stood the vast Temple of Jupiter Capitolinus.

Centering the plaza below stood the funeral pyre of Julius Cæsar, surrounded by priests, centurions and undertakers. On a cloth of purple and gold lay the distinguished corpse, hardly recognizable because the artful morticians had painted him so prettily.

"Ho, ho! Cæsar's going to wear his party clothes when he joins the gods!" It was a small, squeaky voice that spoke this irreverence. Manlius glimpsed a tiny figure, standing beside him, about level with his knees. Hercules, the midget vaudeville actor!

"How'd you get here, flea?" asked Manlius, regaining poise.

"Climbing's a flea's business, nobleman." Hercules laughed some more. "Ho-ho! Funny show! Farce with a happy ending!"

Manlius sobered up, collected his wits and was about to say, "You saw Comma killed. Who did it?" But the little fellow was laughing so you couldn't ask him anything.

"Cæsar was your friend," said the reporter, shaking the midge. "He was your boss's friend, and—"

"Tee-heel You're right, nobleman. Nobody wanted the Big Fella to live more than I did—ho-ho! Say, look who's come! Mark Anthony's going to deliver the *funeral oration!* Oh, that's too much! Oh, I can't stand it—"

Hercules had another seizure of mirth, fell over and rolled off the pedestal into the crowd, which seemed to swallow him. Manlius might have dived after him, but now was no time to play tag with dodging humorists. The mob was beginning to bellow as Cæsar's Own Silver Cornet Band struck up a dirge. Then Mark Anthony, curly-haired and gladiatorial, even in his dirt-colored funeral robes, mounted the Rostra and stood as near the edge as safety would allow. He posed an instant, and with the eye of an archer gauged the mood of his audience which since noon had turned violently pro-Cæsar. Before he opened his mouth Anthony had 'em in the hollow of his hand.

Slowly, powerfully an arm went out and a rich bull voice, broken with sobs, began the immortal oration:

"Friends, Romans, countrymen, lend me your ears;
I come to bury Cæsar, not to praise him. . . ."

"Well, of all the nerve!" muttered Manlius. "The Royal Spell-binder sobs out his heart over the man he killed—"

An astral finger seemed to jab his ribs; and what made him think suddenly of another funeral and of another orator, wringing his heart at the foot of a gaudy bier? Unsteadily Manlius climbed back to Smithicus' shoulders with the dull command, "Let's move."

But as he rode precariously out of the Forum he reflected bitterly on the significance of the magnificent farce which, for some reason or other, had sent tiny Hercules into hysterics. Cæsar was dead, and future generations would grow up with such a fantastic idea of the real story, which lay throttled in the brain of P. Manlius Scribo. Mark Anthony had managed it like an artist, and now he was topping it off with a prize oration. Contemporary historians would consult the *Evening Tiber's* files and get the queer, fanciful version which Anthony, for political purposes, wrote out of his imagination, forty-eight hours before the crime took place. Future historians would copy the bunk, and improve on it. They'd teach it in the public schools, probably. Yes, and some nutty playwright, like as not, would make a famous melodrama out of it!

"Yo hum!" said Manlius. And so to bed.

## XVIII

ROME was flat on its back for a week, recovering from the wine-headache that followed Cæsar's funeral; many of the unemployed, sobering up, began asking why Rome didn't have a few more big political murders, just to relieve the monotony.

A poor time this for a retired journalist to make inquiries. Because of the reign of lawlessness which followed the assassination Mark Anthony conveniently decided to demoralize the Police Department by making Kellius a major general in the new effect which the man on the street called "The Imperial Army." With Cæsar dead, Anthony grabbing all the honors in sight and disgruntled Conservatives referring to the dead Dictator's funny little nephew as His Imperial Majesty, anything could happen again in Rome.

But Mannie Scribo, out of a job, was never out of work. He was his own boss now, although his employee never saw a pay envelope. The detective-sense, insatiable as a lover's desire, egged him on to the solution of a half solved mystery. The hookup between the Comma murder and the Cæsar murder evaded him like the missing link in an otherwise perfect chain.

Never more than a jump ahead of his debts, Mannie soon reached the point where he considered selling his slave. Smithicus, however, saved him this embarrassment by lending him a hundred denarii which, by some quaint trick of British frugality, he had managed to accumulate and hoard in an old sandal. Thus thinly financed, Mannie was enabled to go a little further with his investigations.

Not that they were leading him into any definite path. Mainly he was able to consider the suspicious deadly parallel of circumstantial evidence. For instance, what had four of the principals in the Comma-Cæsar tragedy done with themselves, all of a sudden?

> Disappearance No. I—On the afternoon of the Ides of March the naughty Cleopatra had eased herself into her gilded barge and evaporated downstream. To where? Alexandria, maybe.

Disappearance No. II—On the same day Pompeia, Cæsar's ex-wife, nailed the To Let sign on her house and made her getaway, destination unknown.

Disappearance No. III—Hesiod the actor wasn't at Pompey's Theater on the Ides of March; that morning the new manager got a note from him, saying his mother was sick, and Hesiod was crazy about his mother. So he too was long gone.

Disappearance No. IV—When Mannie went back to the *Evening Tiber* office to collect the last dribble of his salary he found a letter for him, written in girlish Latin and dated March 15th. "P. Manlius Scribo, because you think I'm horrid, you won't be interested to know where I've gone or why—Romula."

Mannie spent too much time, perhaps, considering Disappearance No. IV. Wasn't that like a gal? Even if she had saved his life, he wasn't going to skin himself any more, chasing after her. Not on your grandfather's statue! In the Cæsar murder case, from now on, she was only going to be a piece on his chess-board; not at all a human being. What though she happened to be a cozy little piece to cuddle, what though he happened to fancy red hair with just that kind of eyes—she wasn't getting his goat any more. Look at what happened to Cæsar, after he let another sort of red-head get his goat. Nope. Mannie was simply studying Romula as a piece—a piece on his chess-board.

Wandering with the unemployed through the streets of Rome, our detective had plenty of time to sum up his case and see how near it came to reaching a solution.

In his dizzy interview with Cleopatra it had been clearly revealed to Manlius that Comma had bought and sold the trinkets with the deadly motto, aimed against Cæsar's life. Cleopatra, apparently for the love of adventure and for the love of Mark, had invented the conspiracy. But the conspirators had been such rank amateurs that the plot, and the date planned for the assassination had been passed along Rome's whispering gallery.

Yet, through it all, the generally acute Cæsar had remained deaf, dumb and blind. This might be accounted for by his increasing eccentricity—look at the way he had appeared in royal robes one day and in a shabby tunic the next—or by his intense concentration in his projected

Parthian campaign. But the death-whisper had reached the ears of his ex-wife, Pompeia, who, for some odd reason, had set her heart on marrying him again. Unable to see him alone, she had hit upon the device of prophesying the fatal day as she stood in a booth at the Junior League Fair. Considering this, Mannie remembered Cassius' whispered admission in the Baths of Tamany; the high priest of Jupiter had been bribed to work on Cæsar's superstition, so that the Big Fella would walk up to the knife promptly on the date set, March 15th.

The story, connected so far, made sense; and yet it didn't. At a certain point the plot always seemed to do a Houdini and crawl out of the box. For example; if Anthony, as Cæsar's fake friend, had staged the whole show, even to leading the Big Fella up to the knife-party; and if he had bribed the cops to drag the body to a hiding place under the manhole; and if he had smuggled away the knife which, out of empty air, had stuck the Divine Julius in the back—then why?—

And here again the plot scrammed out of the box.

Why, immediately after that, did Bull Anthony come out and lead a mob-scene against Brutus and Cassius and all their pals? Why the silver tongued oratory that Anthony belched at Cæsar's funeral, turning all Rome into a man-hunt after the runaway Brutus and Cassius? Had Anthony brains enough to plan the whole conspiracy so that he could bump off the tyrant, then turn on his own gang, push them off the lot and grab the whole cheese for himself? Maybe so. But it looked a little fishy. More likely it was Cleopatra, the cute little cobra, who worked it out for her boy-friend. Certainly Mark Anthony's very fancy speech over the man whose death he brought about had been a pretty sardonic thing, come to think it over. . . .

Yes, and Hesiod's fancy speech over the dead Comma was pretty sardonic too. But there was certainly no motive for the actor's knifing his old buddy. And he had a swell alibi—wasn't back from Naples until twelve hours after the killing. Cupidus, the fat *Astra* leg-man, had interviewed Hesiod on the pier that same day, at noon, just as the actor stepped out of Cleopatra's barge. Dozens of water-front bums had seen him come home.

Whew, but this was a screwy-looking mystery. What had Cleopatra been trying to signal that day at Comma's funeral?

Had her w. k. amethyst ring been wig-wagging at Anthony, among the mourners? J. Pluvius! She certainly saw enough of Mark at home, without giving him high-signs in public. What other person, then, was on the watch for the funny flash? Casca? Perhaps. Or Hesiod. From the platform where he was spouting poetry that day he might have been looking right at her. But what in the name of the Sacred Potassium did she want of him? Hm. And why did Hesiod come back from Naples in Cleopatra's barge?

A giant plot was on the fire that day when Comma was buried. A perfect killer was needed to put Cæsar on the spot. Hesiod? *Buncus!* Cæsar had made Hesiod the footlight favorite of Rome. And what actor would be such a nut as to stab himself out of a job?

Where did Cleopatra get off, really? Even if she'd hatched this egg just to bump Cæsar and grab Anthony, why did she let some invisible person, at the last minute, pop out and jab the Big Fella before the conspirators could wiggle a dagger? If she had arranged that magic act she certainly busted her own plot right in the eye. Queer. . . .

Thus Mannie Scribo groped for the lost tack that would pin his clues together; once or twice he almost stepped on it.

A small discovery gave him a deeper insight, if not into his darling plot, at least into the peccadilloes of middle-aged Roman matrons. Putting on a dirty tunic and one of Smithicus' least conspicuous false beards, he had impersonated a brush-salesman at the back gate of Pompeia's deserted villa. The very high walls were plastered with her To Let signs. Only the top of Pompeia's house showed redly through the trees. The back gate was nothing less than a thick oak door; a small look-out window flew open at the ringing of a bell.

"Hail, mister!" said a withered old idiot face, peering. "Nobody home. House closed. What's that? I'm a leetle deef."

"Your mistress is a sudden mover, eh what?" remarked Manlius, trying to make a shout sound casual.

"Sudden? Tee-hee. These Roman ladies *are* sudden nowadays. Of all the doin's!" creaked the ancient.

"And when they travel they don't travel alone," suggested Manlius with a hearty laugh.

"Right, stranger. Some of 'em travels with actors. That feller Hesiod. He ain't been around for a long time. But I says to my brother, 'An actor and an old woman is fire and faggots.' Never too dry to burn. Tee-hee."

"Then Pompeia's traveling with Hesiod?"

But someone or something must have warned the old nitwit; for the barred window closed suddenly with a bang.

Hesiod and Pompeia; things like that were going on every day in Roman society. Queer time for them to get out, though.

A week after Cæsar's funeral, when some of the public buildings which the populace had fired in celebration of a perfect holiday were still smouldering, Manlius went out to Hesperides Avenue. This was his third attempt in as many days. To save litter fare he walked and reached the deserted *bungalorium* at the hour of the siesta. All good citizens snoozed after lunch, and Rome was deader than it would have been at midnight. Roman ghosts, they say, often appeared at 2 P.M., since this was a favorite hour for burglars, firebugs and the simulacra of the unburied dead.

Comma's house was a desolate sight; Manlius went around the side way and gazed into a silent back yard, once noisy with vaudeville actors, practising their turns. Everything had a run down look, as though the place had been vacant for years. He stood at gaze, considering the ethics of lock-picking, when a movement on the kitchen porch brought him out of his dream. An enormous colored man, seated luxuriously, pulled a piece of sugar cane from his ragged tunic and began chewing.

"Law, mistah, I ain't done nothin'," he protested, turning almost white when Manlius appeared before him.

"That's what you're doing now," said the ex-reporter.

"I is and I isn't," agreed the African, chewing. "When Marsta Comma die he didn't do nothin' 'bout me. So hyah I is."

"Oh. So you're Hambonius," said Manlius, striving to look calm.

"I was Hambonius," agreed Hambonius. "But I reckon the next ge'l'man gits me'll call me Jawge. They mostly does, when they don't know a cullud man's name."

"Jawge," said Manlius, slipping a scanty bribe, "I want you to tell me what you saw when you came here to fix the furnace, the morning of Comma's murder."

"Didn't see nothin'," announced Hambonius, without the slightest hesitancy.

"But, Hambonius, your master's corpse was on the solarium rug, right in front of the door. You must have stumbled over it."

"Yessah. Nossah. I didn't see no cawpse."

"Then what made you run out of the house, yelling so that even the police force heard you?"

"Didn't see no police foce."

"No corpse, no police force. Good gods, were you here at all?"

"Nossuh."

"Oh, I see. Somewhere else, eh?"

"Nossuh. Yessuh."

"Who told you to lie like this?"

"Miss Romula and dat li'l boy Hercules done tole me."

Mannie's heart contracted, bumped, stopped for a second.

"When did you see Miss Romula?"

Hambonius shook his bullet head, but his eyes roved hungrily toward four copper coins in the reporter's palm.

"She told me not say nothin'. And I ain't. But the coppers, a good slave's bribe, came closer. "When she come hyah th' othah mawnin' she say, 'You jes' stay hyah an' don't say nothin'.' So I is."

"What did she come for, do you think?" One of the coppers dropped into a black-and-pink palm.

"Dunno. Somp'n out of a box."

Mannie remembered the little wax doll he had discovered that night, searching the crate. He had it now, locked in his room.

"Did she find it?"

"Dunno. She was pretty mad, I reck'n. Said not let nubuddy in dat house no mo'. *Verbum sap."*

"Where is she now?"

"Search me, mistah. When folks from dis house gone, dey long gone. Like li'l Hercules. He done fade away—lookin' foh dat pusson what kill Marsta Comma, he say."

"He lived under the porch, didn't he?" Donating two more coppers.

"Hi, mistah. He say no look da!"

"Fudge!" laughed Manlius. "This isn't breaking into the house."

He was down on his knees, examining the sub-porch kennel where Hercules slept. Now, in broad daylight, he saw something which the moon had not betrayed in his former search. An uncouth roll of white woolen goods. Deftly he reached in, brought it out, shook it till its voluminous folds fell to the ground. A vestal's robe, stiffened all down the front with brownish blood.

Mannie's fingers trembled a little as he measured the garment against his shoulders. It was enormous. Certainly not built for tiny Romula or little Cleopatra. A man had worn it. A man disguised as a vestal. . . . Suddenly the truth clicked into the detective-mind. The Greek who called himself Homer. . . .

"Hambonius," he asked, "did a Greek gentleman named Homer come here often?"

"Nossuh. Didn't see no Greek ge'l'man."

"Well, why do you think Hercules was keeping this bloody rag?"

"Him crazy, I reckon. He say he keep it to rub in de blood of dat man killed Mistah Comma."

"Has he rubbed it yet?"

"Not yit, sah," showing piano teeth, enjoying the ghastly humor.

Manlius rolled up the robe and poked it back under the porch. It hurt him to give the coon a whole denarius, but his silence was worth it. Then he went away and hid between two empty houses across the street. He hid there all afternoon, and far into the night. Nothing happened. Next day and the next he was back at his post and stayed there until the watchman saw him and warned him away.

Something like a week later the person he had sought most diligently was found—and lost again.

All fagged out, Manlius lay between the blankets, trying vainly to find a soft spot in the old oak bed. Smithicus, who could sleep anywhere, occupied a pallet on the floor. A tiny lamp still flickered, to keep away the ghosts which every Roman feared.

Three light knocks on the door. Smithicus blundered to his feet, his hand on his sword.

"Who's there?"

"Me," said a light treble outside.

"Open to her," commanded the master.

Smithicus drew the bolt and a little figure in a heavy brown cloak stepped in. She was hooded to the eyes, but he knew her.

"Romula!" He draped a blanket around him, got out of bed.

"Send your slave away, please," she said coldly. "I won't be long." She was like a little princess, her slim neck proud and straight under the flame of auburn hair. Then, when Smithicus had withdrawn, she said:

"So you went back to Comma's house the other day."

"Mad with me?" he asked, adoring her beauty as she stood there so pale and severe.

"Why shouldn't I be? Why do you keep on meddling where you can't do any possible good?" She was still haughty, but there was pleading in her eyes.

"Romula, I've tried to tell you. It's my business to meddle." He was nonplussed, in spite of himself. "The greatest Roman that ever lived has been butchered in cold blood—"

"And if I told you—" She bit her lip.

"What?"

"Nothing. Only you can't do anything but harm. And Hambonius told me that you'd found the—the robe."

"Yes. Where'd you see Hambonius?"

"None of your business," she flashed.

"Unfortunately, it's all of my business. Romula, I told you quite sincerely that I know you're innocent. Then why can't you be a little candid with me?"

"Do you want to make me hate you?"

"No."

"Do you want me to make it so that you'll never, never, never know the truth?"

"Oh, but I will, if I live. And I'm going to live."

"Yes, I think you will," she said thoughtfully. "You're the kind that fights through anything. Oh, but you must let me alone—"

He was Roman enough to be cruel when he saw his advantage.

"Who was the man that wore that vestal robe?"

"Find that out for yourself, if you can."

"I will."

"Then you'd rather be hateful than wait and let me tell you clearly?" she asked.

"When?"

"Some day."

"Who killed Comma, do you know?"

"Yes."

"Was it that big Greek pansy they call Homer?"

"I think you said you'd find out for yourself."

"Who killed Cæsar?"

"Oh, Manlius!" A tormented cry. He sprang toward her, but she pulled away. "Manlius, this has been a wicked, bloody business. I'd have stopped it, if I could. You believe that?"

"I think I do."

"You *think* you do?" Blue eyes burst into flame.

"Yes, and I think you've lent yourself to one of the nastiest crimes on record. If you'd have consulted me, you'd have kept out of it. Did Anthony kill Cæsar?"

"If you can't wait to be told—"

He stood before her, a ridiculous figure in a blanket, and wanted to shake her, wanted to kiss the haunted look out of her eyes.

"Why did you come here at all?" he asked.

"There's something I wanted. You stole it out of our house."

"Oh, this trifle." He reached to a shelf and took down the little wax doll.

"Thank you." Eagerly she snatched it and hid it under her cloak.

"Why do you want it?" he asked harshly.

"I'll never tell you—now."

"And that's all?"

"That's all."

He unlatched the door for her, and as he opened it, she wheeled suddenly toward him, her face so glorious that his every resolution melted away.

"If only I weren't in love with you," she said. "Damn fool that I am!"

And she was gone.

## XIX

As we recall, it was on the afternoon of March 15th, 44 B.C., that P. Manlius Scribo retired permanently from the newspaper game. On the morning of April First, same year, P. Manlius Scribo ceased to retire from the newspaper game. Not only that, but he went back to the *Evening Tiber.* After all, he was a reporter, and no reporter stays retired more than a couple of weeks.

His return to the most stirring of professions wasn't entirely motivated by hunger, although Smithicus was rapidly eating him out of house and home; as he had a right to do, perhaps, since he had lent the money for the food. Nor was it entirely Mannie's boredom at chasing all day after a mystery, with no place to publish it, even when it was solved. But the more he worked his brain over the Julius Cæsar picture puzzle, and the nearer the pieces came to making a complete design, the more he felt that Mark Anthony was the man, of all men, who would bear watching.

Who killed Cæsar?

During these weeks of unemployment the question had dogged our hero's footsteps, plagued his dreams. He had no money to bribe the police; Kellius had become a wall of silence; and Mannie had about come to the conclusion that he needed a newspaper's prestige behind him before he could advance further with the case. The *Evening Tiber,* of course, would never print the truth. But what was the matter with making a book out of it, a detective thriller with a snappy title . . . *The Julius Cæsar Murder Case. . . .* That ought to make 'em sit up.

Rome had swallowed the *Evening Tiber's* fake account of the assassination, hook, line and sinker. The bedtime story had made a double-distilled hero out of Anthony. Orators, pleading in the law courts, imitated his bull-necked style and copied his funeral oration, referring to Brutus sneeringly as "an honorable man." Society matrons, dallying around the bazaars and making dates with handsome floorwalkers, hissed "Cassius!" when Armenian salesmen tried to fool them about the price of tablecloths.

One morning on the Tiber wharves the ex-reporter heard two old tars dwelling on the case thus:

"Bill, I asks you. Wot price liberty?"

"Liberty's okay, Sandy. Quit yer bellyachin'. Anthony's the best pal Cæsar ever had. Nothin' like a good pal when you're in trouble."

"Specially after you're dead."

"It's the sentiment I admire."

"Aye, mate—Anthony's the only real Roman left—not countin' you and me."

These but fragments out of the mouth of chattering Rome. Anthony, always Anthony. Anthony, the deliverer, the candy kid. Now he was bossing the semi-reorganized government, and would he refuse a crown and sceptre? Oh, boy! What a swell exposure that big palooka would make! Look at him, doing his stuff. His but to do and die, his but to pursue the guilty and avenge the cold-blooded slaughter of—with an appropriate sob—the best pal a man ever had, Julius Cæsar. Oh, yeah?

Such were Manlius' conclusions, together with an unconscious wish to get back on the *Evening Tiber.* Consciously he had sworn never again to stick his nose inside that smutty old door. But one morning he awoke earlier than usual with a gas pain where his breakfast ought to be. Last night Hibernicus, with several happy Irish epigrams, had refused to feed him any longer on credit. And now, looking around his bare bedroom, he saw the good Smithicus, somewhat thinner than he had been, trying to stew something over the last scrap of charcoal in the brazier.

"What sort of a poultice are you making now?" groaned the unhappy master.

"It's not a poultice, milord," replied the slave. "It's food. Something I borrowed from the vegetable market. A great delicacy in Briton, sir. It's called vegetable marrow."

"Smells that way," objected Manlius. "Smithicus, my boy, suppose we hire out as gladiators and pick up a little loose change."

"Oh, sir! It's a bit rough, that work, sir. I mean to say, for a gentleman of your weight—"

A knock at the door, this time easily identifiable as that of Egregius Rector.

"Well," said Eggie, sniffing the mess in the frying pan, "the fruits of idleness."

"Smithicus," ordered Mannie Scribo, "pour some of the fruits down the gentleman's neck. I don't want it. Listen here, Rector, didn't I tell you never to darken my door again? Lend me five denarii till next payday, will you?"

"This is the third time the Boss has sent me around," said Eggie evasively. "And the last time—he says. He didn't put it down in black and white, but he strongly hinted that he's willing to double your pay. But it's a case of double or quits. Now, listen. I'm speaking as to a friend—"

"As Anthony said to Cæsar, stropping his razor."

"Now it's Anthony that's got the Boss all whipped up like an omelet," said Eggie.

"You mean he's sold out again, and wants to soak Anthony?"

"Not exactly. But there's another big story breaking."

"Oh, why worry?" sneered Manlius. "He's got it written up already. High tension journalism."

"No. It's on the level this time. And he wants you to go as war correspondent."

Manlius sat up in bed, forgetting the swollen vacuum in his stomach. The plum of all newspaper jobs was being shaken down.

"Where to?" he asked casually.

"Do you happen to know where Brutus and Cassius have snuck to with something they call an army?"

"I may be starved," said Manlius, "but I'm not numb from the teeth up. They're camping round the Plains of Philippi,[7] scared like a pair of boy tenors on amateur night."

"Mannie, you're wonderful."

"How often have I told you that?"

"Well, do you know this? Night before last Mark Anthony staged a quick fade-out. When last seen he was beating it

---

[7] The reader is requested to discard the theory that the battle of Philippi was fought in Macedonia in the year 42 B.C. The historians are wrong, that's all. Possibly there were two Philippis, or maybe two battles. Be that as it may, our Battle of Philippi was fought somewhere in Italy in the spring of 44. Retain that idea, and this story, as it advances step by step, will be easier to understand.

toward Philippi, picking up regiments of Cæsar's veterans all along the line. They're greeting him as Cæsar's avenger. He'll probably lay Brutus and Cassius so low they'll have to dig for 'em."

"Probably," said the embittered Manlius. "The wicked always prosper."

"Well," asked Eggie in a decisive tone, "are you going to cover that battle for the *Evening Tiber?"*

"No."

"Why not, for Jove's sake?"

"I wouldn't be found dead at such a battle. Probably it's fixed," grumbled Mannie. "Like as not Anthony has bribed Fatty Cassius and Lizzie Brutus to stage a perfectly lovely retreat. Then Bull Anthony can have a big triumph on his march back to Rome. Of course, if it comes to an honest-to-Mars battle, Mark can lick those two amateurs with one hand tied behind him."

"You're smart," agreed Eggie. "But you're wrong this time."

"Am I?" asked Manlius irritably. "Do you want to bet me that Mark doesn't win that battle?"

"Sure. What do you lay me?"

Mannie looked around and saw his only valuable possession, the Briton, industriously ironing a shirt.

"Bet you Smithicus against a hundred sesterces."

"Oh, sir!" implored Smithicus rebukingly.

"Don't worry, *par.* I won't lose you," Manlius assured him almost emotionally. He couldn't think of getting along without his Briton.

"The bet's on," said Eggie. "But I don't know that I can use a gladiator, the way I'm fixed."

"What makes you so sure that Anthony can't win?"

"This is confidential." Eggie lowered his voice. "But I think Bull Anthony's gone crazy."

The detective side of Manlius began pricking up its ears.

"In what way?" he asked lazily.

"He's taken to spiritualism."

"No!"

"Yep. He's spending his time with a priest of Isis—one of those yellowish punk-burners Cleopatra left behind. Mark's gone ga-ga, I tell you. He brought that Egyptian dope around to the office and bullied Old Calamity into starting a column called 'The Great Beyond.' Tie that."

"I can't." But Mannie's awakened mind was searching into a new field of possibilities.

"Mark had given it out for publication that this Hank-am-Ank—that's the guy's foolish name—can raise the dead. And when a general goes out to fight a serious battle with nothing but a spiritualist to tell him how—"

"You mean to say—"

"I mean that the night before Anthony went to war I found him and Old Calamity up in the office, splitting a jug of Falernian. I wasn't supposed to be there. But I'm like you, Mannie—always wondered what Mark wants with the *Evening Tiber.* So I snuggled under a shadow and listened in."

"What were they talking about?" asked Mannie, trying not to be breathless.

"Spiritualism. The Boss was telling him to lay off that stuff or he'd go nookie. Mark got sore and said, 'You're narrow-minded. My priest can materialize spirits. And if you don't believe it, watch the Battle of Philippi. Cæsar's ghost is going to win that battle for me.' How's that for a booby-hatch special—"

"You don't mean to say he's relying on Cæsar's ghost to smack down Brutus and Cassius!" asked Mannie in a half whisper.

*"Dixisti, puer.* You said it, kid. Now do you want to call that bet off?"

"No."

Mannie's head was swimming with wild cogitations. Anthony crazy? Crazy like a fox. Anthony, the open-faced, simple-minded Roman, was always thinking around a corner. Cæsar's ghost . . . and what was this weird development in the rigmarole of crime?

"Oh, well," said Manlius, pretending great languor. "If the paper can't get along without me, I won't be a spoil sport. Smithicus, pass me that shirt. And, Eggie, I invite you round to a hash house where we can eat for a couple of hours. The party's on you."

The return of P. Manlius Scribo to the *Evening Tiber* was like so many of those things. He walked into the city room, as though nothing had happened, and loafed around, listening to Q. Bulbus dictating an editorial on the committee of old gentlemen now running the government and trying to decide whether they'd have another tyrant or a president or a king or a what. Finally, squinting sharply over to the returned prodigal he waggled his thumb toward the little back room and went on dictating.

Everything smelled of paint. In his absence, Manlius noticed, they had renovated the office, given it a new coat of pompeian red, mended the mosaic tiles, done quite a lot toward freshening up and looking prosperous. In the little back room there was no wine on the chipped marble table. The Boss, apparently, had sobered up.

Old Calamity was positively beaming when he came in. Good Medusa! he even shook hands.

"Got something worth your time now, Manlius," he said briskly, chafing his palms till they crackled like dry leaves.

"Yeah. Battle of Philippi."

"Good Graces, boy! You don't miss much, do you?"

Mannie Scribo thought it worth his while to re-quote what he had said to Eggie about not being numb from the teeth up. Q. Bulbus clicked out a couple of chuckles, then wrote a row of Roman figures on a scrap of papyrus.

"There's your back salary, and your raise, just present it to the cashier," he said. "Now figure out your expense account, and don't stint yourself. Mark expects you to be with his army in two days, at least."

"So we're calling him Mark now?" grinned Mannie, unable to stifle this wickedness. But the Boss chose to ignore it.

"Here's a good road map—" producing one from a drawer under the table—"and you'll find fast horses, in relays, every fifteen miles. Can you ride?"

"If you strap me on."

"Good. Anthony will have runners on the field, to send back the news."

"Whose news? His or mine?"

"Your own. I—we're giving you a free hand to write up the famous victory. Now you'll need a bodyguard along the way."

"I have a gladiator of my own," said Manlius proudly.

"Fine. I'll give you letters to staff officers at G.H.Q. and a special one to the general. Everything'll be made easy for you. Only I want you to be ready to leave in an hour."

Manlius stood for a moment, coughing and rubbing his throat.

"What's matter now—choking?" snapped Q. Bulbus.

"No," responded Manlius. "I'm swallowing my ancient Roman pride."

Instinctively he went to the cashier's office before attending to the other important items of his expedition.

## XX

It was the blackest midnight within the records of the Weather Bureau, still functioning in the Temple of Æolus, 'way back in Rome, when P. Manlius Scribo broke another record, but with none to witness save the faithful Smithicus. He had made it from Rome to Philippi in XL hours, XXI minutes, XI seconds, elapsed time. In that tireless ride o'er hill and dale and mossy fen he had forgotten the place where the horse hurt him. It was only when he dismounted that he discovered, to his chagrin, that he walked like a pair of ice tongs.

Dismounted now, and walking astride, he reached out in the darkness and touched the elbow of his British companion; they seemed quite alone, save for a melancholy wind, whistling across the plain; and this of course was no safe guide for two lost adventurers, hunting for a battlefield. A flash of flint and metal; that would be Smithicus, starting his tinder box, a wondrous thing, like its modern descendant, the cigar lighter. In half an hour, according to Manlius' calculations, he'd have the darned thing going, then they could peer around for a guide-post or something to indicate where they were. On a night like this the road map was about as useful as a landlady's moustache.

Occasional little spits of fire indicated the industrious Briton, trying to interest a wad of tinder.

"Smiddy," observed Mannie, "did you ever think that a battle would be so hard to find?"

"They should make more noise, sir," replied the voice of Smithicus. "Back in Britain a clerical gentleman, a Druid priest, sir, once informed me of an invention under way whereby the military might produce quite a noise by—"

"Oh, get your mind off the Patent Office and start that light!" muttered the young master, in no mood for bedtime stories.

He rubbed the places where the horse hurt worst, and managed at last to stand erect. In the haunted solitude a superstitious terror touched him clammily. That wasn't the wind he heard, but a lot of ghosts, complaining. Ghosts are always kicking about something. But tonight he sympathized with their airy grouch. Philippi was certainly no pleasure resort.

Manlius opened his tunic and spat three times on his chest—a dirty trick the Romans had when wishing to change their luck. The gesture brought back his courage, and with it reflection.

Who killed Cæsar?

The rhythm of the question he had asked a hundred times recurred like the catch in a popular song. The evidence still pointed straight at the professional show-off, Mark Anthony. Motive? Power. Method? Undiscovered. Yes, but discovery was the purpose which remained bright in Scribo's mind. For now, with every pang of his disjointed bones, he realized why he had accepted Q. Bulbus Apex's generous offer. Not so much for the glory of strutting around Rome in a war correspondent's uniform—although that was tempting too. Not for the luxury of an increased salary. No, none of these things. P. Manlius Scribo's loyalty to his papyrus had weakened with disillusionment. One driving purpose had sent him, stiff and saddle galled, to the Plains of Philippi; a burning resolve to probe into the very heart of the Cæsar mystery.

And why, shivering in the comfortless dark, did he think again of Romula?

Romula! She couldn't have been a nice girl, the kind one's mother would pick out for a nice young man, after all the funny business she had been mixed up in. Loafing round the night clubs and the Tiber wharves with a Greek nobody knew. Changing her clothes mysteriously in Cicero's office, and slipping away. Preferring to stay in Cleopatra's wicked villa with a notorious *libertinus* like Mark Anthony. Popping into Mannie's room at a time of night when nice girls don't visit around—and for what? A funny little wax doll, worth, perhaps, a denarius in the Public Market.

She'd looked awfully pathetic that night, when he saw her last. Pathetic and offended.

Oh, *bolonia!* With a painful jerk the noble Roman pulled himself together. He was here to report a battle. True, he knew nothing about war, but that should make no difference. Without knowing anything about society he had written a society column that made the Roman matrons twitch and twitter. Just get a few facts and dish 'em up.

Don't try to get things too right. But make it snappy. That's the *tabloidium* idea.

No, Mannie wasn't worrying about the battle. That would be easy enough. But the main idea, deep down in his heart, was to be close to Anthony and probe into the spiritualistic hoax which, Mannie now felt, would reveal the key to the mystery of Cæsar's death.

But Smithicus had at last struck a light, and was holding it to a torch of bundled faggots. Flame blazed up, and the slave, bearing the fire aloft, stalked down the rutty road. Manlius stayed behind with his horse. Noble animal! How our hero wished the plug would choke for the way it and other equally noble animals had churned his innards over every inch of the way from Rome to Philippi.

"I say, sir!" Smithicus' deferential call in the distance. "This is quite odd. Really."

Manlius staggered forward toward the torch and found his slave examining a sign-post, planted at a fork in the road. Smithicus' puzzlement was easy to understand. "To Philippi," said the signboard facing them. "To Philippi," said another signboard, pointing in almost the opposite direction.

"There couldn't be two places of the same name, so close together," said Smithicus.

"Oh, yes there could," puffed Manlius. "In this hick neck of Italy there could be anything but common sense. The way these roads are marked is a disgrace to the Republic."

"When in doubt, turn to the right. That's a little saying we have in Britain, sir."

"Well, take your little sayings and—" But Manlius didn't finish. After all, they were companions in misery, and Smiddy was certainly doing his best, and not kicking about it.

With something like a sigh of relief Manlius hitched his horse to the misguiding sign-post and followed his slave along the turn to the right. For half a mile, perhaps, they plodded on. The walk was doing him good; he could feel his joints growing together again and his digestion becoming unchurned. He tried to think of a merry tune to whistle, but all that came to mind was a Latin version of "A Heart Bowed Down," written by a poet named Catullus, who died of grief. However, he was wetting his parched lips to try it when—

"Halt!"

The unmistakable voice of a sentry, somewhere in the darkness.

"Who goes there?"

"A friend." That was all Manlius could think of, on the spur of the moment.

"Louder."

*"A friend."*

"Advance, friend, and be recognized."

That sounded simple enough, but our hero's feet grew suddenly heavy as he dragged them into the darkness. However, he was comforted by the thought of a scrap of papyrus which Q. Bulbus had handed him upon leaving the office; it contained Mark Anthony's countersign.

He approached the harsh voice until he saw, by another torch, suddenly flaring, that the sentry held a wicked-looking javelin, and behind him stood a giant archer with a six-foot bow; an arrow about the size of a broom handle pointed straight at the intruder's chest. But Manlius had quite recovered from the first shock.

"Give the countersign," demanded the sentry.

*"E Pluribus Unum!"* Jauntily Manlius tossed it off.

But there seemed to be a hitch somewhere. The javelin and arrow still pointed, and out of the torch-lit shadows stepped a natty young officer in a horizon blue tunic and tin kelly the size of a milk pail. For a while he and the sentry held a whispering conference, then with the most likeable smile in the world he signaled the sentry.

"Pass, friend," invited the sentry.

"I see you have Anthony's countersign," remarked the young officer pleasantly.

"Yep. And lucky for us, what? If we'd taken the turn to the left, now—"

"Wouldn't that have been embarrassing?"

"I'll say so. A fat chance we'd have had, bumping into Brutus and Cassius with Anthony's password," said Manlius.

"The party would have been on you, I guess," laughed the sweet young officer. "Mind showing your papers?"

Manlius produced his credentials; the young officer studied them by torchlight, smiled appreciatively and tucked them in his belt. "Newspaper boys, I see. Well, that's the stuff. I'm an intelligence officer myself. Round G.H.Q.

they call us the Committee on Public Misinformation. Joke. This way, please."

As they passed along, behind the handsome soldier, Manlius was aware of other soldiers, marching along with naked swords over their arms.

"We need quite a guard, don't we?" laughed Manlius.

"Yeah. Awfully near enemy country here," sang out the cheerful guide.

"How far's the general's headquarters?"

"No distance at all."

"Think I can see him tonight?"

"Absolutely. He'll want to see you. The *Evening Tiber* is an Anthony paper, isn't it?"

"Yes, it is; or was, day before yesterday."

"Must be great to have a paper to blow your horn for you. Every move a picture, eh what?"

"Sure, it's a comfort," agreed Manlius, liking the young fellow more and more as they advanced.

"Look out," said the happy guide, "Don't stumble over a soldier."

Manlius almost did. At first he thought he was on a stricken field, walking over the fallen. Then he heard snores and saw the soldiers asleep on their shields with their helmets over their faces to keep out the fresh air.

"Ever had any military training?" asked the nice captain of military intelligence.

"Well, not exactly. That is, I drilled with the fire company back home."

"Oh, that's plenty. Get used to handling a fire-bucket, I say. Kills the sense of fear."

Somehow the *Tiber's* correspondent didn't like this last remark; it sounded a bit too cordial. However, there was no time now to analyze refined shades of meaning, for suddenly they rounded a tumbled mass of rocks and came upon a great camp-fire, plainly lighting two large pavilions of striped awning; around them was drawn a cordon of sentries and torch-bearers. Here another sentry challenged them. *"Sic Semper Tyrannis,"* said the young officer, saluting.

"Hey!" objected Manlius. "I thought the countersign was—"

"Oh, we change it as we go along," said the guide merrily. "Just stick around here, will you, while I go in and report to the General."

They were only a few feet from the entrance to the larger pavilion when the officer said this. He turned and went inside, but Manlius and Smithicus found themselves well guarded still. Perhaps a trifle too much so, for the short swords of their escort were pointed pointedly toward the newly arrived guests; a ring of blades, hardly an inch between one edge and another.

"Look here, fella," protested Manlius, addressing a stocky top sergeant who seemed to be managing the spectacle, "is this your idea of entertaining visitors?"

"Sure is, buddy," grinned the sergeant. " 'Specially when them strangers strolls inside our lines givin' the enemy's countersign."

Manlius' jaw dropped with a crash, but he regained it on the rebound.

"Say, Sarge," he asked confidentially, "who's in command here, anyhow?"

"Brutus and Cassius, stranger," said the sergeant with awful gentleness. "If you was a-huntin' for General Mark Anthony, now, you should a-taken the road to the left."

## XXI

NONPLUSSED was the word for it. But had P. Manlius Scribo been of the poor stock that weakens before this nonplus or that, never could he have endured one half hour of the punishment he was obliged to take in solving the fascinating, if baffling, Julius Cæsar murder case. Mysteries are created, some hold, in order to tax the detective's ingenuity in getting out of one tight hole and into another.

"Hey, Smiddy, drop that!" he commanded sternly, for Smithicus had picked up the top sergeant and was about to toss him over the cohorts of sleeping Romans. Dutifully the slave obeyed and set the soldier down just as the young intelligence officer came out of the pavilion, that same optimistic smile on his boyish face. Manlius could have slapped him down, but by an effort of the will he returned grin for grin.

"I hope the visiting fireman is welcome," he said.

"General Brutus will see you now," replied the officer punctiliously. "Just park your gladiator outside and follow me."

Inside the tent stood a large number of staff officers, wearing that tired-foot expression peculiar to staff officers when the general is in one of his moods.

Surrounded by a half dozen Roman lamps, Junius Brutus sat trying to scowl at a war map on the camp table before him; but there wasn't a really good scowl in that face. It seemed all cut up and disorganized like an unsolved jigsaw puzzle. "Cake-eater trying to play fire-eater," was Manlius' mental comment as he stood there, awaiting sentence. Brutus sighed and turned the map over, as if he could make something out of it from the wrong side. Then he handed it to the nearest officer with the comment, "Maybe General Cassius can tell you what to do about it."

At a signal the staff officers withdrew, obviously relieved. All but the youngish one who had brought Manlius in. He stood at attention, waiting.

"Well?" asked Brutus finally, lifting a pair of worried, velvety, drawing-room eyes.

"Sir," said the young officer, "I have brought the prisoner, according to orders."

"Oh—prisoner—to be sure." Brutus' look was far away. He was thinking of more important things, no doubt. "Hm. He was the one found inside our lines with a letter of introduction to Mark Anthony?"

"Yes, sir. When we seized him he was acting in a most suspicious manner."

"What anybody wants to come here for when he can stay with Anthony is beyond me," said Brutus peevishly. "He sets a better table than we can afford." Then with a tired glance at the young officer, "Why do you bother me with such trifles, Captain Milo?"

"Sir, this man—"

"Well, what do you want me to do with him?"

"Sir, according to regulations a spy is strangled without trial."

Manlius shot a poison glance toward the pleasant Captain Milo, then decided that now, if ever, he should put in his oar. The oar went forward with one large sweep, not stopping for commas:

"General-you-will-make-a-great-mistake-by-executing-a-war-correspondent-for-a-spy—I-suppose-you-realize-what-you're-doing."

"So?" asked Brutus, showing real interest for the first time. Now that Manlius had his attention he spoke more leisurely.

"They don't shoot ambassadors, do they, passing between armed camps? A war correspondent occupies a solemn diplomatic position."

"I never heard of a war correspondent before. What is he supposed to do?" asked Brutus.

"He writes up battles," Manlius galloped on. "You'd be surprised if you only knew the finish we can give a battle."

"The finish," said Brutus thoughtfully, looking down at his table. Manlius realized that he'd used the wrong word.

"Whether I write the battle from your camp, General, or from General Anthony's camp is not of the least importance. It's the truth we're trying to get at. We don't take sides—"

But the hellish Milo broke in, "Sir, he represents the *Evening Tiber.*"

"Sir," persisted Manlius, "did you see the write-up I gave you when you mur—I mean, assassinated the Tyrant?

Didn't I make a word picture of you, knife and all, freeing Rome and everything? Didn't I play up the popular demonstration for you? That's me, General. And it's the *Evening Tiber.* Read our slogan: IF YOU SEE IT IN THE TIBER IT'S SO."

This was a desperate play, taking credit for that hideously distorted story. Manlius was fighting for time, but the effect was neutral.

"I never read the newspapers," said Brutus.

"The *Evening Tiber* belongs to Mark Anthony," came in Captain Milo sweetly.

Brutus' look became distinctly unpleasant, and he beckoned in a pair of M.P.'s, waiting at the door.

"Seize him!" he cried. Then as suddenly his mood changed; he held up his hand and commanded, "Don't seize him. P. Manlius Scabio—"

"Scribo is the name," supplied Manlius.

"Do you know anything about battles, really?"

"Do I—do I know anything about battles? What do you think my paper pays me for? It's not a charity organization. You're dead right I know about battles."

"I think I'll keep you," said Brutus in his brooding voice. "Tomorrow's deeds will go down in history. We need a gifted writer to immortalize our famous victory over that political turncoat and arrogant self-appointed Fusionist candidate, Marcus Antonius—"

But his extemporized oration was broken into by the entrance of Cassius, looking peevish and uncomfortable, his fat body bulging from a tight military breastplate.

"General," he said, "I've worked out our plan of attack."

"Sit down, General," invited Brutus languidly. "What's your plan now?"

"General, don't look so dead and alive. We're on the eve of an engagement."

"Holy Gemini, don't I know it?" groaned Brutus. "Stop picking that wart. You give me the willies. What's the plan?"

"Well, General—"

"Oh, cut out the General stuff. There's been too much saluting and not enough head work since we camped here."

"Have it your own way." Ponderously Cassius sat on a creaking stool. "Now this is it. The zero hour is sunrise. That's mutually agreeable, isn't it? My army advances on the extreme left, yours on the extreme right. This manoeuvre is called the Nut Cracker."

"Sounds like it," agreed Brutus, rubbing his hair.

"We advance exactly three kilometers due west, then turn, cavalry leading, and charge."

"Which way do we turn?"

"Toward each other, foolish. You charge toward me, I charge toward you—"

"Don't get you."

"Listen," said Cassius, "I'll try and explain it in baby talk. We're charging toward each other from here to there." His fat finger spotting places on the map. "Thus we're closing in on Anthony, stationed in the middle—"

"Yeah? Suppose Anthony isn't stationed in the middle? What's going to stop our two armies from coming together and starting a fight to a finish?"

"But, my dear boy," Cassius was struggling to be patient, "they can't fight each other. They're practically the same army."

"Does that matter? Did you ever hear of two Roman contingents coming together that they didn't fight?"

"Gosh, they killed Cæsar and let you live," groaned Cassius. "You never seem to think of anything yourself. But you manage to step on every little suggestion I happen to make. Look at the way you scrambled that assassination—"

"Why drag that in?" asked Brutus, shuddering.

"Well, I will drag that in. You bungled it so that the Big Fella was two hours late getting on the spot. . . ."

Up to this remark Manlius sat in his corner, greatly enjoying the way generals behave behind the scenes. But now his ears perked forward like a pair of wings. And Cassius was scolding on:

". . . Then you insisted on putting the conspirators in the wrong place, so that a rank outsider got in his knife before we could say boo. If it hadn't been for me we wouldn't have gotten a stick of credit for the job. Not a stick. And you spoiled the big rally we were going to stage by letting the body just lie there—let it lie there until Anthony—"

"Enough!" broke in Brutus, to Manlius' ineffable disappointment. But for that interruption the captive reporter might have learned Mark Anthony's share of guilt in the assassination.

"Another thing," said Cassius bitterly, changing the subject, "we've got to settle, here and now, who's the commander of this man's army. You or I? You can't get anywhere with two or three heads."

"Cerberus did," objected Brutus. "He went to hell with three heads and they made him watch-dog."

"Which proves my point exactly," sneered Cassius. "Now, get down to brass tacks. I believe I asked a question. You or I?"

"No Brutus ever takes a subordinate position," said Brutus.

"Maybe that's what's the matter with Rome today," said Cassius.

The two generals leaned across the table, eye to eye, glaring. It was a nervous moment. "You or I?" insisted Cassius. Possibly the very tenseness of it stirred the listening Manlius to a rash remark. "Say, why don't you two match for it?" Cassius jumped around, as though the mysterious knife had pierced him in the back.

"How did *you* get in here?" asked Cassius, baring his teeth.

"Listen, Cass." Brutus laid an appeasing hand on Cassius' arm. "He's a war correspondent. I stole him from Mark Anthony."

"Is there any reason why he shouldn't be killed?"

"Oh, I'm using him as my unofficial military adviser."

"Going in for a brain trust, huh?" glowered Cassius. "Well, if I don't get some sleep, I'll be perfectly rotten for the big fight tomorrow. Maybe your pet over there is right—but I'll certainly kill him if I get full command. Let's flip for it and let the gods decide." He reached into a pocket under his breastplate, grunted uncomfortably. "Broke, as usual. Just like this army, no money, no—"

"I have a coin here, sir!" eagerly Manlius stepped forward with a silver piece and stood deferentially between the contending generals.

"You flip it," suggested Cassius. "I'm superstitious about matching with another man's money."

"Your first say," said Brutus mournfully.

"Heads," said Cassius.

It was just a little trick that Manlius had learned around Hibe's speakeasy; for when the coin settled on the table it had turned up tails.

"Best two out of three," said Cassius. "Name it, Brutus."

"Heads," wavered Brutus, always an imitator.

Again Hibe's education. The coin planked down heads up. Cassius picked it up and examined it bitterly, his eyes roving over the face of Cæsar, embossed on the metal.

"Well, Big Fella," he mused, "you're settling my destiny again, eh what?" He brought his heels as nearly together as his fat legs would allow, lifted his arm in the Fascist salute of Rome and asked, "General, what are your orders for the attack?"

"Oh, let's try the Nut Cracker," sighed Brutus wearily. "And in the name of the gods, go to bed."

Therefore Cassius departed, much to the relief of Manlius who, by the expert use of a trained coin, had put Brutus in command and saved his own life.

## XXII

It was the third watch of the night—figure that out if you can. Junius Brutus, looking about as fit for a battle as a poisoned pup for a rabbit hunt, turned restlessly on his pillow. For a long time there had been no sound outside, save for the bellow of a corporal, changing the guard. As official historian of Philippi, Manlius remained awake, nodding over a very dull scroll marked *Army Manual.* Now and then he would rise and peer out over the calm picture of the sentries, fast asleep, some of them lying down, others standing up.

A dull babble, inside the tent, startled him to attention; immediately he realized where it came from. The commanding general, tossing on his rough field cot, was talking in his sleep. Here was such an opportunity as any detective greets with hungry anticipation. Noiselessly Manlius tiptoed over to the couch of care and put his ear close to the sleeper's mouth.

"Cleopatra . . . where does she come in? . . . Not that, Anthony . . . are you running this show, or am I? . . . No, boys, I'll use my own dagger, thanks . . . it's a family heirloom. . . ."

In a moment of silence Manlius looked up and saw a pretty dagger, marked with the Brutus monogram in jewels, hanging on a peg. But the sleeper was burbling again:

". . . *Sic Semper Tyrannis* . . . cheaper to buy 'em wholesale . . . don't monkey with a vestal, I tell you . . . try something simpler . . . hello, are you ready, boys? . . . All the daggers out? . . . Hey! He's down! Who did that? Who put that knife in him? . . . Hey! I saw that fellow. . . . No, it couldn't be Anthony . . . hide that knife . . . give it to me . . . I'll keep it, I tell you. . . ."

Brutus' hand moved from under the bedclothes, stretched out convulsively and something cheaply metallic clattered on the floor. Rapidly Manlius picked it up and concealed it under his tunic, just as Brutus opened his eyes and stared around.

"Hello," he drawled. "I must have been asleep."

Manlius smiled at this bit of original observation and allowed as how maybe they both had been asleep.

"Why don't you go to bed?" asked Brutus, yawning.

"I never go to bed before a battle," said Manlius.

"That so?" asked Brutus and went back to sleep.

Then it was that Manlius crept under a Roman lamp and slyly examined the object he had picked from the floor. A knife, as he had surmised. But what a knife. The kind that cooks buy for two sesterces at any hardware store. Plain wooden handle; thick, single edged blade, made for cutting sausages. But ground to a feather edge. Keenly Manlius' eyes went over the handle and came upon the tell-tale legend, burned into it. "Property of Pompey's Theater."

Hm. Noiselessly he slid the humble blade into his tunic pocket, next to his more effective weapon. So this was the knife that killed Julius Cæsar, the knife that Brutus had pulled from the fallen tyrant's back before planting his own expensive dagger where it would show to the best advantage! A humble kitchen carving knife! Yes, but with a complete enigma burned in the handle. Pompey's Theater did not go in for kitchen knives. The weapons there had brightly painted handles and gilded wooden blades. Had someone—Mark Anthony possibly—gone to the cook-shed where stagehands ate, and borrowed the queer instrument of vengeance?

Where's the connection? thought Manlius, gazing at the vague shadows around the tent. Then he began trying to hook up the ravings, coming out of Brutus' fever dream. A lot of it was no news to Manlius. Cleopatra had as good as confessed that she had fomented conspiracy by passing out the lockets which Comma bought for her. But what had Brutus just babbled? ". . . Hey! I saw that fellow . . . it couldn't be Anthony. . . ." He, at least, had seen the real assassin of Cæsar. And it wasn't Anthony. . . .

The wind began to blow again, an awful sound. Shadows danced. Manlius, no chum of fear, found himself wishing that morning would come and they'd start going over the top. . . .

Wooo-o-o-o-o!

Our hero's scalp felt like a cold toothbrush, his spine like an ice-water spigot as that frightening moan quavered out of lurking shadows above Brutus' head. Manlius gazed, frozen. He was looking straight at a ghost! So Pompey's mystic had made good. For through the thin canvas wall beside the sleeper's cot a pallid head had materialized, bald, narrow-eyed, hawk-nosed. Suffused with a graveyard glow, Cæsar's dead hand went out and touched Brutus on the shoulder.

*"Yow!!!"*

The yell of the haunted man, sitting up in bed, driveling, gawping at the specter.

"Cæsar!" A broken whisper from the lips of Junius Brutus.

It seemed a full minute before the apparition spoke. Then:

*"Veni, vidi, vici,"* quoted the spirit.

"Cæsar—you have come, you have seen—but you haven't conquered—yet." Faintly spoke Junius Brutus.

"Not so fast, Brutus—not so fast!" wailed the spook in a voice like the wind. "In the morning I will keep my appointment."

"Ap—appointment?" Brutus' teeth sounded like ice in a shaker.

"Yes, my appointment." Cæsar's ghost gave the ghost of a smile. "To meet you on the Plains of Philippi."

"But, listen—"

Too late. The spectral head vanished in a cloud of luminous steam, leaving Brutus, paler than the ghost itself, jittering in bed.

"You heard what he said?" asked the general wanly, turning to his war correspondent.

"Don't take it too seriously," said Manlius, being nonchalant. "It was probably something you ate."

"You heard what he said," repeated Brutus inanely.

"I don't see why he should be especially sore at you." Manlius was now reaching out for the secret, apparently within his grasp. "You didn't have a thing to do with killing Cæsar."

"How do you know that?" barked Brutus, jerking around.

"It's my business to know things, General," said Manlius, taking advantage of the opening. Then, after a moment's consideration, "I was there. I saw the whole thing."

"You did?" In a hoarse whisper. "Then, in the name of Jove, tell me. Who killed Cæsar?"

This was discouraging; Brutus' tone betrayed that he was no nearer the solution of the mystery than the young detective at his elbow. But Manlius had one more card to play.

Deftly he flipped the cheap butcher knife from his pocket and held it under Brutus' nose. The general cowered away, as though the thing would bite him.

"There's the knife that did the dirty work," said Manlius coolly. "Who's the owner?"

"Where did you get it?" faintly.

"I picked it up—about the way you did on the Ides of March. Now whose knife is it?"

"I'd give the Roman Republic if I knew," solemnly.

"Is it Anthony's?"

"How could it be—a cheap thing like that? Anthony's famous for his taste in daggers. And can't you see it's marked Pompey's Theater'?" His tone was becoming slightly querulous.

"Oh, I haven't missed that—and it throws a great deal of suspicion on Anthony. When he was leaving Cæsar in the Alley of Statues, two minutes before the murder, do you know what he said?"

"No. Tell me!" cried Brutus.

"He said, *'I'm dropping into the theater to see a sword swallowing act.'* Doesn't that indicate what was on Anthony's mind?"

Brutus sat pondering, his arms around his knees.

"It couldn't have been Anthony," he mused. "Not that he isn't capable of anything. But it couldn't have been."

"Do you mean by that, General, that you saw the real assassin?"

"I had a glimpse—or did I imagine it? Someone had climbed the pedestal of Pompey's statue—a face was looking over."

"What did it look like?"

"How could I tell? It was gone in a flash." Then Brutus grew irritable. "What are you here for, asking questions? What are you, the district attorney, that you should keep me up all night, being cross examined?"

Seeing that his eagerness had taken him too far, Manlius argued rapidly, "I didn't start it, sir. The ghost did."

"The ghost can go to hell and you with him. Between you you've completely shattered my nerves. And look here, young man. You know too much. What do you say to my calling in the guard and ordering you executed as a spy? Dead men tell no tales."

"Oh, yes they do—in this case, anyhow," said Manlius, staying Brutus' hand as it reached toward the bell-cord. Our young reporter was now improvising with all the speed of a fiery imagination. "In the *Evening Tiber's* safe there's a sealed scroll marked 'Open only in case of necessity.' That scroll contains a detailed account of the *real* assassination of Julius Cæsar. It's written by the most talented word slinger in the Republic—myself. It tells plainly how you conspirators acted like a bunch of amateurs, funked the job, never struck a blow. If that story is ever released, a front page spread in one of our enormous editions, all over town, you and Cassius will be the biggest laugh in Rome. You'll never dare go back, even if you do win Philippi and—"

"You'll never publish it!"

"Not if I'm let alone to finish this battle and report to my paper. That's understood between me and my editor. But it's also understood that in case I meet with foul play in your camp there'll be a Manlius Scribo Memorial edition of the *Tiber,* featuring the biggest, truest murder story I ever wrote."

"Huh. Who's to know you didn't fall in battle?"

"Our paper has secrets agents in your army as well as Anthony's. Do you think they'd let as important a man as me go around without protection?" And because Brutus was hesitating again, "I give you my word as a journalist, General, that the minute I'm back in Rome, in my usual health, I'll see to it personally that the story is killed deader than Cæsar."

An anxious moment for P. Manlius Scribo, whose powers of invention were beginning to flag. A still more anxious moment when Brutus pulled the bell-cord, causing a nerve-splitting clang. Curtains parted and the general's orderly entered. "Private Erasmus, what time is it?"

"One hour from sunrise, sir. Already on the Eastern hills the fair Aurora—"

"Can't you report without spouting poetry? Get me my armor—the winter weight suit. And fetch me a pot of hot wine. Hot, do you understand? None of that dish water you served me last night."

"Yes, sir." The orderly saluted and marched away.

The fateful day of Philippi had begun.

## XXIII

SINCE a detailed description of a battle is tedious to the reader and frightfully wearisome to the author, suppose we review Philippi in as few words as possible. Thackeray did the battle of Waterloo in a page or so, and on that scale Philippi should be worth, maybe, one tight little paragraph, or two at the most.

In spite of Cassius' ingeniously planned Nut Cracker Movement, the armies didn't get under way until two hours past sunrise. Maybe it was the fault of General Brutus, who couldn't get his staff to concentrate properly on the advance. More likely it was the fault of the times. Since Brutus and Cassius had made such a fuss about being pro-Freedom, a free spirit had impregnated the ranks, and just before the battle several of the regiments refused to march until they had formed committees and voted on their policies for the day. The cavalry declined to move without the regulation size brass band, and there was some trouble about finding a tuba player. Every now and then panting couriers from Cassius' wing would ride up with anxious inquiries about why Brutus didn't do something about it.

At last they were under way. At exactly ten forty-one, by the handy sun-dial on Manlius' wrist, Brutus had advanced the proper three kilometers and paused by a wooded copse, waiting to give the signal for the famous right-angle charge which was to crack the nut in the center. Sitting his horse now, the fire of battle in his eye, Brutus was every inch a soldier. Sitting another horse, the dust of battle in his eye, Manlius was every inch a cripple. Smithicus had run all the way afoot, and beaten the two horses by several minutes.

"Scabio," began Brutus, only to be corrected again.

"The name is Scribo, sir."

"Perhaps," a little wistfully. "But I shall always think of you as Scabio. Scabio, what you said about suppressing that story was in good faith, wasn't it?"

"General, my word's as good as my bond."

"I hope you're not in the banking business," said Brutus with the first sign of nervousness. "But I appreciate your generous spirit. Now, before we charge, let me say this.

Battles, you know, are a dreadful gamble; one never knows how a battle's going to come out until it's over. One may conquer or one may fall. Suppose I fall. I don't want to die, feeling that I've been unfair to you. Now, get out your tablet and listen carefully. I'm going to reveal. . . ."

All around them the short Roman bugles were braying, getting the line into proper formation. Manlius' fingers shook as he took out a tablet and got ready to write.

"I ask but one concession," said Brutus. "Before I tell you anything you must give me back that butcher knife."

Excitedly Manlius produced the butcher knife and Brutus slid it into his belt. It was a moment of painful intensity when the general leaned forward and began:

"Let me tell you the truth about the man I saw on Pompey's statue. . . ."

But the mystery was destined never to be revealed by Brutus' lips. For just as the key in the whole enigma was about to be released the eyes of Brutus popped from his head and he uttered a horrid shriek. A figure on a white horse, in pure white armor and the pallid equipment of a field marshal, came riding softly up. Within two feet of Brutus it paused and its helmet rattled like a stove lid as sneakily it reached up and opened its visor.

Cæsar's ghost again! In broad daylight the dead white face and scrawny grin seemed more frightening than at midnight.

"Well, old playmate," it drawled, "I'm keeping my appointment."

"How long will you go on torturing me like this?" murmured Brutus, oblivious of his chief of staff, impatiently gesturing.

"Not for long, my boy. Not for long. Ha-ha!"

"Wouldn't it be more decent, sir, to say some word of appreciation over the body before we leave it?"

For a moment Manlius watched Brutus' army, now in full retreat, then he thought of something that would please Smithicus' sense of propriety.

"He was the noblest Roman of them all, I guess," he said. "That's what they usually say at funeral orations, and it goes for Brutus. Now let's clear out of here before we get captured by Anthony and have to do this darned rigmarole all over again."

Hastily he pulled the cheap knife from the suicide's breast, then hurried into the woods which had just swallowed up the retreat of Cæsar's ghost. Manlius was no friend of spooks and horrid apparitions, but now he had far more to fear from a living general than from a dead dictator. And an unformed thought was urging him on. Like a hunting dog, nose to the ground, he was following the trail of a disembodied rabbit.

So they trudged along for a spell, master and slave, Manlius thinking deeply, Smithicus rather burdened down with an odd collection of swords, spears and helmets which he had picked up in the wake of the retreat.

"What do you expect to do with those?" asked the reporter, coming out of his dream. "Going to start a war of your own?"

"In this state of the Republic, sir, one never can tell," was Smithicus' cryptic reply.

In the distance, all too near for comfort, could be heard the braying of more Roman trumpets. Faintly echoed the cry of "Long live Mark Anthony!"

"Oh gosh, Mark's catching up with us!" whispered Manlius.

"Would it not be a good plan, sir, to surrender ourselves to General Anthony? After all, we came here as his correspondents."

"A fat chance we'd have. Anthony caught me once, snooping on Cleopatra. And if he found me here, chumming with the enemy, he'd shoot first and ask questions afterwards. And look at my uniform."

That was bad. For this morning, before going into action, Brutus had lent him one of his old breastplates, marked with the insignia of his own forces. Yes, and he was wearing horizon blue kilts, the colors of Brutus' favorite regiment.

"We'll correct that in a jiffy, sir. A proper disguise is all you need."

Suiting action to words, Smithicus went into his pouch and brought out another mess of hair from the lot he had borrowed from Comma's *bungalorium.* This set was an unnatural yellow.

"With those whiskers on I'll be the human target," objected Manlius.

"They fall in perfectly with the principal of camouflage, if I might say so. They are quite the color of the daffodils blooming all about us. Suppose you remove your uniform, sir, and slip on my tunic. It's a bit large for you, but any port in a storm, as a clerical gentleman—"

"Yes, I know. A Druid priest. Smithicus, it's my policy not to criticize another man's religious views, but that particular cleric was certainly all wet."

Still protesting, Manlius got out of his trappings of war and into the enormous brown garment which flapped about him like a misfit Mother Hubbard. Then he felt the mat of jaundiced hair go over his chin and skull; whatever he looked like, he consoled himself, it was not a soldier in the army of the late Junius Brutus.

The shouts grew louder in the open space outside the wood. Boosting himself into a tree, he disentangled his beard from the twigs and gazed out upon the scene. Horsemen were thundering past. And a swell chance a stranger, whiskered like a comic strip, would have against that horde! Manlius clung there, considering what to do, when Mark Anthony himself, splendid in golden armor, came riding up, surrounded by staff officers. In an open space, only a few yards from the thicket, he drew up his coal black charger and went into a huddle.

"Colonel Bacchus," he shouted in his oratorical voice, "we've wiped out Brutus and Cassius—the dirty quitters—and there's nothing left to do but enlist their armies under the standard of a Free and Glorious Republic—my own. So round up the refugees—no rough stuff, understand. Enlist 'em under the Anthony banner, and this afternoon we march on Rome."

"Aye, sir." Colonel Bacchus gave the Fascist salute, whereupon the staff officers went thundering away in the direction of the refugees. Only Anthony remained, studying a small scroll.

This time, if any, was opportune. Rapidly Manlius slid down from his tree, floppily he advanced toward the golden warrior.

"Well, General," he began, thinking of some cheerful phrase by which to introduce himself, "you had a nice day for it."

"Fair," said Anthony, looking down and taking in the picturesque make-up.

"And you've got 'em on the run, I see."

"A Roman army never runs away," said Anthony, still studying the effect. "Look here, if you've come into this battle as the comic relief, you don't get a laugh out of me."

"Just a minute, General. I'm not what I look like—I mean, I'm here in disguise, representing the *Evening Tiber."*

"Oh," said Anthony, and for a moment he seemed to take his mind off the battle. "So you're the cub they call Manlius Scribo."

"The same," said Mannie in his best detective style.

"Hm. The cub that old fool, Editor Apex, insisted on sending here as a glass blower, or a smoke shoveler, or—"

"A war correspondent, sir," supplied Manlius courteously.

"Something useless, I remember."

"I'd have been here before, but I've been spying on Brutus' army, sir." This sounded better than saying that he'd been captured. "I was there when your ghost materialized, and it worked fine."

Anthony grew red as a beet. "You've done about what you pleased, haven't you?"

"Yes, sir. No, sir. I've come to offer my services, sir. What are your orders?"

"Orders?" thundered Anthony. "Go roll your hoop. Those are my orders. You're here, aren't you? Then why bother me? Git ap, Apollo!" The last command was directed at his coal black charger.

The general went stamping away, leaving Manlius alone with his disguise, wondering if it wouldn't be a good thing to go over and give Smithicus a swift kick in his funny British pants. But he took out his wicked mood in criticizing Mark Anthony. The big, showy exhibitionist. The big Babbitus. One of your success-story favorites. Put him up against a good heavyweight general and he wouldn't last out the first round. Look at the way he ruined the *Evening Tiber* the minute he bought the property. Look at the way he turned a good city editor into a shuddering yes-man. A cheap racket, the whole blooming mess. . . .

One thing, though, gave Mannie a secret delight. He had won his bet with Eggie Rector; Anthony had won the battle. He had won it by summoning Cæsar's ghost from the Beyond. The Egyptian spiritualist had been more useful to Anthony than an extra legion of Gallic archers. You had to hand it to Anthony. In some ways, even if he did give you a pain, he was a whiz.

Great Cæsar's ghost! The interjection came unexpectedly, following a brilliant idea, flooding into Mannie's brain. Suppose—

He was rather terse with Smithicus when he went back to the grove. "Let's get moving," he said.

"Did you give yourself up, sir?" asked the perfect slave.

"He wouldn't take me," grunted Manlius.

"Indeed, sir!"

"Who'd want anything looking the way I do? If you'd throw me into the arena the lions wouldn't touch me. Smiddy, get me out of this wild man effect and gimme back that armor."

"But if you wear it you may be slain as a spy."

"Well, I'll make a dignified corpse, anyhow. Go on. Gimme."

Therefore, after some fussing with nuts and bolts, Manlius was restored to helmet and breastplate and the poison yellow beard torn from his chin. The Battle of Philippi, such as it was, was over.

So master and man plodded along, weighed down with themselves, hoping to steal a horse somewhere; or better still, to hitch hike on one of the chariots returning to the Eternal City. Breaking through the last clump of shrubbery—already they could catch a glimpse of the road to Rome, not far ahead—Manlius stopped dead in his tracks, transfixed, as it were. The prints of horseshoes were sunk deep into the mud at his feet. On a gooseberry bush over yonder several white hairs from a horse's tail were clinging. Yes, but these things led to a far, far more important clue.

For under a shadowy oak, where the violets were trampled down as though someone had stopped there to rest, lay objects which, at first glance, looked like the disjointed parts of a snow man.

"What have we here?" asked our hero appropriately. But upon closer inspection, the true nature of the phenomenon was revealed—*a complete suit of armor, which had recently been painted lily white!*

Tremblingly Manlius picked up the helmet, groggily he inspected it. Yes, it had the very crest, the very visor he had seen this morning when a ghost wore it on the Plains of Philippi! The very crest, the very visor that had adorned a spectral head as it leaned last night, jeering, over the uneasy bed of Junius Brutus! Nay more, on one of the hinges that held the metallic nose-guard appeared the initials which gave it all away. C.J.C.!!

Even in his excitement, Manlius paused to go back over his college chemistry. He smelled the armor. Phosphorus. The stuff that shines in the dark. You can paint your face with it and look remarkably like a ghost. And the face over Brutus' bed last night. . . .

"I didn't think Cæsar would stoop to a trick like that," muttered the detective-correspondent. But here was the solution of the mystery, traced down, as in modern crime you discover a criminal through the laundry marks on his shirt!

"As clear as mud," soliloquized Manlius, holding the helmet the way the gloomy Dane, in a future generation, held Yorick's skull. "Everything is solved now. Everything."

"I dare say so, sir," said Smithicus.

"Who asked your opinion? I'm talking to myself. But it all hooks up. Cæsar isn't any deader than I am. He's been impersonating his own ghost, to scare Brutus out of a battle. Impersonation—whoops! This is how it happened."

"How, sir?"

"I can't say exactly until I know a little more. But I've been a pretty busy lad these past two weeks. And this is how I've worked it out. Either Cæsar was playing dead the day he got a knife in the back, *or some substitute, impersonating Ceesar, was killed in his stead."*

"Extr'ord'n'ry!" cried Smithicus.

"Shut up and let me finish. That Cæsar was stabbed at all seems unlikely; he was in the habit of wearing a knife-proof vest under his tunic. Now let's look into the understudy theory. Did Cæsar know about the plot to kill him? The Big Fella knew everything, as he always did. But instead of arresting the conspirators and having them strangled—the conventional thing to do—he decided to stage his own murder on the Ides of March, with the kind assistance of his friend, Mark Anthony."

"But why, sir?"

"He's getting old. He wanted to retire from public life before the assassins got him. But if he retired openly some other bunch of patriots would begin yelling 'Quitter!' and stick a knife into him. Then see how he worked it. Remember how, during the past few months, a queer-looking Cæsar, overdressed, too pompous, full of gestures, would show up on public occasions? I've been watching him carefully, and I've suspected that Cæsar has been training an understudy for some purpose of his own. That purpose is plain enough now."

"You mean to say, sir," asked Smithicus, "that the Dictator planned to have another person murdered in his stead?"

"Bright guess, Smiddy."

"But who was this other person, may I ask?"

"How in hell do I know? But it wasn't Cæsar any more than I'm a—I'm a—"

The figure of speech faded on Mannie's lips. For he had turned the helmet over, and as he gazed into the crown his keen eyes caught the contour of a little bronze box, set into the apex of the dome. It was equipped with a dial, marked with a series of Roman numerals. But what was the combination? Nervously Manlius spun the dial this way and that. Nothing, of course, happened.

"What do you think's inside it?" he muttered.

"The papers, I have no doubt," said Smithicus brightly.

The ex-gladiator took over the helmet and pulled it apart as easily as you'd peel a banana. The little box flew open, and out of it fell a tiny roll of papyrus, such as Romans used before note books were invented; tremblingly Manlius unrolled it and gazed upon a long column of names, dates and figures, written in Cæsar's crabbed hand. A memo of personal expenses, running from the Nones of February almost to the Ides of March. Most of the figures—although they ran high—meant nothing. Then this significant record:

To Pompeia .............................. V talents
To Comma ................................ D sesterces
To mfg. jeweler ......................... CM sesterces
To Pompeia .............................. X talents
To Pompeia .............................. XV talents
To Hesiod ............................... V talents
To Pompeia .............................. II talents
To Hesiod ............................... VI talents
To wigs, costumes, theatrical
props, etc .............................. MDCCL sesterces
To extra size vestal robe and
special wig ..................... .......... CXLVI sesterces
To Comma ................................ CLXXX sesterces

And on the reverse side of a sheet a few scattered notes, abbreviated so that they read like cipher:

Cl get reg. sz. vest. rb. from Cm. Cm sup. Sic to Cl in dis.

Hd. get lrg. vest, rb me pers. Cl. barge stop down Rv. Hd return aft. job.

Cm gd. mk-up Hd. to me. Hd in vest. rb. get Cm knows too mch.

Pom. ag. to Ides also exit with me.

Under this was scrawled in perfectly legible Latin, "A nice surprise for the boys."

Manlius sat among Cæsar's trick armor and concentrated upon the algebraic problem which, if he could conquer it, would be the last step, he thought, in solving the colossal mystery.

Hm. The list of expenses. Pompeia, for an ex-wife, had cost the Big Fella a lot of money lately. Thirty-two talents, which would be thirty-two grand. What for? It was well known that he paid her off in a lump sum when they were divorced. Comma wasn't so well paid, according to the expense account, as the sesterce, at par, was only about four cents—but there was that rather large item for wigs, costumes and make-up—MDCCL sesterces. To the manufacturing jeweler CM sesterces. And Hesiod; certainly eleven grand was a pretty liberal dividend for an actor already overpaid in Pompey's Theater.

Yes, and what about that item of CXLVI sesterces for an extra size vestal robe and wig—paid for out of Cæsar's own pocket?

Feverishly, a letter at a time, Manlius began dissecting the abbreviated notes. Then words began to come in fine, round Latin:

"Cl get reg. sz vest. rb. from Cm. Cm sup. Sic to Cl in dis."

"Cleopatra will get regular size vest ribbon—" No, that couldn't be it. Vest rb. Vest rb. Ha! Vestal robes! "Cm sup. Sic to Cl in dis." "Comma will supply Sic Semper Tyrannis lockets to Cleopatra in disguise."

Then the other notes, fully interpreted, flowed across the detective's vision:

"Hesiod will get the larger robe from me personally. Cleopatra's barge will stop down the river until Hesiod returns after the job."

"Comma is a good person to make Hesiod up to look like me. Then Hesiod, in vestal robes, will get Comma, who knows too much."

"Pompeia agrees to make the Ides of March warning, and on that date she will exit with me."

"Eureka!" cried Manlius, tossing Cæsar's notes in air and catching them again. "Eureka—practically, anyhow."

"Thank you, sir," commented the Briton.

"Don't mention it. Here it is, Smithicus, all in a shut-nell—nut-shell, I mean. Gosh, I'm so excited I've forgotten my Latin constructions. If Cæsar had gotten tight and confessed the whole thing he couldn't have done better. Now listen to this plot. Anthony and Cleopatra are in love, and Cæsar's willing to oblige, because he's tired of that Egyptian deity. He's crazy to run away with Pompeia and get out of public life. He knows all about the conspiracy, of course. He decides to fool Brutus and Cassius so that they'll murder somebody else, thinking it's him. His job is to keep up the conspirators' enthusiasm. So he gets Cleo, the little trouble momma, to pretend she's in the assassination plot, dress up as a vestal and peddle the *Sic Semper* trinkets—which Cæsar is paying for himself. Didn't the Levantine Squaw admit, the night she gassed me, that Comma kept the lockets for her in his *bungalorium?*

"Cæsar has a date with Pompeia to get out of Rome on the Ides of March. But Brutus and Cassius have been dawdling along, changing the date of the murder every week or so. Cæsar's job is to make 'em stab on schedule. Cleopatra coaxed 'em into settling on March fifteenth and even gets Cassius to bribe the priest of Jupiter so that he'll predict good luck for Cæsar on the Ides. The Big Fella, of course, knows every move that's been made. That's why he and Pompeia play that little farce at the Junior League Fair. Pompeia yells, 'Beware the Ides of March!' and Cæsar answers, 'You're foolish. The Priest of Jupiter says it's my lucky day.' It's all rehearsed, of course. But it makes Brutus and Cassius think their man will be on the spot, on the minute. You follow me, Smithicus?"

"No, sir."

"Good. Because you're not much of an observer, probably you didn't notice how Cleopatra, in vestal robes, was signaling somebody at Comma's funeral. I thought at first that she was wig-wagging Mark Anthony. But the high-sign was really for Hesiod, who was looking right at her. The signal meant, 'Come to the rehearsal.' "

"Rehearsal?"

"That afternoon, at the Fresh Air Fund Gladiatorial Show, Cæsar came in all dolled up in imperial robes, strutting and gesturing. Not himself. Why? Because it wasn't Cæsar at all, but Hesiod putting over another impersonation. Cæsar's plan, you see, to get the public used to thinking that he sometimes looked that way."

"Very clever of you, sir," said Smithicus. "And might I ask if you have solved the Comma mystery also?"

"Let's go back to that, merely as a step toward the so-called Cæsar murder. See what Cæsar's own notes say. 'Hesiod in vestal robes will get Comma, who knows too much.' Also, 'Cleopatra's barge will stop down the river until Hesiod returns after the job.' I found the blood-stained vestal robes, a very good fit for Hesiod, under the back porch. Yes, but Hesiod's perfect alibi—didn't get back from Naples until the noon after Comma was killed. There were plenty of witnesses to his arrival. Well, the notes here explain that too. Cleopatra's barge, coming up the Tiber, late at night, stopped at some little port to let Hesiod off. Hesiod got off, finished the murder, came back. The barge, under orders, loafed along and made the Tiber wharves at noon. Hesiod, a wonderful female impersonator, had time, in that little stop-off, to put on the vestal robe and red wig which Casar had furnished. Comma came home plastered. Fake vestal waited with knife. Simple, when you know how. And the whole show was under the personal direction of C. J. Cæsar."

"Would you call that cricket, sir?"

"Hell no. Not even good football."

"But why should Csesar wish to get rid of Comma?" asked the Briton.

"There you go!" said Manlius, losing some of his exaltation. "Cæsar's note says, 'He knows too much.' He knew about the *Sic Semper* racket and Cleopatra; also he was the artist who made Hesiod up to look like Cæsar. He had to be shut up. But it seems to me that it would have been simpler for the Big Fella to hush him with a large wad of money. That's the usual way among us noble Romans."

"It was unsportsmanlike," insisted Smithicus, "for Cæsar to have put Hesiod, his trusty friend, in such a false position."

"Trusty? Slave, I'll tell you something I've learned about Hesiod. Pompeia's janitor hinted very strongly that Hesiod had been the lady's *homo amatus*—boy-friend, you know—for quite some time. Cæsar decided to remarry his ex-wife, disappear and pay off an old score, all in one stroke. Hesiod must die. It wouldn't do to have an actor bragging all over Rome that he'd first vamped Pompeia, then impersonated the Dictator on a dozen public occasions. So along comes the Ides of March. Everything ready, conspirators waiting with daggers—but no Cæsar."

"But what detained Cæsar—or Hesiod, I should say—so long?"

"That was characteristic of Hesiod. At the theater they complained that he was often late coming on—fussy about his costumes. But that's not so important as another point. After the alleged Cæsar fell dead you remember how we followed a trail of blood to a man-hole and found two cops guarding the place where the body had disappeared?"

"Then Chief Kellius—"

"Mark Anthony was bossing Kellius. Anthony wanted the corpse put out of sight before the conspirators and the general public got a good look at it and discovered it wasn't Cæsar at all. Hence the big hurry about having the body burned. Almost indecent haste, considering that the dead man was the conqueror of the world. And the cremation was so far away from the crowd that nobody could really make out who it was. Anthony, you see, took charge of the comedy from the Ides of March on, because Cæsar, probably, was out of Rome by then.

It was Anthony who escorted the fake Cæsar right up to the butchery, then left him to stroll along the Alley of Statues and get stabbed without seeing the point—"

"And without seeing the assassin, sir, if I might say so," put in Smithicus mournfully.

"Oh, for Jove's sake, why bring that up!" Mannie was all worn out with his slave's interlinear annotations. "You kill-joy. You realist."

"But I've always had a vulgar curiosity about that knife in Cæsar's—Hesiod's back. Where did it come from?"

"Smithicus," grumbled Mannie Scribo, "I paid forty dollars for you and there are times when I'd trade you in for a second hand chariot."

"I should hate to see you cheated, sir," objected the slave with something like a show of spirit.

So they straggled up to the road to Rome, and went as far as the sign marked "To Philippi" in both directions. There they stood, jabbing their thumbs over their shoulders as one vehicle and another went by. At last a near-sighted farmer on a load of hay stopped his oxen and let them aboard.

Thus gradually they crept toward Rome. The hay was a comfort, and Manlius managed to unbutton the hardest part of his armor so that he could have room enough to utter a few more weary sighs. Then he stretched himself out and went on considering the Julius Cæsar murder case. He had cracked the shell of the mystery, but the tenderest kernels of the nut still clung inside. Smithicus had been right when he said that Hesiod, in dying, hadn't seen his assassin. Only Brutus had recognized the killer; and Brutus was dead too. Who, then, had managed to dig a knife into the imitation Dictator as he walked a dozen feet or more out of arm's reach?

Yes, and there were other points to clear up. Who was the Greek who had been so devoted to Romula? And why? Why had Anthony and Cleopatra been entertaining her as their guest? Did she know of the death-drama that Cæsar was working out, with Hesiod as star? More than likely. Certainly she had resented Mannie's every attempt to investigate. Yet that night when she visited his room she had said in a voice that was half tears, half temper, "Manlius, this has been a wicked, bloody business. I'd have stopped it if I could." Would she have stopped the slaying of Hesiod, who killed her father? Queer business, this Romula situation. And what did she want of that old wax doll? Vaguely he wondered if she could be in love with Mark Anthony.

"With that big Babbittus?" sneered Mannie, and went to sleep.

## XXIV

ABOUT a couple of thousand years before timetables were invented nobody arrived anywhere on schedule. It is close enough to the facts to say that Mannie got back to the *Tiber* offices ten days after the battle. Without even changing his travel-stained toga he reported to Q. Bulbus Apex that he was ready to write the story, as per contract, but of all the war games he'd ever reported Philippi was the most heavily laden with cheese.

"Play up Anthony," smiled Q. Bulbus, disregarding Manlius' personal opinion. "Give him a hand. Give him two hands. Have a drink." Out of a washbasin Old Calamity produced a jar of something really good—wine of Præneste, none better anywhere.

"Tuck some of that between your teeth and get busy, boy," he commanded. "We'll get out a late edition—shoot it all over town at about 11 P.M.—time the drunks begin coming home. Battle of Philippi. Butchery of traitors. Mark Anthony, the new Father of his Country." Q. Bulbus lowered his voice. "See anything of that ghost?"

"See him? I was close to him as I'm to you."

"Well, just give the spook passing mention, will you?"

"Hell, but he won the battle."

"Oh, no. Anthony won. Stress that point."

Manlius smiled grimly. So Anthony had sent his instructions. He had created a ghost, and now he was jealous of it. Wanted all the credit, as usual. Mannie wondered how much Old Calamity knew of the inside story about Cæsar. What was the difference? Anthony owned Q. Bulbus now, and Q. Bulbus was nothing but Anthony's mouthpiece.

"Aw, gimme some tablets," snarled the sports reporter, and when these came in he put his gifted stylus to work.

> The Battle of Philippi has come and gone—principally gone. In the estimation of this humble scribe it was about the saddest piece of ping-pong that has offended our nose since the management frisked the customers at the notorious Fresh Air Fund Gladiatorial Show.

"Look here, young man!" Q. Bulbus was severe; he had been reading over Manlius' shoulder. "You can't do that. Not with one of the greatest battles of history—"

"I just wanted to get your slant, Boss," said the artist diplomatically, discarding the tablet and reaching out for another one. "You furnish the words, I furnish the music. How does this lyric go?"

With as great facility as he had shown in the first account he tackled the second:

> At last we've seen a battle, folks. Philippi is going down in ring history as the spot where the heroes took it on the chin and came up for more. Brutus and Cassius, whom this writer used to call palookas, developed remarkable class; who would have thought they had it in them to stand the constant rain of blows.

"Don't give it all to Brutus and Cassius," prompted Q. Bulbus.

"Good Juno," said Manlius irritably, "what do you want 'em to think? That Anthony was fighting a pair of fainting swans?"

"Well, get Anthony into the first paragraph," insisted the Boss. The stylus moved again.

> . . . constant rain of blows showered on them by the undoubted champ of champs, Mark Anthony—

"Better put in something about his popularity—savior of Rome, popular after-dinner speaker, another Moses, sent to lead us out of the wilderness," suggested Apex.

"Go easy on Moses," said Mannie. "That's Hebrew stuff. Next you know they'll be saying we're not a good pagan paper—then where'll our circulation be?"

"Anyhow, make it strong," said Q. Bulbus.

The account went on:

> You've got to be in a battle, folks, to realize what confidence it gives the forces to know that they're being led by the savior of Rome and a popular after-dinner speaker. Yes, Mabel, when it comes to generalship Mark is good. Good to the last drop. That fighting face of his is

enough to make any opponent wish he had died before he went in there to go up against it.

"Go easy on his face," cautioned Q. Bulbus. "We're working up a special feminine appeal this week, and ladies don't like faces that scare 'em. 'Terrible in his manly beauty' would fit in better."

Therefore Mannie erased the line about the fighting face and wrote on:

> . . . terrible in his manly beauty, what opponent would dare go up against a face like that? Don't think Brutus and Cassius weren't game. But you can't stand up against genius—that's the very thing Big Mark demonstrated every minute when he sailed into that famous Nut Cracker and tore it up like a yard of rotten cotton—

"Genius! That's fine. Fine." Q. Bulbus rubbed his dry palms. "Here, you'd better have something about Mark meeting the two traitors and killing 'em in a hand to hand conflict."

"Yeah? He didn't do anything but ride around on a black horse and give a lot of wind-bag orders. Brutus would have been alive now if he hadn't committed suicide, and Cassius—"

"Oh, it couldn't have been like that!" objected Q. Bulbus.

"Was you there, Carolus?" asked Mannie.

"No. But a battle can't possibly be so tame. You've got to have high spots. Write some high spots—and give 'em to Anthony."

"Say, are you running an all-fiction magazine?" snorted the reporter.

"We're pioneers in tabloid journalism," replied the editor with dignity.

Manlius was tired of arguing; a romantic way of introducing Cæsar's ghost struck fire in his imagination, so he wrote:

> Before the battle it was quite apparent to your correspondent that the traitorous expedition of Brutus and Cassius was doomed to failure. The two conspirators spent the evening hen-pecking over the ethics of friendship. Brutus even descended to accusing Cassius of

squeezing drachmas from the poor. Then Cassius got dignified and Brutus sneered, "When love begins to sicken and decay it affects a high headdress." Whereupon Cassius threatened to throw the battle to Anthony, and went to bed.

A disagreeable hallucination seemed to bother Brutus that night. Always something of a spiritualist, he complained that the ghost of the late Dictator appeared to him, promising to meet him on the field. Next day, according to superstitious soldiers, a spectral Roman did ride up to Anthony and whisper in his ear. The Brutalists had an attack of nerves, that's all.

But the real fight, when it came, was all Anthony's. Oh, boy, how he rode 'em down. The big moment in the battle was when he came upon Brutus and Cassius, defied them to meet him, two to one, and beheaded them both with a stroke of his sword.

"Now you're hitting your pace!" chortled Q. Bulbus Apex. "Don't let it cool on you, kid."

In an hour Manlius—with frequent interpolations from the Boss—filled three closely written tablets and handed in the story.

"It's so different its own mother wouldn't know it," said he.

"That's the very spirit I'm trying to get into the *Evening Tiber,"* said Old Calamity. "Don't choke your story up with facts. Give 'em lure. This is your masterpiece, Mannie. This last paragraph, especially." Gloatingly he read the line under his thumb. *"Then Mark Anthony, never failing in his big generosity, leaned over the fallen Brutus and spoke feelingly. 'He was the noblest Roman of them all,' he said, and his great voice trembled!"*

"That's live journalism, my boy," said Q. Bulbus, his funny eyes shining with tears. "It's beautiful. It comes darned near being poetry."

On the way out Manlius caught up with Egregius Rector. They locked arms and started over to Hibe's to drink a cozy dinner.

"How's the battle?" asked Eggie.

"Limburgius," said Mannie.

"But the *Evening Tiber'll* work a miracle," said Eggie.

"Sure. Put in Limburger and it comes out ice cream."

"Yeah. Or vice versa."

*"Semper veritas in vice versa."*

*"Dixisti,"* agreed Mannie. "Anything happen while I was away—except a lot of ham speeches?"

"Nothing much," said Eggie. "Rome's gone on and off the gold standard twice. Off again, on again."

"I know. Same principle as the water wagon." Mannie made his voice sound careless when he said, "I guess a lot of the old steadies have left town. Cleopatra, Pompeia—"

"Yeah? Shouldn't wonder if Anthony has a future date with the Levantine Squaw. Probably Pompeia got so sore about losing Cæsar by assassination that she just faded out of the picture. Rome's deader than Cæsar. They've padlocked all the arenas. Chief Kellius is back at his desk, and he got his orders from Mark, I guess. No more gladiatorial fights until Anthony comes back and blows himself to a ten-mile triumph—at public expense, of course. Pompey's Theater's closed. No star. Guess Hesiod lost his taste for acting."

"And where do you think Hesiod went?" asked Manlius innocently.

"Dunt esk. Where do actors go when they retire? To Greece, maybe, or to hell."

"Make it hell," said Manlius softly. "By the way, you owe me a hundred denarii. Anthony won, you know, in spite of spiritualism."

"Let me pay you five on account," said Eggie Rector.

They paused, because they had reached the door of Hibe's.

They found themselves places in the corner where reporters ate; since Manlius, with magnificent cunning, declared that the dinner was on him, Eggie ordered three dozen oysters, a large variety of roast game and a jug of vintage Falernian. Because there was method in Mannie's generosity, he waited until his friend had finished eighteen oysters and quaffed a large share of the Falernian straight, before he slyly advanced the king-question on his chess-board.

"Poor old Pompey's Theater," he said sentimentally. "I hate to see the old house dark. Losing Hesiod put the place on the blink, of course. But Comma was really the brain trust there. When they killed that guy they killed the theater. It was a pretty lousy trick, the way they cut his throat. A murderer, before he commits a crime, ought to think of what he's doing to a man's family. Look at Comma, the natural protector of a beautiful daughter—"

"Hey!" broke in Eggie, who up to then had been indifferent, eating oysters. "If you're talking about that *puella* Romula, you should worry about natural protectors."

"We published Cæsar's will last week. He didn't leave as much as folks thought he would. He left Calpurnia enough to pay her board bill, provided she stays out of Rome. His slaves got a cut on the rest; Tamany of Athens has a claim on his real estate. But there was a whale of a fortune, held in trust—"

"Held in trust," prompted Mannie, because Eggie was eating.

"—held in trust, to be delivered at his death to Romula, only daughter of the late J. Romulus Comma."

The room seemed to slip one way, the table the other. Frantically Manlius reached out for the Falernian jug and tried to pour himself a drink. Too late. Eggie had finished the wine long ago. Unsteadily Manlius beckoned for another one.

"Did—did she get the money?" he gasped.

"I'll say she did. Five thousand talents—"

"Zowie!" Five thousand talents; and had Mannie possessed the futuristic knowledge of Mr. Morgenthau he might have computed it to be some five million uninflated dollars.

"Yes, five thousand talents," mused Eggie, reaching for the horse-radish. "Delivered in a check by Cicero himself, right in his law office. Front page spread. But I thought, for a minute, that the deal was off. There was a hitch in it."

"What sort of a hitch?"

"You know Cicero has hated Cæsar's guts ever since the Big Fella helped get him exiled. But a long time ago they were perfect boy-friends. Cicero was Cæsar's lawyer, and he made Cicero trustee over this money, so I guess when it came to paying out the coin the old bird tried to make it hard as possible. The will was read—it was short enough. Then when the time came to sign the check Cicero said to Romula: Not a sesterce do I pay until you have produced the proof."

"What did Romula do then?"

"Just dipped down into her shirtwaist and brought out a bum little wax doll. Ain't that somethin'? Cicero took it and stood it up and sat it down—imagine Cicero playing with dolls! Then he took a piece of papyrus out of his desk, studied it, looked at one of the doll's legs—naughty old man—and chirped, 'What did you call this doll when you were a baby?' 'Sweetie,' said Romula promptly. 'All right,' said Cicero, 'the money's yours.' "

"Did you interview Cicero?"

"Did you ever interview the Sphinx? And that gal Romula can keep her trap locked too. But we got out the story—Prize Peach Cops Cæsar's Coin. And is she an eyeful? I'd give the Roman Republic with a red ribbon around it to—"

"How was that bequest worded—I mean—"

"Short and snappy. 'Provided she can produce the proof mentioned in the instructions I furnish separately, I bequeath the sum of five thousand talents, with love and affection, to Romula, daughter of my old friend, J. Romulus Comma.' "

So that was what Romula had been searching for that night when Manlius found her in the *bungalorium.* Proof. A wax doll. Proof of what? The bequest might have been conscience-money, paid out to the girl whom Cæsar's assassin had orphaned. But five thousand talents! What orphan, however deserving, is worth that dole?

All worn out with mysteries, Manlius poured liberally from the new jug of Falernian, hoping to stimulate his powers of concentration. But just then his eyes, slanting toward the door of the little back room where gladiators took their nips, caught a vision more amazing than the midnight appearance of Cæsar's ghost. A little man, something under three feet, stood like an elf, slyly beckoning. Hercules the midget!

Manlius sat weakly unable to move anything but his speechless mouth. Meanwhile Hibernicus came blustering up with, "Hi, you slave, git back on yer own side. Whaddaya think ye are, a gintleman?"

Hercules dodged out of sight, but not too late for Eggie to see him and have a good laugh.

"That's the thumb-nail sketch," he burbled, "that's been at the office every day, asking for you.

He used to work at Pompey's Theater, and I guess he's looking for some kind of job."

Regaining his strength, Manlius went into the back room.

He found Hercules, a toy terrier, running around the legs of giant man-killers who drank like savages, standing up, their feet against a rail.

"Nobleman!" cried the midget, leaping on a table beside Manlius, to be close to his ear. "I told her I'd find you. Bully for me! She said she'd hire detectives—she can afford it now. But who ever heard of a detective finding anything? Oh, we're so rich, nobleman. We have a villa and fifty eunuchs. How's that?"

"Pretty good," said Manlius, his heart sinking. A little poorer than when his story opened, he found himself in love with a girl who had a villa and fifty eunuchs.

"What does she want of me?" he asked dully.

"So many things to be explained, nobleman."

"She's got around to that, has she?"

"Oh, but there *are* things to be explained," twinkled the little man. "If you look at it that way, you'll be surprised."

"Lead me," said Manlius.

Eager as a pup, the midge had him by a corner of his toga and was dragging him toward an outer door. Manlius had a momentary picture of Eggie, left alone to pay the check. But that was all right. Eggie never paid for anything, if he could help it, and his credit was still good at Hibe's.

## XXV

THEY were walking along the streets, toward the Janiculum Hill. Smithicus, who had been waiting outside, carried a torch.

"Hercules," said Manlius, bending down until his back was tired, "there certainly are a lot of things to be explained."

"Oh, you think so. That's great. That's fine." Elfin eyes twinkling up. "I suppose you want to know who killed Comma."

"That's an old story. It was Hesiod, the actor."

"Ain't you smart. But I bet you can't guess who killed Cæsar."

"Nobody. Hesiod was killed in Cæsar's place."

"My goodness—ain't you bright! Now here comes a hard one. Bet you give this up. Tee-hee." Very slyly. "Who killed Hesiod?"

"I didn't—that's about all I know."

"Well, I did!" giggled the dwarf.

"What?"

"Honest. Cross my heart."

"Look here, midge." Roughly Manlius picked up the pint-size and stood him on a convenient doorstep, so that they could talk face to face. "How in Hellas did you come to do that?"

"I hid behind Pompey's statue that morning when Hesiod came along pretending to be Cæsar."

"Yes, but he was a dozen feet away from the statue."

"Did you ever see my knife-throwing act in Pompey's Theater?" asked the dwarf proudly. "I can hit a pin at twice that distance."

"I see, I see." Manlius bit his nails. "But every crime deserves a motive. What was yours?"

"I knew that the dirty Greek butcher killed my boss," said Hercules. "At that time I thought of Comma as the finest man I ever knew. Maybe I've changed my mind a little since then. I seen him murdered by that fake vestal—they was struggling together in his room—ahem—"

"I appreciate your embarrassment," agreed Manlius. "But for the gods' sake, go on."

"Then I seen she had a dagger against his throat. He was putting up an awful scrap. First he tore off her veil, then he got his fingers in her hair—it was a wig—"

"What color?"

"Red. Off comes her wig, just as she sliced him. And I seen who it was. Hesiod. I just hid. I couldn't do nothin' because slaves ain't allowed to carry weapons, and the knives I use in my act I'd left at the theater. I seen Hesiod take off his vestal robe, it was so bloody. Then he dragged my boss to the sun-porch, maybe thinking he'd hide the body. Finally he give that up, put on his wig and went away."

"What did you do then?"

"Next day at the Theater I got one of my knives—if I had a knife I'd show you—"

"Take this one," said Manlius, producing the clumsy butcher knife with "Pompey's Theater" stamped on the handle.

"The very one!" Little eyes bulged. "Where'd you get it?"

"On the Plains of Philippi."

"Bad news travels fast," said Hercules. "Well, I took this knife and swore the acrobat's oath by passing the edge across my thumb nail. I swore that point would go into Hesiod's heart, if I follered him a thousand years. It didn't take that long. But I had to tag him several days. He didn't go to the theater no more, but spent a lot of time at Cleopatra's house. At first, when he'd come out, I wasn't sure which was Hesiod and which was Cæsar; he was that cute at make-up, from what Comma taught him. Then, the day before the Ides of March I got so I knew the real man from the phoney. Hesiod, as Cæsar, looked a little too much like Cæsar, you understand.

"The rest was too easy. The morning of the Ides I snuck behind Pompey's Statue, because I knew that Hesiod—if he was play-acting Cæsar's part—would come that way. I seen him come in. I poised my knife. I let him have it under the left shoulder blade. Not too far to the left." With the air of an expert.

"Neat," said Manlius.

"Oh, it's just knowing how. Looky." A little dog was trotting along, about twenty feet away, and had just come into the light cast by Smithicus' torch. "Watch his tail," whispered Hercules slyly, holding his knife by the blade and poising it.

A flash of steely lightning. The end of the dog's tail dropped off so suddenly, so painlessly that the little animal, unconscious of his loss, went jogging along, wagging the stump.

"Perfect," admitted Manlius. "What did you do after you did that to Hesiod?"

"Went out looking for Romula, mister. I thought of Cleopatra's house, on account of how thick the lady had been with Comma. And I wanted to tell Romula that her father's blood had been avenged. Just as I come up to Cleopatra's door, who should come out and step into a fine, gilt carriage but Romula herself. . . . Maybe you'll think this story's a-getting queer."

"Oh, I'm used to that," said Manlius.

"Because it's going to get a lot queerer as it goes along. I ast her how she come to be there in such style, and she told me Cleopatra had moved suddenly, so Anthony was going to take care of her for a while at his wife's house. I was going to tell her how I'd just avenged Comma's blood, but the mean way she talked about Comma shut me up."

"Unnatural girl," said Manlius appropriately.

"I thought so too, until she told me what was the matter with Comma. Then I began sort of wishing I hadn't took all that trouble, throwing a knife into his murderer."

"What did she tell you?"

"You'll never know, mister, if you wait for me. If she wants to give it away, all right."

"What was the idea of her running around with that Greek and getting so thick with Anthony and Cleopatra?" asked Manlius.

"The Greek," said Hercules, "was Mark Anthony in disguise."

"What?"

"Sure's you live. When Anthony and his girl and Cæsar decided to bump off Comma, then stage the big killing, they wanted to keep Romula away from harm, as much as possible."

"Why?"

"I promised not to tell why. She can tell, if she wants to. But Anthony didn't want her mixing in the Comma case, so he put on the Greek make-up and started taking her round to parties. On the night of Comma's murder he took her to a banquet, dropped something in her wine and put her to sleep. Next day he pretended to rescue her, made a date to meet him at the Tiber Wharves, then took her to Cleopatra's house and told her what was up."

"And what was up?"

"She'll tell you, maybe. I promised to shut up. Only she stayed in Cleopatra's house as her guest until the big assassination was over. She wasn't supposed to talk to anybody. She was in a queer fix. Anthony was responsible for her."

"How responsible?"

"Ast her. She can tell you now."

"You're going a lot out of your way, little feller," said Manlius, "to make another mystery. Does she know that Hesiod was killed, instead of Cæsar?"

"Sure, but I didn't dare tell her that it was my knife instead of Brutus' that done the work. It seemed so fresh of me, spoiling Anthony's fine conspiracy. She was glad as anybody to get Hesiod out of the way."

"Why?"

"She was scared of him, that's why. Once Comma offered to sell her to him, to pay off his debts. Gosh, I'd never took all that trouble if I'd knew what a stinker Comma was. But I'm glad I got Hesiod, anyhow. He was crazy 'bout her, but she wouldn't look at him. Twice he tried to kidnap her. And Comma just looking on like a yeller dog."

"That's a new light on the case," mused Manlius. "But why did Cæsar want Comma dead?"

"Tired of paying blackmail, for one thing."

"What for?"

"If you want to see Romula, you'd better hurry," said the midge. "She may be rich, but she don't set up all night."

## XXVI

THE little man had leaped ahead of Smithicus' torch of close-wrapped faggots, and in the glow was trotting along the quiet streets, leading up Janiculum Hill. The three of them, giant, dwarf and average-sized hero, passed in to a narrow lane; with something akin to uneasiness Manlius recognized the high walled alley. It was here he had rolled himself in a rug, only to be rolled in turn by Cleopatra. He recognized the deep oak door, built in the wall, and experienced some relief when Hercules led him past it. It was at the door beyond this, a cheerful-looking one, painted bright red, that the midget stopped and knocked three times with his powerful fist.

Noiselessly, as though by prearranged signal, the door slid open and the party entered to thread their way through a pleasant garden, planted with statues mostly. Then they approached a façade of fine white marble where a big white dog bounded out at them, but only managed to bite Smithicus twice before the gentle gladiator kicked him senseless. A slave, chained to the door by a ring around his waist, proclaimed cheerfully, "Don't be afraid. He won't hurt you."

A truly Roman welcome. And now, at a whispered word from Hercules, a major domo—sex undetermined—bowed gracefully with the suggestion, "May I take your shoes and toga, sir?" This, of course, was the usual ceremony when you made a call; and Manlius was glad to get rid of his dusty outer garments. He was on the point of asking for a bath when the major domo summoned the fattest of the fifty eunuchs who slipped a pair of number eight sandals on the caller's feet.

More eunuchs showed up, prettily clad in Nile green shirts, suggesting Romula's taste in color. Two of them crowned Manlius with laurels, two more strewed his progress with rose petals, two more played flutes as they led him into the atrium, requested him to be seated, and disappeared. The room was so full of statues, mostly representing ancestors, that Manlius couldn't turn round without knocking his crazy-bone against somebody's stone elbow.

Sculptured eyes frowned down on him from every nook and corner.

Romula was certainly throwing on a lot of dog, he reflected with a panicky resentment. It didn't look honest to him. How come? Instead of putting on mourning for a father foully butchered in a midnight *bungalorium,* here she was accepting untold millions, left in the will of a man who wasn't even dead. Probably she was like all the Roman girls, a gold digger by nature, destined to grow into another Fulvia or Clodia. . . .

Anyhow, argued Manlius, she's too rich for my blood. Now that she's got the jack she's gone daffy over the Palatine Hill set, probably, and next week Q. Bulbus will be asking me to write up her engagement to one of the big guns in the Remus Club. Yeah, even if she got mushy and took me I'd turn her down flat as a hall carpet. 'Cause why? 'Cause you don't catch this baby marrying a *puella* for her coin. Come what will, I'll guard the inner shrine of my personal integrity. That's me.

I wish she'd come on, if she's going to, he thought. Because I want to ask a few brief questions, calling for brief replies, and then walk out of her life forever and forever. Her unearned wealth, her guilty splendor, have erected between us a wall which can never. . . .

In the midst of this reflection he saw something pink and female flutter out from behind a particularly repulsive statue of the late Appius Singularius. Absent-mindedly Mannie reached out and took her in his arms. For a busy man he wasted a good deal of time on a kiss, which seemed to taste better the longer it lasted. Suddenly he let her go.

"Listen, *puella,"* he said severely, "that's not answering my questions."

"You oughtn't to ask so many," she retorted. "It's a horrid habit, and I'm going to break you of it when we're married. You're too beautiful and lovely to have people calling you the Human Question Mark."

He stepped back and took a melancholy pleasure in looking her over and realizing that the girl he must relinquish forever was a whole lot prettier than his dream had made her out to be. But she had changed into something gayer than the tragic little thing who had visited him that night. Now she stood before him, looking like a *puella* who expected something else.

"Oh, all right!" he snarled, and kissed her five times, rapidly.

She sat down beside him, and after she had recovered her breath she said, "So we're engaged!"

"We're nothing of the sort," said Manlius sternly.

"No?" His decisive tone had, apparently, made no impression on her. "Of course we are," she said. "We're in love, and you've come back to ask me to marry you. Why didn't you ask me before?"

"Fat chance I had, didn't I?" he asked. "Last time I saw you you gave me a mean look and asked for a doll."

"Oh. Doll." As if she'd never heard of it before.

Then he started in bitterly, "And that didn't mean anything to you but—"

"The doll's what it's all about," she said in a whisper and looked nervously around the palace room with its pillars of ivory and walls painted with heroes jumping actively all over Troy.

"Aren't you a little old for dolls?" he asked.

"Manlius," she said, eyes big and innocent, "the first time I saw you, the Greek warned me not to talk about dolls or anything."

"He would. Your Greek was nothing but Mark Anthony with fake whiskers. Why in Helvetia did he warn you?"

"Because he said you were so darned inquisitive. He called you the Human Question Mark."

"The big Babbittus!"

"Please, Mannie! He's been so good to me."

"Wow! Him?"

"Yes, dear. And Cleopatra's sweet, too."

"So's arsenic. Go ahead."

"Well, she was lovely to me—both of them were. If they hadn't protected me I think Hesiod would have done—something horrid. He planned to kidnap me, really he did, after he killed Comma. Anthony and Cleopatra were darlings, too, helping me get my fortune. Anthony stuck to me for weeks, a sort of bodyguard, you know—"

"Yeah. I know what sort of bodyguard Mark is with a pretty gal—"

"Manlius!" She straightened up.

"Sorry, darling. Honest, I am." It required another demonstration to calm her down, then she went on with her story.

"He had to put on that funny Greek kimono and all the ringlets and bracelets and things so that no-body'd guess who he was. I had to promise to keep perfectly silent until Cæsar's estate was settled . . ."

"Holy Mercury!" shouted Manlius. "Where do you come in on this Csesar estate, anyhow?"

Her eyes were on the floor when she said, "He had to do something about me. It was only decent."

"Look here, *puella!"* With sudden suspicion Mannie took her by the shoulders and frowned down on her. "If you mean to say that bald old sugar-daddy's been playing round with you—"

"You're horrid," she said, shaking him off.

"Well then, how come Cæsar to dump five thousand grand right in your lap? Love and affection?"

"Call it that." Her eyes were purer than any vestal's ever dared to be.

"But why, Romula?Why?"

He could hardly hear her soft answer, yet somehow it cracked in his ears like a thunderbolt:

*"I'm Cæsar's daughter, that's why."*

Manlius, proof against most surprises, took quite a while to think up a reply. "Well," he said at last, feebly, "you don't look a lot like your old man, and that's something. Cæsar's daughter! Say, I've had to do some tall guessing in this case—"

"I was surprised, too, when Anthony told me," she admitted mildly.

"But look here," he insisted, "the way I learned it at school, Cæsar had two kids. Julia, she's dead. Then Cleopatra popped up with that baby they call Cæsarion. Of course he's ille—"

"—gitimate," she supplied. "And so am I." Holding up her sassy little red head.

"Great Cæsar's ghost—excuse me." Mannie was holding on to the bench. A red-headed girl, a roomful of assorted statues, fifty fat eunuchs seemed whirling round in a senseless circle.

"My mother was a German waitress, owned by Cæsar's first wife," he heard a sweet voice saying through the jumble. "He found us a house in the suburbs, and she died when I was six years old. Cæsar couldn't afford another scandal then—the Democrats were making an awful drive on him—"

"Did you know he was your father?"

"No. I remember his coming to see mamma once. He gave me a little wax doll and showed me a sort of star-shaped mark, stamped on its leg. 'Don't lose that doll,' he said, 'and some day it'll make a great lady of you.' When my mother was dead a man named Comma came to get me. He said he was my father, but I never believed it, he was so darned mean. And I didn't know Cæsar was giving him an allowance for me—"

"Huh. You never saw any of it?"

She shook her head. "When Comma wasn't at the theater, or locked away with his wigs, he was playing the chariot races. The slaves taught me to read and write. I ran in the streets, and that was fun—"

"Strikes me that the Big Fella didn't make so awful good as a daddy," broke in Manlius.

"Let him alone!" She was prettier than ever when she got mad. "If you were busy as he was, conquering the world, you wouldn't have much time for an ille—" Her lip trembled. Red-headed *puella* cry easily; to stop the shower Mannie had to do things that made them more and more engaged.

"Ever see him again?" he asked, after she had calmed down.

"Yes. The night of that first horrid murder—Comma's." She made a face, but went on, "Anthony took me over to Cæsar's big house on the Palatine. We had to go late to see him at all. Cæsar was very busy, packing to go. Do you know he got out of Rome the day before the fake assassination?"

"Trust C.J.C. to steal a march!" chuckled Manlius, now very pro-Cæsar.

"Yes, isn't he perfectly adorable! He just saw me a minute, and said he hoped I hadn't been neglected, so many other things were on his mind, you know. And he said, 'Tomorrow I'll be dead—officially—and you're remembered in my will. Too bad it's Cicero that holds your fortune in trust. I'd have taken it away from him, but I didn't want that sort of publicity. Old Kick (that's what he calls Cicero) will demand every possible proof of your identity. I'll leave that to Anthony. Get the documentary proofs of your birth out of Comma's effects—right away. And don't forget that wax doll.

I mentioned it as positive proof in a letter I gave Old Kick thirteen years ago.' Then my father kissed me good-by."

"That clicks," said Mannie. "Next night I found you and the Greek—Anthony, I mean—pawing over the Comma papers in the *bungalorium.*"

"It was a pretty close shave for you, Mannie," she said. "If Mark had caught you there—oh, boy!"

"Well," said Mannie philosophically, "he caught me in Cleopatra's cellar—"

"Horrors! All those executioners coming at you with hot tongs!"

"You were a good egg, Romula. The way you yelped and saved my life. You know, I thought for a minute we were both goners—"

"Wasn't it fun!" she tinkled.

"Yeah, it was rollicking," he grunted.

"I mean, I felt like a star in a melodrama. Suddenly I heard your voice. It couldn't have been any other voice—"

"Come here," he said, and gathered her up. "Now I guess we're engaged for keeps." But the reporter in him was still astir. "Did Cæsar have Comma bumped off just because he wasn't good to you? Or because he knew too much inside stuff about the conspiracy? Or because Comma was the one who dolled up Hesiod as Cæsar's understudy?"

"My father would have let him live," she said, "only Comma asked him for a thousand talents to hush up about me."

"Sweet team of blackmailers, Comma and Hesiod. Then Cicero tried to hold back on Cæsar's bequest, did he?"

"Yes. He just puckered up and stood pat. No proofs, no money. And I'd lost the doll. Anthony tried bluffing Cicero. Nothing doing. When Mark was called away to Philippi I had to work the rest out for myself. One day I found Hambonius at the *bungalorium,* and he told me you'd been around. 'I'll bet Manlius picked up my doll,' I thought, so I got your address at the *Tiber* office and went round to see you."

"And I gave you the doll."

"Next day I showed it to Cicero, the old meanie, before witnesses."

"That must have been the day I started for Philippi."

"The minute I got my money," she said, "I tried to find you, Mannie. Really, I did. I knew how horrid you must have thought I was, not telling you a thing. But now I could talk, and I wanted to holler it all to you. And I wanted you to get a cut on my good luck—"

"No cut!" roared Manlius very positively, holding up his hand. "What do you think I am, a *homo amalus* chiseling in on a woman's bank account? No. I'm just a poor simp who's fool enough to like earning his own living. If I'm in love with you, that's just too bad. Well, good-by, *pulcherrima.* I've got a date with Destiny." He sprang to his feet.

"When'll I be seeing you again?" she asked cheerfully.

"In Eternity." With a heavy scowl.

"All right. Come around in the morning, about ten."

"Romula," he said, "you're very young, and I don't think you know about the facts of life."

"Yes, I do. A girl in Cicero's office told me."

"I don't mean—well, you're practically a princess now, even if you were born in the suburbs. You're reeking with money. And look at me."

"I love to," she smiled. "Do lots of girls tell you how handsome you are?"

"Let's stick to our subject. I'm a plain stylus-pusher. But I don't have to come around for spending money to any woman alive. No! I earn my sweat by the bread of my brow—shucks, you know what I mean. I'm self-supporting, thank you. My wage may be a pittance, but that pittance upholds my self-respect."

Quite an oration for Manlius, but it sounded well in Latin. Romula just raised a little motherly hand to stroke his hair.

"Nice hair," she sighed. "Do other women tell you so?"

"No." He winced at the fib, remembering where Cleopatra's fingers had strayed a minute before she gassed him. But Romula's hair-stroking was deliciously different.

"I've been thinking about your work," she said, "and reading the *Evening Tiber.* Poky old sheet, isn't it? Now, the *Daily Astra*—"

"Speaking of bright papers, nobody was ever struck blind, looking at the *Astra.*"

"Oh, Mannie," she pouted, "I thought you'd like being editor of the *Astra.* You could buy it for practically nothing."

"Yeah. That's what I've got."

"But listen. You could borrow the money."

"Who from, may I ask? Tamany of Athens?"

"No, angel. From me."

"Pawnbroker."

"That's all right, presh. What's a pawnbroker's rate of interest?"

"Twelve per cent."

"Twelve per cent is fair enough." He was beginning to smile. For the last year he'd been thinking about what a really live citizen could do with the *Astra.* Twelve per cent was steep, but he could make fifty, once he got the sheet going. Give the *Evening Tiber* a bump that would send Q. Bulbus into a decline; run the *Astra's* circulation up to some tremendous figure like four, five thousand. But Romula was waiting for a definite reply.

"Sure, honey," he said.

"But you could never touch the real story of my father," she said.

"No. That's out. Every newspaper publisher begins life with his hands tied. But I could shoot some stuff that would shake Rome down to its very sewers. How 'bout running a serial called 'The Dictator's Daughter'?"

"Mannie, you wouldn't!" she screamed.

He shook his head rather wistfully. "I guess Q. Bulbus was right when he said, 'It's not what you publish, but what you suppress that makes a great paper.' "

So after one of those lovers' farewells that bring wealth to waiting taxi drivers, Manlius departed to join Smithicus, that staunch representative of a race which, according to an age-old hallucination, never, never, never shall be slaves.

Together they strode away into the pagan night.

THE END

# RAMBLE HOUSE's
## HARRY STEPHEN KEELER WEBWORK MYSTERIES

(RH) indicates the title is available ONLY in the **RAMBLE HOUSE** edition

The Ace of Spades Murder
The Affair of the Bottled Deuce (RH)
The Amazing Web
The Barking Clock
Behind That Mask
The Book with the Orange Leaves
The Bottle with the Green Wax Seal
The Box from Japan
The Case of the Canny Killer
The Case of the Crazy Corpse (RH)
The Case of the Flying Hands (RH)
The Case of the Ivory Arrow
The Case of the Jeweled Ragpicker
The Case of the Lavender Gripsack
The Case of the Mysterious Moll
The Case of the 16 Beans
The Case of the Transparent Nude (RH)
The Case of the Transposed Legs
The Case of the Two-Headed Idiot (RH)
The Case of the Two Strange Ladies
The Circus Stealers (RH)
Cleopatra's Tears
A Copy of Beowulf (RH)
The Crimson Cube (RH)
The Face of the Man From Saturn
Find the Clock
The Five Silver Buddhas
The 4th King
The Gallows Waits, My Lord! (RH)
The Green Jade Hand
Finger! Finger!
Hangman's Nights (RH)
I, Chameleon (RH)
I Killed Lincoln at 10:13! (RH)
The Iron Ring
The Man Who Changed His Skin (RH)
The Man with the Crimson Box
The Man with the Magic Eardrums
The Man with the Wooden Spectacles
The Marceau Case
The Matilda Hunter Murder
The Monocled Monster
The Murder of London Lew
The Murdered Mathematician
The Mysterious Card (RH)
The Mysterious Ivory Ball of Wong Shing Li (RH)
The Mystery of the Fiddling Cracksman
The Peacock Fan
The Photo of Lady X (RH)

The Portrait of Jirjohn Cobb
Report on Vanessa Hewstone (RH)
Riddle of the Travelling Skull
Riddle of the Wooden Parrakeet (RH)
The Scarlet Mummy (RH)
The Search for X-Y-Z
The Sharkskin Book
Sing Sing Nights
The Six From Nowhere (RH)
The Skull of the Waltzing Clown
The Spectacles of Mr. Cagliostro
Stand By—London Calling!
The Steeltown Strangler
The Stolen Gravestone (RH)
Strange Journey (RH)
The Strange Will
The Straw Hat Murders (RH)
The Street of 1000 Eyes (RH)
Thieves' Nights
Three Novellos (RH)
The Tiger Snake
The Trap (RH)
Vagabond Nights (Defrauded Yeggman)
Vagabond Nights 2 (10 Hours)
The Vanishing Gold Truck
The Voice of the Seven Sparrows
The Washington Square Enigma
When Thief Meets Thief
The White Circle (RH)
The Wonderful Scheme of Mr. Christopher Thorne
X. Jones—of Scotland Yard
Y. Cheung, Business Detective

## Keeler Related Works

**A To Izzard: A Harry Stephen Keeler Companion** by Fender Tucker — Articles and stories about Harry, by Harry, and in his style. Included is a compleat Keeler bibliography.

**Wild About Harry: Reviews of Keeler Novels** — Edited by Richard Polt & Fender Tucker — 22 reviews of works by Harry Stephen Keeler from *Keeler News.* A perfect introduction to the author.

**The Keeler Keyhole Collection:** Annotated newsletter rants from Harry Stephen Keeler, edited by Francis M. Nevins

**Fakealoo** — Pastiches of the style of Harry Stephen Keeler by selected demented members of the HSK Society.

**RAMBLE HOUSE**
**Fender Tucker, Prop.**
**www.ramblehouse.com fender@ramblehouse.com**
**318-455-6847 443 Gladstone Blvd. Shreveport LA 71104**

## RAMBLE HOUSE's OTHER LOONS

**Slammer Days** — Two full-length prison memoirs: *Men into Beasts* (1952) by George Sylvester Viereck and *Home Away From Home* (1962) by Jack Woodford

**The Organ Reader** — A huge compilation of just about everything published in the 1971-1972 radical bay-area newspaper, THE ORGAN.

**Dr. Odin** — Douglas Newton's 1933 potboiler comes back to life.

**The Chinese Jar Mystery** — Murder in the manor by John Stephen Strange, 1934

**The Julius Caesar Murder Case** — A classic 1935 re-telling of the assassination by Wallace Irwin

**The Contested Earth and Other SF Stories** — A never-before published space opera and seven short stories by Jim Harmon.

**Freaks and Fantasies** — Eerie tales by Tod Robbins, collaborator of Tod Browning on the film FREAKS.

**Vixen Scandal** — Two sleaze masterpieces from the 60s by Jim Harmon: *Vixen Hollow* and *Celluloid Scandal.*

**Maniac Siren** — Two more sleaze marvels by Jim Harmon: *The Man Who Made Maniacs* and *Silent Siren*

**West Texas War and Other Western Stories** — by Gary Lovisi

**Marblehead: A Novel of H.P. Lovecraft** — A long-lost masterpiece from Richard A. Lupoff. Published for the first time!

**The Secret Adventures of Sherlock Holmes** — Three Sherlockian pastiches by the Brooklyn author/publisher, Gary Lovisi.

**The Universal Holmes** — Richard A. Lupoff's 2007 collection of five Holmesian pastiches and a recipe for giant rat stew.

**Tales of the Macabre and Ordinary** — Modern twisted horror by Chris Mikul, author of the *Bizarrism* series.

**The Gold Star Line** — Seaboard adventure from L.T. Reade and Robert Eustace.

**The Werewolf vs the Vampire Woman** — Hard to believe ultraviolence by either Arthur M. Scarm or Arthur M. Scram.

**Black Hogan Strikes Again** — Australia's Peter Renwick pens a tale of the outback.

**Four Joel Townsley Rogers Novels** — By the author of *The Red Right Hand: Once In a Red Moon, Lady With the Dice, The Stopped Clock, Never Leave My Bed*

**Killing Time** — New collection of short novels by Joel Townsley Rogers

**Night of Horror** — A short story collection of Joel Townsley Rogers

**Twenty Norman Berrow Novels** — *The Bishop's Sword, Ghost House, Don't Go Out After Dark, Claws of the Cougar, The Smokers of Hashish, The Secret Dancer, Don't Jump Mr. Boland!, The Footprints of Satan, Fingers for Ransom, The Three Tiers of Fantasy, The Spaniard's Thumb, The Eleventh Plague, Words Have Wings, One Thrilling Night, The Lady's in Danger, It Howls at Night, The Terror in the Fog, Oil Under the Window, Murder in the Melody, The Singing Room*

**The N. R. De Mexico Novels** — Robert Bragg presents *Marijuana Girl, Madman on a Drum, Private Chauffeur* in one volume.

**Two Hake Talbot Novels** — *Rim of the Pit, The Hangman's Handyman.* Classic locked room mysteries.

**Two Alexander Laing Novels** — *The Motives of Nicholas Holtz* and *Dr. Scarlett,* stories of medical mayhem and intrigue from the 30s.

**Two Wade Wright Novels (and counting)** — *Echo of Fear* and *Death At Nostalgia Street*, with more to come!

**Three Rupert Penny Novels** — *Policeman's Holiday, Policeman's Evidence* and *Sealed Room Murder,* classic impossible mysteries.

**Five Jack Mann Novels** — Strange murder in the English countryside. *Gees' First Case, Nightmare Farm, Grey Shapes, The Ninth Life, The Glass Too Many.*

**Four Max Afford Novels** — *Owl of Darkness, Death's Mannikins, Blood on His Hands* and *The Dead Are Blind* by One of Australia's finest novelists.

**Five Joseph Shallit Novels** — *The Case of the Billion Dollar Body, Lady Don't Die on My Doorstep, Kiss the Killer, Yell Bloody Murder, Take Your Last Look.* One of America's best 50's authors.

**The Best of 10-Story Book** — edited by Chris Mikul, over 35 stories from the literary magazine Harry Stephen Keeler edited.

**A Young Man's Heart** — A forgotten early classic by Cornell Woolrich

**The Anthony Boucher Chronicles** — edited by Francis M. Nevins

Book reviews by Anthony Boucher written for the *San Francisco Chronicle,* 1942 – 1947. Essential and fascinating reading.

**Muddled Mind:** Complete Works of Ed Wood, Jr. — David Hayes and Hayden Davis deconstruct the life and works of a mad genius.

**My First Time:** The One Experience You Never Forget — Michael Birchwood — 64 true first-person narratives of how they lost it.

**The Incredible Adventures of Rowland Hern** — Rousing 1928 impossible crimes by Nicholas Olde.

**Don Diablo: Book of a Lost Film** — Two-volume treatment of a western by Paul Landres, with diagrams. Intro by Francis M. Nevins.

**The Charlie Chaplin Murder Mystery** — Movie hijinks by Wes D. Gehring

**The Koky Comics** — A collection of all of the 1978-1981 Sunday and daily comic strips by Richard O'Brien and Mort Gerberg, in two volumes.

**Gamefinger** — Incredible 1966 sado-sleaze from Clyde Allison (William Knoles).

**Dime Novels: Ramble House's 10-Cent Books** — *Knife in the Dark* by Robert Leslie Bellem, *Hot Lead* and *Song of Death* by Ed Earl Repp, *A Hashish House in New York* by H.H. Kane, and five more.

**Stakeout on Millennium Drive** — Indianapolis Noir — Ian Woollen.

**Dope Tales #1** — Two dope-riddled classics; *Dope Runners* by Gerald Grantham and *Death Takes the Joystick* by Phillip Condé.

**Dope Tales #2** — Two more narco-classics; *The Invisible Hand* by Rex Dark and *The Smokers of Hashish* by Norman Berrow.

**Dope Tales #3** — Two enchanting novels of opium by the master, Sax Rohmer. *Dope* and *The Yellow Claw.*

**Tenebrae** — Ernest G. Henham's 1898 horror tale brought back.

**The Singular Problem of the Stygian House-Boat** — Two classic tales by John Kendrick Bangs about the denizens of Hades.

**The One After Snelling** — Kickass modern noir from Richard O'Brien.

**The Sign of the Scorpion** — 1935 Edmund Snell tale of oriental evil.

**The House of the Vampire** — 1907 thriller by George S. Viereck.

**An Angel in the Street** — Modern hardboiled noir by Peter Genovese.

**The Devil's Mistress** — Scottish gothic tale by J. W. Brodie-Innes.

**The Lord of Terror** — 1925 mystery with master-criminal, Fantômas.

**The Lady of the Terraces** — 1925 adventure by E. Charles Vivian.

**My Deadly Angel** — 1955 Cold War drama by John Chelton

**Prose Bowl** — Futuristic satire — Bill Pronzini & Barry N. Malzberg .

**Satan's Den Exposed** — True crime in TorC New Mexico — Award-winning journalism by the Desert Journal.

**The Amorous Intrigues & Adventures of Aaron Burr** — by Anonymous — Hot historical action.

**I Stole $16,000,000** — True story by cracksman Herbert E. Wilson.

**The Black Dark Murders** — Vintage 50s college murder yarn by Milt Ozaki, writing as Robert O. Saber.

**Sex Slave** — Potboiler of lust in the days of Cleopatra — Dion Leclerq.

**You'll Die Laughing** — Bruce Elliott's 1945 novel of murder at a practical joker's English countryside manor.

**The Private Journal & Diary of John H. Surratt** — The memoirs of the man who conspired to assassinate President Lincoln.

**Dead Man Talks Too Much** — Hollywood boozer by Weed Dickenson

**Red Light** — History of legal prostitution in Shreveport Louisiana by Eric Brock. Includes wonderful photos of the houses and the ladies.

**Gadsby** — A lipogram (a novel without the letter E). Ernest Vincent Wright's last work, published in 1939 right before his death.

**A Snark Selection** — Lewis Carroll's *The Hunting of the Snark* with two Snarkian chapters by Harry Stephen Keeler — Illustrated by Gavin L. O'Keefe.

**Ripped from the Headlines! —** The Jack the Ripper story as told in the newspaper articles in the *New York* and *London Times.*

**Geronimo** — S. M. Barrett's 1905 autobiography of a noble American.

**The Compleat Calhoon** — All of Fender Tucker's works: Includes *The Totah Trilogy, Weed, Women and Song* and *Tales from the Tower,* plus a CD of all of his songs.

**The Naked Trocar** with **The Best Revenge** — Two misdemeanors by Fender Tucker from 2007

www.ingramcontent.com/pod-product-compliance
Lightning Source LLC
LaVergne TN
LVHW090937080826
845145LV00003B/782

*9781605430379*